Meltdown

Sam Silver

Chapter One

"The bowels of hell are ready to let loose."

Kimie recalled the magazine quote as she ran out the front door, her school bag over her shoulder, knowing it was all too true. Morning always came way too soon for her liking, especially on a school day, and she'd once again slept in, thanks to her stupid alarm clock having stuffed up. The worst-case scenario had hit, and she knew that the bowels of hell were gearing up for an almighty blow out.

The cool breeze brushed through the ripped knees of her jeans as she headed for the bus that was pulling up with a hiss. She boarded, scanned her card and made her way down the aisle, past a leering boy.

"Hey Kimie, ready to shake 'em for me later?"

"No, just knee 'em," she shot back.

The boy grinned. "Oooh! Feisty!"

She went to the rear of the bus, sat down tiredly next to a dark-haired girl, leaned forward, and rested her head on the back of the seat before her.

"Your old lady still giving you a hard time?" the girl asked.

"Yuh-huh," Kimie replied.

"Thought so," the girl said. "You didn't spend as much time on your hair this morning."

"Rub it in, why don't ya?"

"Relax. My maths test sucked too. Looks like we're both screwed."

Kimie looked out the window at the houses. Most were rundown, old and battered. Some even had screaming coming from inside.

"God," Kimie said glumly, "there's got to be more to life than this, Xandi."

"More to life than being dumped on by boys, bullies, teachers and parents?" the girl scoffed. "Yeah, right. It's just us against the world."

A spitball flew past their heads.

Kimie leapt up, punching a nearby boy in the arm. "Try that again, dipstick, and I'll ram it so far down your throat you'll be blowing it out your butt, along with your brains!"

He glared at her and raised his fist.

"Try it!" she snapped, raising hers and staring him down.

"Screw you," he scowled, and faced the front of the bus.

"See?" Xandi pointed out.

Kimie took her seat and drew a sharp breath, still seething.

"How's your old man?" Xandi asked, changing tack.

Kimie sighed. "Still in hospital and getting worse. Hasn't worked in ages and can't keep up with what he owes Mum from the divorce. If this crap goes on, I'll have to leave school and get a job."

"You serious?"

"Got no choice. Too many bills and not enough breaks, Xandi. It's not getting any easier, that's for sure."

A spitball hit her.

"Oh, you sh—!" She dived on the boy.

The bus screeched to a halt.

"Just us against the world," Xandi said again.

Kimie arrived at school half an hour late. The bus got there exactly on time. Not her. She'd been kicked off and forced to walk, thereby missing part of her first class. She was then yelled at by her teacher before having to listen to him crap on to anyone interested about economic theory. It was boring as hell. She tapped her pen against her pad throughout the lesson, whilst gazing wearily out the window.

The next class, English, wasn't much better, then came recess, which was way too short. Maths followed, where her teacher was especially tough on her for her recent test results. He scolded her for not trying hard enough and told her to come back at lunchtime. She didn't.

Art was the final class of the day. Cathy Terry, the butt pain from hell, kept making sniggering comments about her. Kimie had nicknamed her 'the Catheter', because she was always drawing out the worst in her.

After one ultra-nasty comment, Kimie snapped, throwing a tin of paint at the Catheter, which erupted into a full-blown scuffle that overturned several tables. The room exploded into chaos as the kids encircled them, screaming for a fight.

"Why are you here, Kimie?"

The principal, who everyone thought of as Old Grogan, because he always looked so long and drawn, leaned forwards from behind his desk.

Kimie folded her arms defensively and crossed her legs.

"Are you going to answer me or are we going to sit here all day?" he pressed.

"Up to you," she replied.

He tapped her file. "Three fights in a fortnight. Several complaints from your teachers and failing grades too. Not impressive, is it? So I'll ask you again, Kimie, why are you here?"

She kept her mouth shut.

"You clearly don't want to be with us, so why waste our time?"

"Maybe you're wasting mine," she retorted.

"There's no call to be rude."

"Oh, really? You're telling me to put more effort into a place that doesn't give a stuff about me! Why should I come here every day to try and make the school look good when it's screwing me over?"

He stared at her, unmoved. "What is it, Kimie? Trouble at home? I know that your parents are divorced and your father's not well."

She shifted a little. "Trouble everywhere."

"If it's financial trouble, have you thought about getting a job?"

"Thought it, tried it, didn't get it. Happened a few times."

"Then I don't know what else to say. You're a smart girl, you just have a problem with your attitude."

"You can talk!"

His tone hardened. "Unless something changes, Kimie, you're going to have a lot of problems from here on in. It's not too late."

"For what?" she asked gruffly. "To become what you want? What this crappy system wants? What about what *I* want?"

"Freedom of expression is fine in the appropriate place and time, but without the proper discipline—"

"Then what? Feral kids running around in a drunken stupor, right?"

"That's not what I meant—"

"Like hell, you didn't!"

"Language."

"I don't do drugs and I never drink—sir!"

"Still leaves us with a problem, doesn't it?"

"No, you have a problem, this school has a problem, everyone in it has a problem! It's sick, and for some reason, some god-awful reason I just don't get, I get the blame for it! Blame the victim, right, sir?"

His stare gave nothing away.

"Right, sir?"

He stared at her for longer than ever. Finally, he said, "I think that's all we have to say on the matter, Kimie. I can see no course of action but to suspend you indefinitely. I'll inform your mother."

"Get stuffed!"

She stood up, threw her bag over her shoulder, kicked the chair away and stormed out the door, slamming it behind her.

"What happened, Kimie?"

Xandi ran after Kimie as she strode across the oval.

"Just got kicked out of school," came the glum reply.

Xandi gasped. "That fight was *not* your fault ..."

"Tell that to the infected mongrel's ballsack sitting behind the principal's desk," Kimie retorted, wiping her eyes. "It's okay, I don't want to go back."

"What are you gonna do?"

"I'll think of something." She turned to her. "Thanks for ... you know."

"Yeah, I know."

They hugged.

"Look after yourself," Xandi said.

"You too."

They parted.

"Your mum's so gonna freak," Xandi warned.

Kimie inhaled sharply. "Tell me about it."

"Maybe if you got a job first it'd lessen the blow."

"That's if someone'll hire me. I'll see ya round."

Xandi nodded sadly. "Yeah."

Kimie turned and walked off the oval.

Kimie headed as far from school as possible. It would soon be out for the day and she knew that the Catheter and her designer brand of toxins would be after her with a vengeance, but right now that was the least of her worries. Her thoughts were a mess as she gazed sadly at the rundown houses, listening to the wailing police sirens in the distance. She wondered what to do next. She'd no idea where to go from here.

Her heart was heavy as she passed several people in the street. Some looked down on her. Others looked up from where they sat in the alleys, roused from their drunken dream worlds. She held her bag tightly as she hurried through the brown bits of old newspapers drifting in the breeze, making her way to the small café on the corner.

Xandi had been right. Her mum would go mental at her for getting kicked out of school but might ease off if she knew money was coming in, even if it meant working for a dump like this. The place felt as old as hell, even more so when she pushed open the creaking door.

A big man stood behind the counter. Apart from him, the place was empty.

"Uh … hey," Kimie said, approaching him.

He frowned, suspiciously.

She shifted awkwardly. "I was, uh, sorta wondering if we could help each other. My name's Kimie. Kimie Walsh. I'm looking for work. You got anything?"

He crossed his arms. "What? You just get kicked out of school or something?"

Kimie averted her gaze.

"Yeah, that's it, isn't it?" he pressed. "I can tell. They gave you the flick."

Kimie shrugged. "Just want to help, that's all. I'll work hard for as much as you think I'm worth."

"I got nothing. Sorry, kid."

Kimie's face hardened. This loser wasn't sorry at all. She could see it. Anybody could. Somehow she kept her anger in check and turned away, ready to storm out. Her hunger got the better of her and she sighed, turning back.

"How 'bout," she began with great restraint, "a burger and chips, then? Would that be okay? Not that I can afford it, but the last of my money should be good enough for you, even if I'm not."

He indicated a booth. "Sure, take a seat."

She walked over to a table, dumped her bag down, caught a glimpse of herself in the window's reflection and grimaced. No wonder he didn't want to give her a job. She looked like the spawn of Queen Kong.

She turned to him. "Hey, uh, where's your bathroom? Have to look good if I'm going job hunting."

He pointed to a small corridor running past the counter. "Right there. Where the signs are."

"Thanks."

Leaving her bag behind, Kimie headed past him and entered the restroom.

"Moron," she muttered, walking over to the mirror.

She'd barely started fixing her hair when she heard the café door open and the man behind the counter call, "What the hell are you doing here? You wanna get your head shot off?"

A woman spoke coolly. "No, just shot at. Could do with a burger too."

Her voice caught Kimie's interest. It was hell rebel. She went to the bathroom door and pulled it back a little, peering through the crack. Three people stood by the entrance. Two were men in suits. The third was a woman in a long dark trench coat, wearing sunglasses, and with striking blonde hair.

The woman observed the area. "Place still looks crude, rundown and stinking of god knows what, with food that looks like it's just fallen off the back of an animal." She nodded, satisfied. "It's got potential."

"No!" Counter-Guy yelled, pointing at her. "No way! You are *not* bringing your work in here! Half—no, scratch that—*all* of the city's out there gunning for you. On both sides of the law!"

Kimie gasped.

The three newcomers ignored him, went over to a booth and sat together on one side, with the woman sandwiched between the men.

"Why do you do this to me?" Counter-Guy cried. "Why not just disappear? You can do it. You got enough to set you up for life."

"Play dough," the woman replied.

"So what have you got planned this time?" he asked.

"You'll know soon enough." She counted down. "Five, four, three, two …"

There was a screech of tyres.

"Right on time."

Counter-Guy cringed.

Kimie tensed, preparing for the worst.

The blonde woman, however, sat like a statue.

Kimie heard a car door slam, then watched as a man in black with his hair tied back enter the café. He approached the woman, placed his hands on the table, leaned over her and spoke in a dangerously low tone.

"I gotta respect you." He moved in closer. "You got guts."

"Brains to go with it," she quipped. "Unlike some."

Kimie grinned with admiration.

The man's glare grew. "You steal my money, call me here, throw insults at me and then think it's smart? You want to die, don't you?"

The woman shrugged. "No, just flirt with death. Hear it has a nice kiss."

To Kimie's astonishment, the woman sat forward, staring back at him.

"You see," she continued, "you're an animal. You kill, you gamble, you go on instinct. I, on the other hand, am an artist. Everything I do is out of choice and helps paint a bigger picture. You got the potential to be put in it. Course you won't make as much of an impact but at least with me you'll never be framed."

He pulled out a gun, aiming it at her forehead. "You talk too much!"

Kimie froze.

The woman didn't budge. Neither did her men.

"Do it," she said, without a care in the world. "Nothing's stopping you." Motioning to her men, she ordered, "All hands on deck."

Six hands were laid on the table.

"Why not just shoot us in cold blood and walk right out of here?" she asked the gunman. "You'll be as a hero of the underworld. Go ahead."

"Don't tempt me …" he warned.

"So why you taking so long? You got doubts?"

He sneered. "I don't like this."

"I love it."

Kimie watched, transfixed. Even from the bathroom, she sensed his thoughts churning.

"No," he said suspiciously. "Something's up. What?"

Silence.

"What the hell are you up to?" he pressed.

"What's wrong?" she asked. "Feeling like you're missing out?"

"Damn you!"

The tension in his gun hand grew.

Kimie pulled out her phone. The screen flickered, bringing up her worst fear. She hadn't topped up her credit, meaning there wasn't enough to make a call. She cringed, fully expecting Gunman and his weapon to explode together.

Gunman slammed his gun on the table, making Kimie jump. He drew a sharp breath, then slowly sat opposite the blonde woman.

"So," he said, clasping his hands together, "what's the deal?"

"Got a job," she answered. "It's big. Far bigger than anything you've ever done. You help out, you get your money back. Two million. Just for you. Won't be missed until at least a decade down the track. If ever."

He gave a hollow laugh. "You are kidding me."

Her face gave nothing away.

"What is it, a bank job?" he asked. "Rumours are out there."

"Rumours are true," she confirmed. "This is a beauty. A cyber attack. Courtesy of my platinum card, which, incidentally, stays hidden for the moment."

He stared at her, as if trying to dig deep into her psyche, but found nothing. "So I get two million. What's in it for you?"

"Nothing," she stated firmly.

"Nothing?" he repeated sourly. "Isn't there supposed to be a bigger picture?"

"I've always believed there's more to life than economics," she replied. "No one agrees with me."

This confused him. "If your platinum card's so good, then why not pack up and leave? Why do a cyber attack, take nothing and give two million to me?"

"It's half a million more than what I owe," she told him. "You want more? Fine, you'll get it, but there's a higher chance you'll get caught."

"What are you playing at?"

"Waking people up," came the simple reply. "That includes you. Everyone's so attached to things these days. Money, phones, the net, and everything else controlled by this ugly system we live in. You take away all that and you get people's real sense of self-worth. I mean, look at you without cash. You're a mess. You got nothing. No standards. A stabbing, a shooting, robbing a store … it's all so low. It's brutal, it's horrific, it's ugly and it's cheap." She gave a flicker of a smile. "Crime can be so artistic, just like life. It doesn't have to be bad. It can prove a point too."

"You're insane!"

"So my shrink keeps saying. You in?"

He stayed silent, considering her words.

"So what are you going to do?" she pressed. "Pull the trigger, or take the money? Your choice. I'm fine either way."

From the bathroom, Kimie moved to get a better view. Her elbow hit a can of air-freshener on a shelf, sending it clattering to the floor and rolling loudly over the tiles.

Gunman's gaze snapped towards her.

Kimie slammed the door shut and looked around quickly. A small window above a sink was slightly open. Maybe big enough for her to squeeze through, with a bit of a struggle.

Only one way to find out.

She hurried to the window and pushed it back. It didn't open easily, or far. She climbed onto the sink, crawling into the gap. It was tight but she could fit in. Barely.

Gunman entered the bathroom.

Her phone slipped from her hand, falling onto the tiles and smashing open.

She swore and pushed herself through the gap. The move worked and she fell outside, tumbling over and thumping next to a dumpster in the alleyway. Groaning, she rose to her feet and staggered down the street, glancing back to see Gunman peering out the window.

Ignoring the pain, she rounded the corner and fled.

Her first instinct was to run to the cops. She was seriously freaked out by what she'd seen but knew if she ran to the police wailing about psychos in a café planning a cyber attack, she'd be thrown in the nuthouse for sure. Besides, that crazy blonde lady would probably have contacts everywhere. No, she determined, home it would be.

She'd no money for the bus and her house was way on the other side of town. That meant the walk home, although doable, would be long. Her mother wouldn't exactly be happy with her getting thrown out of school, losing her phone and topping it all off by running into the mob. Still, she didn't have a choice.

Great, she thought, trudging along glumly. Perfect end to the Crappiest. Day. Ever.

Night had fallen by the time she reached her street. She headed for her house, then stopped dead in her tracks.

A man stood in her doorway talking to her mother. Kimie recognised him straight away. He'd been with the blonde lady in the café and was holding up, what she guessed, was a police badge in one hand, and her school back in the other. The badge was either fake or he was as corrupt as hell, she figured.

Her mind whirred. Gunman could have shot the blonde lady and re-cruited her people, or they could now all be working together. Either way, they'd tracked her down.

She hid behind the tree near her front gate, watching as her mother took the bag from him.

"She's not in any trouble," the man said. "We'd just like to ask her a few questions. The security cameras picked her up in a café this afternoon. We think she might have seen something that could help us out."

Kimie saw her mother's lips purse and shuddered, knowing she was ready to blow. She knew that look all too well—the death glare. It was horrifying.

"Were you aware of her dismissal from school today?" the man asked.

"Yes," her mother replied. "Her principal rang."

"Do you have any idea where she might be?"

"None," came the reply. "I can give you some numbers to try …"

"No, that's alright. She dropped her phone in the café. We've already retrieved its contact list."

Kimie fumed.

Her mother did the same, only on a superior scale.

The man continued. "Let me know if she comes home. I'd like to see her."

"So would I," her mother said bitterly, "but you might want to put her behind bars first. She'll be safer there."

The man smiled. "Now, you're the kind we'd like to have working for us." He handed her his card. "Here's my number. If anything happens …"

"I'll call," she finished, taking the card. "That's if you're not called back here on a murder charge first."

This time he couldn't help but give a light laugh. "Thank you. Good night, Mrs Walsh."

"'Night." She closed the door as he turned away.

Kimie watched him make for his car. She wondered why it was parked so far away and not in her driveway, then decided she didn't care. Things sucked big time. Her life was melting. These losers had found out where she lived and sent her mother into volcano mode. One way or another, an eruption was coming. Her only instinct now was to get out of Dodge and leave all this garbage behind.

She took a step backwards.

A hand clamped over her mouth.

She yelped and struggled wildly.

A gun click made her freeze. Her heart pounded as its cold nozzle pressed into her neck.

"Take it easy, kid."

She didn't recognise the voice. At least it wasn't Gunman from the café, so that was good, although there was nothing to say this nutcase didn't work for him. She thought about biting his hand and screaming for help but knew it would only make things worse. After this crappy day, she wasn't expecting any miracles. Besides, she was too on edge to fight.

He shifted her so that she faced the other man's car. Now she knew why it was parked so far down the street. These ferals had been staking out her house, waiting for her to come home.

"Over there," he ordered. "Nice and relaxed, like we're walking on the beach. Fun times, sweetheart."

He guided her onto the road, keeping them both to the shadows while concealing the gun.

The cop who'd spoken to Kimie's mum saw them approaching.

"Jackpot!" he said, grinning.

Kimie was whirled around, pressed up against the car and cuffed.

"What the hell is this?" she snapped. "This is wrong! This is so beyond wrong!"

She saw the man who'd caught her. The blonde lady's other goon. No surprises there.

First Cop, the one who'd spoken to her mother, said, "Believe me, kid, you're better off with us than at home right now."

Kimie scowled. "Yeah, and your mum must have been a street slapper to screw you up this bad—mmmf!"

A gag was placed in her mouth and she nearly hurled. It tasted of engine oil.

"You're easier on my ears this way," Second Cop said.

Kimie swore at them under the gag. The door opened and she was thrown into the back seat. Second Cop entered, sitting next to her, while First Cop got in the driver's seat.

The car came to life and she watched helplessly through the window as she was driven away.

The journey was sickening. The gag tasted awful in Kimie's mouth and she felt gross from both it and the ride. She rested her head glumly against the window, feeling like crap. Angry too. She should be at home, chilling in front of the TV like any normal teenager, not being kidnapped by two psycho freaks who seemed way too relaxed about this whole thing.

The cops said little throughout the journey, not even to each other. She had a mountain of questions and no idea where they were going, only that it wasn't the police station. All she knew was that they'd just emerged from an industrial area and were now travelling down a long straight road, heading into the countryside.

Second Cop, who she'd inwardly termed the Sherriff of Dodgy City, sat next to her, gazing out of his window. She looked at him wearily, then saw what lay on the seat next to him.

A set of keys.

They'd fallen from his pocket and were within her reach. She figured it must have happened when they'd gone around a bend a short while ago. One of them had to be for the handcuffs. There weren't that many to go through and it wouldn't take long to find the right one. She didn't know what she'd do after the cuffs were off but had to take a chance. Anything was better than sitting here with a gag over her mouth and a hangman's noose practically on her neck.

She shifted slowly, keeping her eyes on the man next to her. Thankfully, he kept staring out the window, lost in the world outside, and in a song on the radio too. Some old tune, she couldn't put her finger on, was relaxing him to the point of nodding off.

Fighting against her growing car sickness, she stretched her fingers out for the keys. She didn't look down. That would only raise suspicion, so she kept looking out the window. Finally, her fingers wrapped around them. She couldn't move fast, despite wanting to. It was hard work keeping quiet and her rising nausea didn't help either. Slowly and carefully, she brought the keys closer to herself, turned one around and placed it in the lock.

It went a short way in, then stopped.

Wrong key.

She swore silently.

Two keys rubbed against each other, making a small clink.

The man's eyes opened.

She froze.

The car went over a bump. She clutched the keys tightly to stop them from clinking again. The move worked, and he closed his eyes once more.

She worked carefully, getting hold of a second key and cautiously placing it in the lock. It didn't go very far.

Now she was jittery. Her hands were almost sweating. They'd been travelling for a while and would have to be stopping soon. Either that or her luck would run out and the deadhead next to her would wake up and see what she was up to.

She tried with the third key.

Nothing.

Her heart sank.

"Nearly there," she heard the driver say.

She froze.

Dodgy City's Sheriff beside her shifted tiredly. "Can't wait. Getting hungry."

"Me too."

Much to her relief, the Sherriff returned his gaze to the window.

She shifted another key around, placed it in the lock, felt it enter smoothly, then heard a small click as the cuff came free. Without thinking, she pulled the handcuffs away.

The Sheriff gave a long stretch.

"I'm dying for a burger—" he began, then saw what she was doing. "Oi!"

Kimie threw the cuffs at him, clicked her belt open and reached for the door. She didn't care if the car was speeding. If the door opened it might attract someone on the road—that's if she was lucky enough for anyone to see it.

She grabbed the handle and found it locked.

The Sherriff pulled her back. She shoved him away, pulled the gag from her mouth and went for the door again.

"What's going on?" the driver called.

The Sherriff leaned over, grabbing her by the hair with one hand and pulling his gun out with the other. She leapt on him, pushing the weapon up with both hands. She didn't know what she was doing, only that she was filled with anger. Pure, burning rage for every crappy thing that had happened today. Getting kicked out of school, her mum's temper, and now these two morons with all the brains of a dead monkey's butt kidnapping her. Fury overtook her and she smacked the Sherriff's hand out of her hair before biting into his wrist near the gun.

The Sherriff cried out and clasped his free hand over her face. She grimaced, feeling her guts heave and thinking it was the same hand he used to go to the bathroom with. Through his fingers, she saw the gun come down for her. It twisted to one side and—

Bang!

The shot hit the windshield.

The car screeched, veering to the side of the road.

The gun fired again, hitting the dashboard and blowing out the central locking system. She kicked the Sherriff back, opened the door and hurled herself outside. A fresh gust of forest air hit her, bringing much-needed relief from the car's sickening atmosphere.

She hit the ground hard. A flash erupted behind her eyes and the world swirled as she heard the car skid away. Gravity took hold as she rolled over the gravel and down a slope into the darkness below, turning head over heels before smacking her forehead against a rock.

Another sickening flash followed and everything went blank.

Chapter Two

Kimie opened her eyes.

Her vision was hazy and her head throbbed. Everything was cold and dark, making it impossible to tell where she was. A night bird hooted in a tree high above, meaning she was in bushland.

She sat up, wincing.

A mist had risen, breezing through the crisp night air. This wasn't bushland, she realised. The natural smells were too fresh for that. No, it was a forest. A weird one too. There were tree roots almost as big as her whole body. She tried thinking and came up with more questions than answers. Yes, her name was Kimie and yes, she'd been in trouble. She recalled being in a car before coming here, yet everything else remained a dark, ugly mystery.

Fighting against her aching back pain, she rose to her feet and staggered along. One step at a time, she thought, easy does it. Bit by bit, she limped over the small mounds of earth and nearly tripped on a rock. Disorientated and confused, she pushed on, stumbling into the night.

She'd only gone a short way when she noticed that the ground was quivering. She wondered if it were a natural tremor, like a small earthquake. No, she concluded, it was too gentle for that. Far too gentle. If anything, it felt … mechanised?

She made her way deeper into this forest of God knew where until she came to a clearing and stared ahead in awe.

"Whoa …" she whispered, raising a hand to her head in disbelief.

A city stood in the distance. It wasn't familiar in the slightest. A spectacle of pristine perfection, with unblemished towers appearing brand new. The ground tremors, she realised, came from the city itself. It was beautiful, she observed, truly it was, but didn't seem like a city at all, more like a giant, living organism that had conquered the land around it.

She rubbed her temple, confused.

"Talk about the ultimate breakdown," she murmured.

The sound of running water caught her attention. She moved towards it, came to a river, and stopped in her tracks. Dazzling moonbeams were dancing on the soft ripples before her, as if in a mystical ballet. She gazed at them in awe, until a whizzing noise broke through the air, followed by a plop, like a line had been cast.

A wave of relief swept over her. Someone was here. Even though it was quite loud for a fishing line, she didn't care. Maybe now she'd get answers.

She followed the river down a slope, came to an underpass beneath a concrete bridge, and crept in cautiously.

A figure was seated beneath that bridge, fishing. A man, who seemed ordinary enough. He took the line out of the water, pulled a fish off it and put it into the bucket beside him. At the sight of Kimie, he looked up proudly and said, "A good night's work, I'd say."

Kimie didn't know where to start with her questions but didn't trust him. Her memory may have gone, but her instincts hadn't.

"Dodgy old con," she muttered.

He threw his line back into the water.

"Times are hard, aren't they?" he prompted.

His tone resonated deeply within her, like it held an undercurrent, and he understood more than he should.

Kimie found herself nodding. "You have no idea."

He gazed at the city. "Oh, I might have some. Towers are going up. Wages are coming down. Now we're being made to work twice as hard for half as much. It isn't right."

"Way of the world," Kimie said wearily. "Guess that's why you've got this little side venture, huh?"

"Oh, it's no side venture, I assure you," he replied. "Yes, the work's hard, but the rewards pay off, especially when I find what I'm looking for."

"Which is what?" Kimie wondered.

"Good company at times." He peered into the water. "As well as a decent piece of fish every so often."

"That's just sad."

"Speaking from the heart, are we?"

Kimie shrugged. "I don't even know what I'm doing here."

"Do any of us?" came the reply. "I guess that makes us both soul searchers, although since I like to fish, I'm what you call a *Sole*-Searcher." He chuckled. "That's s-o-l-e—"

"I know how you spell it!" Kimie cut in irritably. "You really have lost it, haven't you?" She sighed and looked around. "Think I have too."

"Actually," he began, "I'm always finding things. Sole-Searcher was a name another lost girl gave me a long time ago. Before then, I was just a plain fisherman." He paused. "My guess is that you've been hooked into a situation you can't get out of. Am I right?"

"Dead right," she confirmed. "I'm in trouble. *Real* trouble. I know that much. Now I've got to figure out what to do. Maybe I can get help here. A job even. I remember wanting one."

"Money isn't everything," he cautioned. "Look at this place. It's become obsessed with it and things have taken a turn for the worse." He indicated ahead. "Still, there's an inn down the road that's always accommodating. Take the first street on your right, then turn left, and the building you'll want has a small star over its door. You'll find it has a spirit that goes beneath money. That's why it's called the InnerCent. You'd best get there quickly if you don't want to be spotted."

"Talking to you, you mean?" Kimie asked.

"That too," he replied. "The last thing I want is my job taken away with all this downsizing going on. Better hurry while no one's around and surveillance is down, thanks to a resistance faction on the move."

Now Kimie knew this guy was nuts. He had to be on drugs. Utterly screwed up on heroin or something. Then again, with the way she felt at the moment, maybe she was too.

"Thanks," she said, confused. "See ya."

She moved past him and headed to the other side of the underpass.

"Just be careful," he warned. "It's getting dangerous in there."

She walked on, exiting the underpass and muttering, "Random. Real random."

Kimie expected things to get easier after leaving the happy hobo behind her. Much to her annoyance, they got even weirder. Everything was so quiet. Too quiet. In a city this size there should surely be people around, she thought. Some life, vitality, humanity. Loud noises were expected in a city twenty-four-seven. Instead, it reminded her of a newly built mansion that was empty. Yes, she could hear strange-sounding vehicles whooshing overhead, rather like small planes, but they weren't visible. There were countless hotels, shops and other businesses too, yet they were spotless, and also dead silent, with no vibe or spirit. Just a hollow shell of the utterly superficial.

She strode through the deserted streets, looking for someone, anyone, to help her out. The only familiar sound was a single car revving in the distance, as if on a raceway. The noise rose, then faded and vanished. She almost hoped it would come back.

She followed the Sole-Searcher's directions as best she could until music came from up ahead. It wasn't like the mechanised humming she'd heard upon arriving. This melody had life in it. Passion too, with the sounds of flutes, fiddles and laughter flowing like a gentle breeze onto the street. At least it *seemed* human, thankfully.

She let herself be drawn in, only to find the harmonies emanating from an old inn tucked between two towering buildings. True to the Sole-Searcher's words, a star hung over the entrance. She picked up her pace and entered.

A fireplace's warm embrace was the first thing to welcome her. The people seemed friendly enough, maybe even old-fashioned, but the kind she could tolerate, and not the icky Grandma-smell type that sprang to mind.

She went to the fireplace and sat on the couch by its side, sinking into its cushions. They were so soft that she just wanted to curl up into them, like a snuggling cat.

"Can I get you something, miss?"

Kimie looked up at who'd spoken. A young man, who appeared to be a waiter.

"Uh, no," she replied, sitting up straight and thinking fast. "It's fine. I don't have any money. Have you got a phone?"

She wondered why she'd asked. She'd no idea who to call. Try as she might, she still couldn't recall a damn thing about herself before waking up in the forest. This god-awful mind-blank made her question her sanity even more.

The man shook his head. "No, miss. I'm afraid there's a bit of a mis-communication with the City at the moment. Nobody can get a signal out, unless it's through the City's wavelength."

"That's fine by me."

"Not us, it isn't. Newcomers like yourself are scarce here."

"In a city this big?"

"Yes." He looked her over. "At least you're not a Hooker. That's a relief."

Kimie gasped. "Oh, you're so asking for it! Do you normally talk to people like that, ya suckhole?"

He was undeterred by her outburst, staying as formal as ever. "I'm sorry, miss, but we need to be on guard. If a Hooker were to enter here—"

"What, are you guys that snobby?"

"No, miss, Hookers aren't people."

Kimie's jaw dropped. "You are a feral pig, you know that?"

"My apologies," he said hurriedly. "It's been a while since we've had a newcomer here and I'm new to this role myself. Still learning the ropes."

"Yeah, I can tell!"

"We're a bit low on staff," he continued. "Two of our waitresses left to go travelling with friends. Smart girls. I wish I'd gone with them."

"I don't care, ya chauvo, I'm gettin' out!" She moved to stand, pushing deep into the cushions.

His hand rose, stopping her. "Not a good idea, miss. You're new to the City and the perfect target for a Hooker."

Kimie was horrified. "Oh, you are seriously asking for a twist and rip!"

"Our Hookers are different from what you think," he told her. "You'd best stay here while I get the manager. He'll explain everything. I'll send you a lemon, lime and bitters as well."

He hurried away.

"A phone would be better!" Kimie called after him. "I need to make a call real bad!"

Her first instinct was to ask someone else for a phone, but none were in sight. Not anywhere. Weird, she thought. They should be out everywhere, especially with this many people absorbed in conversation.

She stood up and called to a girl, "Excuse me?"

The girl didn't respond, headed to an open space on the floor, and started dancing with a man. The music grew louder and several cheers went up as the couple swirled in a dazzling display of flexibility. Kimie watched them, impressed, and recalled a vague memory of a talent show she used to like on TV, but this was so much better. This place felt wholesome and welcoming. Nevertheless, she had an inkling that it could also be part of a psycho religious cult and was hesitant to let her guard down.

"A drink, miss?"

She looked at the waiter. He held a tray with a drink upon it.

"How much will this cost me?" she called over the music.

"Only your time," he called back. "Try it! It's good!"

His tone reassured her and she sniffed the drink, then sipped it. It was better than she expected.

"Okay, that's cool!" She took another sip.

A much deeper voice spoke from nearby. "All natural ingredients too."

She turned to see who'd spoken and her eyes nearly popped out of her head. Standing there was a man with sandy blond hair and stubble. She swooned inwardly, even though he was old enough to be her father.

Somewhat smoothly, he sat on a couch by the fireplace. Kimie stepped back automatically and sat where she'd been before. Its cushions hugged her like a friend and she didn't know whether to call it the seat of heaven or to give that title to the couch opposite her where the heavenly guy now sat.

The music softened, allowing the couple on the floor to move in for a slow, close dance.

"That brew's famous for putting colour in people's cheeks," Heavenly Guy said.

"You certainly put some in mine," Kimie blurted out, and regretted it instantly. Embarrassed, she put the drink on the table beside her.

He glanced at her sternly. "A girl your age shouldn't be talking to a man of mine like that."

Kimie fumed. "I can do what I want!"

"Exactly, and that's why you're here," he pointed out. "You're in trouble."

Kimie folded her arms defensively and sat back, annoyed that her cover had been blown. "Sure am with you around. Where's your phone? It's urgent."

"Who are you calling?"

She was about to say that it was none of his damn business, then frowned. Everything before waking up in the forest was still a big blank in her mind. Thankfully, the music was relaxing her to the max.

"I never take advantage of trouble," he continued. "I always think of it as my duty to help, especially when it's just us against the System."

The music slowed further. The need for a phone faded from Kimie's mind. Realisation dawned as she finally said what she'd been feeling deep down for a long time. "What if you can't be helped?"

"Haven't met a soul yet who couldn't be," he replied.

"Yeah, well, this one's just scored a touchdown in hell's superbowl," she said sadly. "Something bad's happened to me, but I'm not sure what. It's like I've had a meltdown and switched from hardcore hell into fantasy land. Now I've ended up in snob central where your mummy's boy waiter's got a thing about hookers."

He wasn't affected by her snipe. "We're all wary of Hookers here, but they can't enter this building. Nor can the DeciMauls."

"The wha—?"

"Not for the moment anyway," he cut in. "The stronger the City becomes, the sooner they, and the Hookers, will be allowed to."

Kimie was aghast. "What is your damn problem with streetwalkers?" An ugly notion hit home. "Oh, I get it! I totally get it! You bait underage kids into your bar, you swear on the almighty Bible that you're not going to screw 'em over, you offer 'em a way out, then bam! You turn 'em into junkies and pimp 'em!"

"Wrong," he stated. "We don't do that here."

"Oh yeah?" she shot back. "You know what I learnt today, you slimy rat's nutsack? You can't trust anyone. The only difference between you and the rest of the garbage outside is that you're good at faking it."

He was unfazed by her outburst and his voice slowed as he spoke, growing gentler. "Listen to the music. It never fails to heal."

Kimie was about to give him some music of her own when she stopped dead. He was right. The soothing tones, simple as they were, resonated within her, breaking through her tough exterior. She listened, and for the first time in her life, *really* listened. The pent-up tension that had been bugging her for so long eased off, and before she knew it, there was only the fireplace, the harmonies and the man sitting opposite.

"What's your name?" she found herself asking.

"Orion," he answered. "*The* Orion Sentry to be exact."

"What kind of dodgy name is that?" she asked, tensing once more. This time, the music kept her in check.

"It's not a name, it's my role," he corrected. "Generally, however, I'm referred to as Orion."

"So you're not the boss?" she pressed.

"That I'm not," came the reply. "He is around, though."

Kimie nodded. Something about him, and the music, made her feel safe. Her tiredness grew, and as her mind drifted and reality blurred, she wondered if this whole thing was a dream, and after the day she'd had she didn't blame her head for acting out. Nevertheless, she desperately wanted to ask for a phone, but the music was sending her headfirst into zonk central.

Orion spoke just as soothingly. "I have a feeling that the Boss has a great deal in store for you. This is your journey, and it's not towards me, or this inn."

His words rang true, yet Kimie remained stubbornly defiant.

"You make a lotta sense," she said, "but I still think this is dodgy as …"

Her insult trailed away as her head rolled to the side and into sleep's soft embrace. She struggled one last time against it, but her attempt was futile and she drifted into oblivion.

Kimie's eyes flickered open.

The smell of the dying fireplace was the first thing she noticed. The cushions beneath her felt comfortable, along with the warm, heavy blankets she was curled under. She snuggled into them, feeling more relaxed than in ages.

She savoured the moment until an awkward feeling hit her. She knew she should be somewhere else, *doing* something else, only she couldn't think what. Her thoughts churned. How did she get here? In fact, just where *was* here?

She sat up, finding herself on the couch where that Orion guy had left her. The place was now empty. No people, no dancing, just the shadows from the fire's fading glow. Still, she was grateful for the blankets, the warmth and a place to rest.

Her gaze moved to the window. Orion stood before it, staring out into the silence of the night where the city remained as stagnant as ever. The clock tower was in sight, telling her it was almost midnight.

"The sleeper awakes," he murmured.

Kimie blinked. "You must have eyes in the back of your head."

"I'm all eyes actually," he responded. "Insight's a wonderful thing." He turned away from the window and moved past her. "Sometimes it's better than looking out."

He sat on the couch opposite.

"Thanks for being so nice," Kimie said, indicating the blankets over her. "I was sure you were going to screw me over."

"You're welcome," he answered. "Are you hungry?"

"Starving."

"What would you like?"

"Some chips'd be great."

"Princeton!" he called.

The waiter she'd met earlier called back from the kitchen, "Yes, sir?"

"Fetch this young lass a bowl of chips, would you?"

"Right away, sir."

Kimie eyed Orion suspiciously. "If you are a con then you're damn good at it. If I even thought you were screwing me over you'd have two black eyes and be hobbling by now."

"I believe you," he replied.

She turned, looking outside to the clock again. "Bit early for closing time, isn't it? Shouldn't this place be partying all night?"

His gaze darkened. "New regulations. The cost for staying open has blown out to far more than we can afford. Our energy levels are falling."

"Chips, miss," said Princeton, carrying in a bowl from the kitchen. "Some were left in the oven."

Kimie found their smell intoxicating. "Thanks." She took the bowl, delved straight into them and her face lit up. They were the best she'd ever tasted. "Oh, this is so good!" she said around a mouthful. "So, so good! Mmm, god! Best chips *ever*, Orie!"

"It's Orion," he corrected, "and you'll do well to remember that."

Princeton looked at Orion, who nodded discreetly at him. The waiter moved quietly away.

"Hey, don't chuck a sad," Kimie said, still with her mouthful. "I'm grateful … Orion. Thanks for letting me crash on the couch too. Appreciate it."

He nodded again. "Eat up. You've had a rough trot lately, I see."

She took another mouthful, devoured it hungrily, then wiped her lips with a napkin from the coffee table. "So, you got a vacancy for a waitress? I'd love to help out if the food's this good."

"That's not an option," he told her. "Things are growing worse, I'm afraid."

She frowned as vague memories surfaced. She didn't know where they came from, only that she found herself saying, "It's like that everywhere. Mum's struggling with house prices going up. Cost of living's going through the roof too. So many of my friends' parents have been laid off. What we need is someone to stand up to the nutcases up top and tell 'em where to go." She put a hand to her head. "Whoa! That's weird."

She'd no idea why she'd said all that, but knew it was true.

"You're right," Orion agreed. "Here, we refer to the System's financial sector as the EconoMe, because it's so self-centred. It's not as inclusive as our Village that preceded it."

Kimie munched on her chips. "Small is better in some ways. Less politics, but then less help with day-to-day stuff too. Can't win."

He spoke carefully, like he didn't want to reveal too much. "Our Village did very well for a time. That was our home until the City expanded and swamped it."

"So your inn's all that's left since those corporate psychos took over?"

"Alas, yes. The Village was special. You could say it was a Nexus point. More than that, it was part of …" He paused, then spoke cautiously, wary of her reaction. "A Vine."

Kimie almost laughed. "Are you for real?"

"That's the problem with the System," he said. "There's too much information. Everyone seems to know everything and nothing. Sometimes it can even lead," his voice lowered, "to insanity."

"Yeah, with the way you're talking," she scoffed. Inwardly though, he was freaking her out.

"In any case," he continued, "the System has grown, blocking our Vine's path and cutting us off from the natural world, leaving us confined to the City."

Now Kimie was convinced she was caught up in a cult. She felt the urge to get up and bolt, only the chips were telling her otherwise, along with the cushions beneath her and Orion's presence too.

He leaned forward. "I don't expect you to believe me. You're already disturbed enough by my words, aren't you?"

Kimie shifted uncomfortably. "A little."

"That's understandable. I'll let you know upfront that I don't intend to keep you here. You can't stay for long anyway. The InnerCent's soon to become the victim of an economic takeover."

Kimie tensed. "So what? You want to recruit me as your terrorist just so you can keep your business open, is that it? Is that why your fishing guy sent me here?"

Orion remained calm. "Yes, he's more than just a fisherman. He's a Sentry, like I am. He does his job well by keeping watch for newcomers and sending them to us."

She fumed inwardly. Even though she couldn't recall much of her life before entering the City, she felt no desire to go home in a hurry. She didn't want to fight the law in this dodgy psychoverse either but vowed not to be screwed over by anyone. She opened her mouth to give him a right serve, but he cut in quickly.

"I can see how it looks, lass, and I understand your suspicions. You weren't prepared before entering the System and should have been briefed prior to your arrival. It seems your recruitment didn't go as planned."

Kimie was stunned. This guy was sounding crazier by the second, but also stirring up memories she couldn't see clearly. Still, she decided to give him the benefit of the doubt. For the moment anyway.

"You're not the first girl this has happened to—" he began.

Kimie tensed again. "Lots of 'em came before me, then?"

He stayed infuriatingly calm. "Only one. A very special girl." His face filled with sadness at the memory. "She was much younger than you when she arrived in our Village, just as the trouble with the City began. When the System took over, decimating our home, she led the fight against it."

Kimie almost laughed. "A kid? Leading a battle against billion-dollar thugs? No wonder she's not around anymore. What'd she do? Run at 'em with a slingshot?"

"She used her brains," he answered. "Sabotaging equipment with only the simplest tools was her forte. Her youth gave her the advantage of being overlooked as a threat, initially."

"She'd have been a little ratbag in class. Bet you were glad she was on your side, huh?"

"Indeed we were, lass. Her deviousness could outsmart any team of corporate planners and, for a while, that's what she did. While others fought openly against the System, she sneaked around behind the scenes, bringing a child's spirit into the fight for a better tomorrow. Ultimately though, the System grew too powerful and discovered her."

Kimie listened intently. Even though this whole conversation was nuts, and she was sure she was being baited for terrorist recruitment, she went with it and asked, "What happened to her?"

"Nobody knows," came the reply. "She won quite a victory in the end. Not enough to stop the City's expansion, just sufficient to cause a major setback. Our celebrations had barely begun when she suddenly vanished. It was exactly six months ago, System time. The time she spent with us before that was much longer."

Kimie was confused. "What's System time? Is it different to normal time?"

"No one argues with the System," he told her. "It's adjusted things considerably since taking control, and yes, that includes time, which has slowed down even more since our young friend left."

"Maybe she found a way out," Kimie speculated. Her hopes rose at the prospect of finding a quick exit from crazyland. "Where was she last seen?"

"The EpiCentre," he revealed. "An underground club a few streets away. She was seen running from its office."

"An underground club?" Kimie asked in disbelief. "What's an under-age kid doing in a club?"

"The EpiCentre welcomes all who resist the System, lass. That's what makes it illegal. It's best not to judge it without seeing what lies below the surface. I imagine you've wished people would do the same with you at times. Am I right?"

Kimie made a face at the hazy memory of a classroom.

"The true purpose of the EpiCentre," he continued, "is to keep our Village's spirit alive. Only a handful of clubs remain hidden from the System now. They'll fall if we don't stay alert, just like this inn's about to."

Kimie wasn't swayed by his argument. "I get that these clubs would have to be underground if the System's so bad here but I swear, you guys are a cult."

"Think what you will," Orion said. "We're the last line of open resistance. We won't be for much longer. Someone's got to make a stand, and it takes the focus off our allies doing the groundwork, or in their case, the underground work."

"Yeah, wait till the cops find out about this setup …"

"There are no police here."

Kimie's eyes nearly popped out of her head. "What? You're kidding me, right?"

"There's only an empty police station," he revealed. "It's the same with the hospital and firehouse. The City doesn't employ any emergency service personnel. Everything's unified under one System that's supposed to take care of us all. It's done that by making severe cutbacks for the so-called good of its economic growth. You saw how barren the streets were. They're almost mechanised. Only those who the System deems worthy are allowed in. Everyone else has either been assimilated as its prisoners, or forced to leave, keeping the City's people to a minimum. That's what makes it economically viable."

"Surely there'd have to be some phones around?" Kimie pressed.

"None," he replied. "The City's law is that if we can't talk to it, then we shouldn't be talking at all. No technology's allowed, except what the System provides. Tech-wise, there's only our illegal *battlelines* to assist us now."

Kimie was astounded. "What is this? A Nazi hellhole?"

"It may as well be," came the reply. "Bluey thought so right from the start."

"Hang on, Bluey? Who's she?"

"The girl I was telling you about," he reminded her. "That's what she called herself when she arrived, apparently after a dog she once had. She carried its leash around for luck, and used to lay all sorts of traps with it too." His face fell. "The unity of the resistance crumbled when she disappeared, while barriers were set up around our Village to stop us returning. Now the resistance has formed into factions to fight against the System, which devours anyone who tries to change it. Anyone who doesn't join a faction is kept as a slave in economic subservience. These factions work together at times, but are also bound by loyalties to their superiors."

"What about the children here?" Kimie wondered.

He paused. "Bluey vanished and the rest were forced underground. Literally."

"You mean they're dead?"

"Far from it. They've shifted to the only place where they can survive. It's another form of downsizing."

Kimie wanted to question this. He continued before she could do so.

"Bluey was an outsider, like you, who nobody knew much about, yet her passion united all resistance factions. Her origins were somewhat obscure, giving her an advantage. That same advantage applies to you."

Kimie put her empty plate down. "Nice story, but I don't buy it. Any of it. All I know is that I'm in trouble and I need a phone to call the cops and get help. I'm sorry for you, really, but this, all of this …" she indicated the surroundings, "is not my problem. I've got enough to deal with and I'm not gonna dig myself any deeper into this schizo delusion, you got that? Seriously? Have you got that?"

Orion nodded. "Yes. Completely."

Kimie nodded back. "Thank you."

He paused thoughtfully. "Despite your reluctance to assist me, I'd still like to help you. Alas, my options are somewhat limited, and you'd be much safer in the club I've spoken of. The EpiCentre. Luckily for you, a resistance faction's provided us with valuable information as to the Hookers current whereabouts. Not only that, they've also ensured that part of the City's surveillance network's still down. I can give you a path to the EpiCentre to get you there safely."

Kimie could only think of getting to a phone, or the police, whichever came first. Even though this crackpot sounded convincing, she didn't believe a word. She couldn't. This was all too weird, totally nuts, and she didn't get what he wanted from her either. She only knew that she needed sanity as fast as possible.

She looked out the window again, to the clock outside. Strangely, the time hadn't changed.

"Thing must be busted," she murmured.

"No," he countered. "It's correct. As I told you, we're on System time."

She shook her head, confused. "The sooner I get out of this mental ward, the better, if you don't have a problem with that?"

"*I* certainly don't."

She was unsure about his tone. He seemed way too sure that she wouldn't leave.

"Sorry I can't help," she said, "but I really, *really*, want this to be over."

"So do I," he replied. "More than you think."

Kimie shivered, not liking any of this, and watched the fire dim slowly beside them.

Chapter Three

The night had grown colder.

Kimie walked away from the inn and into the moonlit street. Nothing had changed and there were still no signs of activity. No cars, trains or buses were around, no cafés or shops were open and, strangest of all, there were no people. The place looked perfect, but dead. Completely and utterly dead. Then again, she concluded, everything about it was out-of-the-ballpark nuts.

She headed into the night, going in the direction of the EpiCentre, and keeping a lookout for anyone else. She turned a corner, made her way down the street, and caught sight of a building. A police station.

"Thank friggin' god!"

She ran up the steps and pulled on the door.

Locked.

The lights were off too.

She pulled the door again in frustration, then banged loudly. "Hey! Let me in!" She banged harder. "Open up!"

No response.

She rattled it a few more times.

"What kind of crap is this? Get out here!"

She gave another bang.

Still nothing.

She kicked the door irritably and ran down the steps onto the street, looking for a brick to throw at the window, but there was nothing around. Everything was spotless.

"Healthy economy, no humanity," she muttered. "Typical!"

Orion's words returned to her. "*There are no police here.*"

She shivered.

What if he's right? she thought. *What if he's telling the truth? What if...?*

The roar of a car engine jolted her back to reality, or whatever the hell this was. It was the same car she'd heard earlier. Closer this time, which also made it louder. Violently so. It would have attracted the attention of the police if this were a normal city, yet there were no sounds of anyone chasing it, which messed with her head even more.

A figure stepped out from an alleyway.

They were her height and wearing a hood. Their head rose and she caught a glimpse of their face in the dim glow of a streetlamp. It belonged to a youth, a few years younger than herself, whose eyes widened at the sight of her.

Before she could say anything, he bolted.

"Like hell!" she cried, running after him.

Fuelled by desperate energy to prove that Orion was totally wrong about absolutely everything, she picked up speed, caught up with the youth, whirled him around and threw him against the wall so that he faced it, cop style on her part.

"Nuh-uh!" she said fiercely. "I want answers!"

"Okay, okay!" he said back quickly. "Enough already! I'll spill!"

"Damn right you will!" she snapped. "What's the deal with this place? No, don't answer that. Where's your phone?"

He paused, then spoke in realisation. "You're not a Hooker!"

Kimie turned him to face her, pushing him up against the wall. "I have had a *really* bad day. Seriously bad, okay? I don't know what's going on, I don't *care* what's going on, and everyone around here seems to be on drugs, or maybe it's me who's gone nuts. You want to throw insults, fine, I'll rip your funnies off later. I just need ... a phone. Have you got one? Say yes."

The kid looked at her curiously. "You *are* new here, aren't you?"

"Yeah, and you're getting old fast," Kimie retorted.

The kid shuddered. "I knew I shouldn't have come out tonight." He swallowed hard. "I don't have a phone. No one here has. They're banned."

Kimie frowned in disbelief and thought of her conversation with Orion.

"Surely there'd have to be some phones around?"

"None. The City's law is that if we can't talk to it, then we shouldn't be talking at all. No technology's allowed, except what the System provides. Tech-wise, there's only our illegal battlelines to assist us now."

"Oh no," she whispered in horror. "No, no, no! He can't be right. No way …"

"Who?" the kid wondered.

She stared at him aghast, searching his gaze for something, anything, to give her some logical answers in this crazy nuthouse of a world. "So you're saying that phones really are banned? In a city like this? Are you seriously kidding me?"

"You think I'm dumb enough to be out here for the hell of it?" he countered. "It's only 'cause the EpiCentre's hacked into the City's surveillance systems and a whole stack of us can get to the club and—"

Kimie thumped her fist against the wall and turned away. "Oh my god, you're one of them."

"One of who?" he wondered.

"Maybe it really is me," she continued. "Maybe I am lost in an inner-meltdown nightmare. I so want to wake up right now." She ran a hand through her hair, then pulled herself together, trying to recall her life before the City. All that came up were god-awful feelings. "Or do I? Maybe I should just go with all this instead of running around like a mad dog getting a moontan." She inhaled sharply and did her best to gain some perspective. "Guess I've got no choice if the EpiCentre's the only place with people around, apart from the inn-crowd."

The lone car's engine revved again, this time from a street nearby.

"Better than going after that thing anyway," she said. "What is that?"

The kid opened his mouth to speak.

"No, don't tell me," she cut in. "I just want a phone to get out of here." She clasped his shoulder with one hand and pointed at him with the other.

"*You* are taking me to the EpiCentre, got it?"

He gazed at her in awe. "Is this a date?"

She smacked his shoulder angrily. "No, it's not a date! Of course it's not a date! I'd like nothing better than to get away from you and go back to my own problems but I can't do that 'cause this place is so mental! God, what are you, twelve?"

"Yes."

She blinked. "Oh, right." A thought struck her. "Hang on, aren't the kids here meant to be underground or something? Or are you part of a different resistance faction or whatever they're called?"

"I'm just out of the house for the first time in ages," he replied.

"Yeah, I can tell," she retorted. "The EpiCentre's not far from here, right?"

"Three blocks down," he told her. "We better move fast. The streets aren't safe." He started to go, then stopped. "But you better not be working for the City."

"Why would I work for this psycho ward?" Kimie cried, throwing an arm up. "There's no people!"

"Keep your voice down!" he hissed.

"Why?" she shot back. "What's everyone so afraid of?" She brushed him off. "No, this is garbage. I'm getting a phone, getting help and leaving this dump. Understand?"

"It's not me who doesn't understand!"

"Move!"

She grabbed his arm, pushing him along to an alleyway. They headed through, reached the end, and she asked him which turn to take. He pointed, and they made their way down another alleyway before approaching a door.

"This it?" Kimie asked.

He nodded.

"Get us in," she ordered.

He raised his hand and knocked three times.

Nothing happened.

"Wrong place?" Kimie wondered.

She looked back, then jumped at the sight of two figures wearing skeleton masks.

"Oh sh—!" she began, but was cut off as one pushed her up against the wall. The other pulled out a metal device, scanned her and the kid, then nodded.

"They're clean," he reported.

The first, also male, spoke. "Doesn't mean they're not City agents."

A voice came through their earpieces that Kimie heard loud and clear. *"They're not. We've just got word from the Orion Sentry. She's legit. So's he."*

"Understood," First Skeleman said.

Kimie scowled bitterly. "Yeah, but if you can track me, what makes you think others can't, ya walking boner?"

"Experience," Second Skeleman replied. "We've been monitoring you since you entered the City. You might be a newcomer, but if you're good with the Orion Sentry, you're good with us."

"What am I, a football to be passed around by a bunch of tossers?" Kimie snapped. "I want to go home!"

"First you need to go downtown."

"You mean there really are cops here or are you just shaking my—"

He kicked the wall. A hum came from below them, a hatch opened and Kimie cried out as they dropped a few metres. The Skelemen landed on their feet while Kimie and the kid crashed in a heap.

"Get off me, ya perv," she grumbled, kicking him away.

The hatch above closed, locking in place.

Faint synthesised music came from up ahead.

"This way," First Skeleman said, walking into a thin corridor.

With no other choice, Kimie and the kid rose and went with him. The walls narrowed as they walked along, forming a tight squeeze.

"Talk about getting out of your comfort zone," Kimie muttered, straightening up as much as possible.

"It's designed to stop anyone from entering too quickly," Second Skeleman explained. "We also need a warning if we're about to be busted."

"Oh great, drug central," Kimie scoffed. "Doesn't matter, I already feel totally out of it."

The music grew louder and the corridor widened as they approached a door. They moved in, an overhead sensor scanned them and the door slid to the side.

A strobe light hit Kimie in the face, along with a blast of electronic music. The light passed her and her eyes adjusted, widening at the sight of a dance floor where a mass of people stood. Her first instinct was to dive right in and party with the best of them while thanking god that all her prayers had been answered at last, yet she sensed a dark undercurrent too. Yes, this place had the appearance of a club and yes, people had drinks in their hands, but no one was dancing or partying. They were deadly serious and talking intensely.

At least there was a bar, and that meant a phone, but it was the man behind the bar who caught her attention more than anything. Her face lit up at the sight of him and she gazed across the room, breathtaken. He was good-looking. More than that: god-like, prime-hunk meat with irresistible tenderloins. He might be about five years older than her, but god, he looked like something hot off the internet. She found herself swooning as if nothing existed but him, and she watched, completely blown away, as he turned to a bunch of women at the end of the bar and began serving them.

Forgetting herself and the Skelemen behind her, she headed straight for the bar. She was almost there when a voice called over the music, "Ha! You got stung!"

Kimie stopped and saw who'd spoken. A blonde girl, slightly older than herself, holding a drink.

"Excuse me?" Kimie called back.

"We call him the Dragonfly!" the girl said loudly. "He stings girls' hearts!" Her face fell. "Only our hearts, sadly. Nothing else."

Kimie stared at him in wonder. "He taken?"

"Yeah!" the girl answered. "By me and every other girl round here! You got no chance, babe!"

"That sucks!" The reality of the club hit her. "This whole thing sucks! What is this? A rebel base or a party?"

"Both," the girl told her. "The music drowns out any bugs if we've been infiltrated, tech-wise. Funky wavelengths distort enemy signals."

"Let me guess, no phones," Kimie concluded.

The girl nodded. "That's right, newbie, no phones. We're not sure who we can trust nowadays, but you must be alright if they let you in." She sipped her drink. "The City's wavelength's the only form of digital communication up top. We call it the Freakquency. Emphasis on the *freak*!"

Kimie raised a hand to her forehead, feeling dizzy. The club's pulsating rhythms were making her head swirl. She went to the empty end of the bar, steadying herself on it.

"You okay?" the girl asked, following her.

"Yeah," Kimie replied, blinking as the world returned to focus.

"Dragonfly hit you that bad, huh?"

"That too."

"You need a drink. I'll see if I can get you one. I'm more than happy to, with him up there."

"I thought you said this was a rebel base."

"Sure is," the girl confirmed. "That's why we're partying as well as plotting. Back soon!" She moved to join the mass of other girls who were eyeing off the Dragonfly as he served their drinks.

Kimie wanted to go with her but knew she'd be lost in a crowd of strong competition if she did. She watched a couple of people go by and, as expected after this crappy day, no one was carrying a phone, nor was there one in sight. Surely in a club like this someone would be texting or taking pictures, she thought.

"Hey, Glow Worm!"

She looked up and nearly fainted. Facing her, from behind the bar, was the Dragonfly. He'd left several fuming girls to come over and talk to her. Now they were giving her death glares. Kimie ignored them and gazed at him in awe. Everything about him was perfect, from his looks to his aroma to his hair.

She shuddered. "Oh my god!"

"Not quite, but I'm working on it," he said smoothly. "Haven't seen you in here before. You're new, right?"

Her heart pounded. He had all the charm of Hollywood, and she couldn't think of what to say.

"Can see you got spark," he continued. "It's why I called you Glow Worm. How 'bout we stick with it. What do you say?"

Kimie found herself beaming.

He grinned back. "There you go, glowing away again." He poured a drink, handed it to a girl and said to Kimie, "So what do you think of our little hidey-hole here?"

"I love it!" Kimie blurted, getting even greater glares from the girls at the end of the bar.

"You should see us on a good day," he replied. "How long have you been in the City?"

"Forever," she answered automatically, then shook her head and focussed. "I'm told there are no phones here. I'm hoping you can change that."

"You mean a hotline? Right here, babe."

Kimie smirked. "No, I'm serious. I really need one."

"We have a lot of things," he told her, "but a phone to anything that's not the City ain't one of 'em. That's still a work in progress."

Kimie indicated the nearby girls with a nod. "Some things are working on you too. Or at least trying to."

"More so than you think," he said, indicating Kimie herself. "Goes with the job. I, however, prefer quality over quantity."

Kimie blushed, for the first time in her life. "And you think that's me, huh?"

"Maybe if you were a little older," he said, moving back. "Glad you came, though."

"Didn't have a choice!" Kimie snapped, angry that she was losing him. "I'm new here and the other place I was at didn't have a phone either. From what I heard there was a kid called Bluey who hung out in this dump and was last seen running from it. What happened? You brush her off too?"

His face hardened. Even like that, Kimie realised, he was still irresistible, and it took effort to keep her feelings in check.

"You are new," he confirmed, "and you know way more than you should. You found our club, you're filled in on Bluey, and that makes me edgy. Your glow's dimming."

"Believe me, man, you're starting to look like total crap right now and what I really want, more than anything, is to ditch this place! If you've got a phone, I can get out of your botoxed face, okay?"

"Sorry," he said, as infuriatingly cool as ever. "No phones."

Kimie glanced at the nearby girls. A few were smirking that she was getting the brush-off.

She scowled at him. "I bet that Bluey kid was over everything too. No wonder she split. See ya round!"

She smacked her hand on the bar, turned away and stormed off.

The girl she'd spoken to earlier hurried over, grabbed her arm and stared at her open-mouthed. "Did you just sting the Dragonfly right back?"

Kimie realised what she'd done and shifted awkwardly.

"Guess so," she mumbled. "He looking over?"

"No," the girl replied. "He's got plenty of distractions."

Kimie's fists clenched tightly. "I'm gonna bust his face!"

She started to turn but the girl stopped her. "Forget it. He's got plenty of eye candy at the end of the bra."

"You mean bar?"

"Not with what's down there. Or padding it up, rather. What'd you say to him?"

"Only wanted a phone," Kimie said. "He went nuts when I brought up Bluey."

The girl's face dropped. "Uh … yeah."

"What is it?" Kimie asked. "He have a thing for her?"

"What, are you kidding?" the girl scoffed. "Look at his age. She was only twelve and he's got enough competition from dial-a-bimbo over there, but they're nothing compared to Bluey. We all loved her. The kid stood out. She had a really great vibe."

"So where's she now?"

"Don't know," the girl answered. "Last I heard she was running out of here for her hideaway about eight blocks up. A place in the streets that kept her down to earth, or so she said. She had a lot of knick-knacks there, like her trademark dog leash she used to help her out of scraps. That little hidey-hole was her safe haven after the Village went out of bounds for everyone." She frowned. "We never saw her again after she split from here. A few of us tried to get to her hideaway to look around but it wasn't easy, not with all those extra patrols in the area. The place was turned into a junkyard after that. We've never got near it since."

Kimie sighed wearily. "Hope she found a magic portal that'll get me home. That'd be the best thing."

"Yeah, for us too," came the reply. "Then we wouldn't need an attack plan for later tonight."

Kimie was taken aback. "For what? To take down the City?"

"If only," the girl said. "Nah, we just wanna knock it around a bit so we can grab some stuff for our buddies back at the big base."

Kimie blinked in disbelief. "What base? The one in the forest? Your old village or whatever?"

"You really are new here, aren't you?" the girl pressed.

"I wish I wasn't here at all."

"We're all wishing that. About ourselves I mean. No, the Village is a no-go area that's shut up tightly and no one can get to now."

"What sort of attack have you got planned?" Kimie asked. "Cyber?"

"No," came the flat-out response. "Real one."

Kimie grimaced. "So what? You're gonna hit them with your …" she indicated the surroundings, "… club?"

"Got it in one."

"Then count me out," Kimie said firmly. "I don't want to take part in a hippie rebel protest that's gonna get ugly."

"We're not gonna sit back and let it get any uglier," the girl told her. "We need—"

A deafening siren blared around them, killing the music, and a voice echoed over the PA system. A Skeleman's, Kimie realised.

"Perimeter breach! We fff—!"

He was cut off by a sickening squelch. More screams erupted, this time from partygoers, who ran for the rear door, opposite the one Kimie had entered. They'd barely made it when it swung open to reveal a silhouetted figure in the shadows.

The girl next to Kimie turned as white as a sheet.

Another figure entered through the club's main door. Kimie recalled the cramped corridor on its other side and murmured, "How'd they get in so fast?"

The girl spoke shakily. "Club's been sold out and not in a good way." She swallowed hard. "This your work, golden girl?"

"I've been asking for a phone since I got here so think about it, genius."

"They could have seen you on the street and followed you here, *genius*."

"Uh, yeah, there is that," Kimie mumbled.

The two newcomers strode in from opposite directions. Kimie expected them to be ugly monsters by the way people were reacting. Instead, she saw two of the most beautiful women she'd ever seen in her life. They were over seven feet tall and flawless. One had long blonde hair and a red dress, while the other was a brunette in black, but apart from their clothes and hair, they were identical.

They came together in the middle of the floor and stopped.

A man turned and ran.

The blonde woman's arm snapped up, a metal line blurred from her palm and rammed savagely into his back. Kimie's stomach heaved and she went green, even more so when a long spike in the middle of a four-pronged hook burst up through his rib cage, pulling him backwards and casting him against the wall like a rag doll.

Kimie shuddered. Murder! That was cold-blooded murder! The woman was a damn robot! She had to be! This was too weird! Way beyond weird! Now, Kimie figured, her brain had shot light-years past insane, and she could only watch as the line, and the hook, retracted smoothly into the blonde woman's palm, vanishing into a small slot.

"Oh!" Kimie suddenly realised. "So that's why they call 'em Hookers!"

A chill went through her as reality hit home. Everything Orion had said, everything that everyone had told her since entering the City, everything that she'd so casually dismissed because this place seemed full of terrorist lunatics, was true. All of it. This was no pack of cult-crazed psychos. This was real. Unless she was somewhere god-awful in the real world dreaming it all up, of course, and she seriously doubted that. Things were so intense that she could physically feel every sensation, painful or otherwise, meaning that she really was in a crazy asylum dimension where the bad guys were in control. Either she'd ended up here by a freak accident or someone had dumped her right in it.

The arrival of a third woman caught her attention, along with everybody else's. The crowd watched in stunned silence as the newcomer emerged from the entrance that Kimie had come through. Proudly, they strode onto the floor to be illuminated by the strobe lights. This woman was taller than the others, and had flaming red hair that trailed past her flawless features, onto a dark dress.

Kimie heard the girl beside her whisper, "Now we're screwed."

"Who is she?" she whispered back.

The girl's voice was shaky. "Barbie Q. The Moneyarch's head InnSinerator." She indicated the Hooker's smile at the blood on her subordinate's hand, left by the hook. "And I think she's just been turned on!"

The blonde and the brunette clicked their necks to one side.

People bolted.

Kimie dived over the bar, falling behind it as two hooks zipped past her, hitting the glasses on the shelves and then retracting. She peered around the side of the bar, grimacing as the hooks shot out again, mashing two people together. Both were thrown at the red-headed woman who raised her arm, decapitating them in a single swoop.

The blonde and brunette leapt into the crowd, flowing with the music in a deadly dance. Hideous screams ignited as their hooks ripped into several people, severing heads, limbs and other body parts while the rest of the crowd fled in a stampede.

The brunette retracted her hook and punched another head clean off a woman. Kimie rose to run, then ducked behind the bar as that head flew over her, hitting the bottles on the shelf. She peeked up cautiously to see the blonde Hooker grab a man, crush him, discard him, and fire a hook through another man's neck.

Kimie felt sick to her stomach as the Hookers cut down people ruthlessly amid the multitude of colours from the strobe lights. She saw a speaker on the stage by the brunette, along with a microphone on a stand, probably there to keep up appearances, she guessed. Unless they were for something else, like …

"A weapon," she whispered, as a memory hit her. Somehow, through the insanity of hell's vomit around her, she recalled what she'd seen a feral runt of a kid do in a shopping centre once. She didn't know how he'd done it, she just had to copy him as best she could and take a chance.

She ran out from behind the bar and raced for the stage, just as a click came from the brunette's arm. Kimie took a flying leap, dodging the soaring hook over her head and knocking the microphone stand over in midflight. She crashed in front of the speaker, right on target, and the microphone landed before her. A piercing resonance burst over the surroundings and the crowd screamed, covering their ears.

The Hookers, however, staggered backwards, jerking up and down as if in a macabre dance.

"Dance to that!" Kimie hissed over the noise. "Ya disc-ho queens!"

The pitch increased, becoming unbearable.

With no choice other than to save her ears from exploding, Kimie pushed the microphone away from the speaker. The noise ceased abruptly and all three Hookers suddenly flopped over, their arms dangling in front of them. She knew they wouldn't be down for long. Their bodies were twitching, and making loud mechanical whirrs, like they were charging up.

Kimie sat up sorely, rubbing her shoulder. "Talk about a leap of faith."

Silence followed, then panic erupted and the stampede ignited once more.

Frustration welled within her. Not just towards the Hookers, but for everything here. She rose angrily, went to a wall, ripped off a fire extinguisher and stormed at the Hookers, ready to bash their heads in.

"Uh-uh!" someone said, stepping in and stopping her.

The Dragonfly.

Even in this madness he still made her knees weak, and for a moment she forgot she was holding the extinguisher.

"Their alloy's hardcore," he explained. "Bashing 'em won't do any good. Good trick with the microphone though. We were going to do a similar thing tonight on a wider scale up top. Looks like you taught us something new."

Kimie's heart jumped.

"Doubt it'll work a second time," he finished. "They adapt quickly."

He grabbed her free hand. His touch was warm. Exciting too. Almost tingling. Her whole body felt like jelly as she dropped the extinguisher, letting it clank to the floor.

The whirring grew from the Hookers as they slowly rose.

Kimie sensed people rushing by, then was smacked from the Dragonfly's grasp and wrenched away. She swore as she became disorientated, and when she regained her senses there was no sign of him, only a final group of youths fleeing from the Hookers.

She made for the rear door, ran through it freely and headed down a passageway before bursting into an alleyway. She rounded a corner and heard a Hooker's laugh from the club behind her.

They were back online.

She ran across the street, into another alleyway. When she reached the end, a whooshing sound came from the sky, like something mechanical was flying overhead. It had barely faded when footsteps rose nearby. She whirled around to see the girl she'd spoken to in the club running past.

Kimie moved to follow but the girl turned, pointing at her.

"No! You stay away from me! Stay the hell away!"

"That wasn't my fault!" Kimie snapped back. "And I just saved your butt in there!"

"Don't trust you," the girl said tearfully. "Get lost. I mean it!"

She ran into the night.

Kimie was about to call out after her when a searchlight, from high up, swept over the alley. She fell against the wall, evading it, before hurrying away and running for a while until the chaos behind her dissipated.

Silence returned, then anger got the better of her and she kicked a spotless drainpipe, feeling completely and utterly screwed. The whole damn world was out to get her and nobody, absolutely nobody, could be trusted. Right now she was fully prepared to leave this craphole by walking home, even if she didn't know the way.

She slumped against the wall, sliding to the ground in defeat and mumbling, "At least things can't get any worse."

A can clattered to the ground from the top of a stairway.

She looked up with a start. A figure stood in the darkness above her.

She rose slowly, holding her breath, then inched along the wall as the shadows shifted around her. Bit by bit, she made her way to the corner of the alley. She'd almost reached the end when a hand stretched out, tapping her shoulder lightly.

She yelped and lurched forward. A snap followed, a rope net engulfed her, and she found herself being scooped up, before coming to a jolting stop. She struggled in the net, twisting in a tangled heap, then heard a cry as a dozen or so kids leapt out of the shadows, brandishing crude weapons made of street junk. They were her age, dressed in rags, and looking like they hadn't washed in ages.

"Oh, you bastard!" Kimie sighed, swearing at life in general as they gathered below. "You complete and utter bastard!"

Chapter Four

The kids' faces were stained with dirt. Their hair, even more disgusting, as they held crudely made weapons. There were baseball bats with protruding nails, sharp-edged chains, and broken bottles with spikes sticking out from their middle like primitive swords.

A bat jabbed at her. She pulled her hand back as snickers rose. Another prodded her side, making her flinch.

"See the roofer jump!" a boy mocked, in a voice that had barely broken. "Jump, roofer, jump again!"

The bat jabbed harder.

A bottle flew in, rebounding off the net.

"Enough already!" Kimie snapped.

"So feisty!" a girl hissed.

"Razor pain and be done with it!" a boy scowled.

The rest of them closed in. "Razor pain, razor pain!"

Kimie cringed and made eye contact with a girl slightly younger than herself. The girl peered at her curiously, then suddenly ran in, leapt onto the net and hung from it, pressing her face close to Kimie's.

Kimie flinched and had to stop herself from gagging. The girl stank of dirt, grime and god knew what else, yet Kimie also felt an affinity with her. The girl had been struggling for a long time, and no doubt believed that the whole world was against her too.

The girl dropped from the net and faced her people. "This one is an innocent. A newborn."

A boy stepped in. "You are certain?"

"I am," came the reply. "She has much fear in her."

"Oi!" Kimie snapped.

"Anger too," another kid said. "No matter! She has passed our Into-Net security system. Release her!"

Kimie felt the net slacken and yelped as she dropped to the ground. She'd barely regained her senses when the kids ran in, pulled the net away and hoisted her up.

She grimaced. "Get off me, ya rodents!"

"Only the boys," a boy corrected. "We're Sewer Rats. Girls are Alley Cats."

"Oh, great, street kids."

"More than that," the boy continued. "We have found a way of living apart from the System. We are now natives who worship at altars the System refuses to believe in, making us, Altar-Natives."

Kimie recalled her talk with Orion.

"Bluey disappeared," he'd said, *"and the rest were forced underground. Literally."*

"You mean they're dead?" she'd asked.

"Far from it," he'd replied. *"They've shifted to the only place where they can survive. It's another form of downsizing."*

Now Kimie understood what he'd meant. The kids around here were street trash, apart from the one who'd guided her to the EpiCentre. He really must have been a loner, she figured.

"Come," the girl ordered. "You are expected."

"What—?"

A loud giggle ripped through the night.

Kimie turned to see the silhouettes of Barbie Q and her Hookers rounding the corner.

A boy hissed, ran to a manhole cover, aimed a device and flicked a switch. The cover flew up, attaching itself to the device with a fierce clamp. Only then did Kimie realise that he held a powerful magnet that could be turned on and off.

The girl who'd been on the net with Kimie grabbed her arm and pulled her to the opening. Kimie tried to pull away but the girl wouldn't let go, forcing her along.

The kids ahead of them leapt into the manhole. Kimie felt sick as she jumped in after them, praying that she could take the horrors below.

The rest of the kids entered until only Magnet-Boy was left. He too leapt into the opening, holding the cover over his head, then let go of it upon entry, dropped into the sewers and landed smoothly on his feet. A short way above, the cover fell into place, sealing the hole perfectly.

Kimie groaned and pushed herself up. Things didn't smell quite as bad as she'd expected. Made sense, she thought. In a city with hardly anyone around then of course the sewers would be a whole lot cleaner. What's more, the walls were fluorescent.

She stood up. A patch of slime rubbed off on her hands and she went as green as it was. "Eeew!"

She wiped it on the wall and watched as Magnet-Boy went over to a long chain lying on the ground. One end was attached to a thick handle bolted into the wall. The rest lay in a heap with an open padlock. He picked up the chain, climbed the ladder, reached the magnet under the manhole cover, looped one end of the chain through, then padlocked the two ends together. Just as he finished, the cover shook, like someone above was pulling on it.

He jumped from the ladder, landing before Kimie.

"Into the Labyrinth!" he ordered, running into the tunnel.

Net-Girl ran after him.

Kimie had no choice but to follow. Magnet-Boy vanished rapidly from sight but she managed to keep up with Net-Girl. They turned a corner, then rounded a few more. Surely the tunnels couldn't be this short, Kimie thought. Then again, maybe these rodents had been working hard down here, turning it into a rat's maze. Before she knew it, she was zigzagging everywhere, and utterly disorientated. She was about to call out when Net-Girl suddenly stopped.

Kimie nearly crashed into her.

A rat-like squeak came from ahead.

The girl cupped her hands and squeaked back.

Another squeak came in reply.

"One of our Scouts," Net-Girl told Kimie, and walked along. "This way, while all is well."

Kimie followed her. "Where we going?"

"To our Queen," came the answer.

Kimie struggled to comprehend this. "You mean, queen of the sewers?"

"Yes."

"Sounds fantastic."

"Do not mock her," the girl warned. "She holds great power."

Kimie was baffled.

Net-Girl continued. "We have been watching you since you left the Orion Sentry. We saw you enter the EpiCentre and then flee it when the attack began. We were still suspicious of you, which is why we hooked you into our Into-Net security system. Now we know you are a friend. I am Alley-Money."

"Sounds feral."

"I chose it."

"Seriously?"

"Yes. I broke away from the City and now I feel it owes me something like …"

"Alimony!" Kimie realised. "Okay, that makes sense. Hey, if girls are Alley Cats, then Alley Chicks might be a better name." She smirked and said, "Running around the neighbourhood would make you a *chick off the old block*!"

Alley-Money frowned, confused, and led her on through the Labyrinth.

Kimie and Alley-Money came across the occasional Scout, either male or female, who gave them updates. Kimie learnt from them that Barbie Q and her Hookers had also entered the tunnels and that the Scouts were doing their best to keep them occupied. It brought her little comfort.

They soon arrived at a great archway with a cat's head carved into its centre. A Sewer Rat and an Alley Cat were on guard.

The Alley Cat addressed Alley-Money. "Our Queen awaits." She looked sternly at Kimie. "For both of you."

"Bite me," Kimie retorted.

The Alley Cat hissed loudly, baring her teeth.

Kimie recoiled. "Last time I'll ever say that."

"This way," Alley-Money said, leading Kimie along.

The sentry sneered, watching Kimie inch around her, following Alley-Money into the archway.

Kimie found things a touch brighter inside. Several torches hung on the wall, illuminating the many youths who were crouching on the ground, looking up at her suspiciously. A few were eating scraps off dirty plates, while the remains of fish bones were littered nearby.

Kimie grimaced. "Ugh! How can anyone live like this?"

"If the System treats us like animals then that is what we become," Alley-Money explained. "There was no future for us in the sky realm so we descended to the underworld, and into the rule of our Queen."

"Talk about going down the drain," Kimie quipped.

Alley-Money frowned again. "Yes. I was."

"You're just kids," Kimie said. "Where are your parents?"

"Where are yours?" Alley-Money asked back.

"Good point," Kimie agreed, "but I asked first."

"They are old," came the reply. "The City could not afford to keep them and they were downsized."

"Which means what? Killed?"

"They were taken from us," Alley-Money stated. "We never saw them again."

Kimie shivered. "Now I know this place is run by Nazi freaks."

They walked in further, approaching a small brick platform where a figure sat upon a tatty old chair. As they came closer, Kimie saw it was a girl her age. She was dressed in rags with what seemed to be a tiara made of tin over her slimy hair.

Kimie almost burst out laughing at the sight of her but knew better, courtesy of that Alley-Cat's hissy-fit in the archway.

Alley-Money stopped a short way from the girl. Kimie did the same.

The girl spoke. "You may approach."

Kimie had to bite her lip again. It was almost like this girl was play-acting in this loony bin. *Bin* being the operative word.

Alley-Money moved in, with Kimie following.

Alley-Money spoke. "My Queen, I bring you one who has fallen from the sky. She seeks sanctuary from the predators above.”

“Yeah, not quite—” Kimie began.

The girl let out a cat-like hiss.

Kimie froze.

“I really have to stop doing that,” she muttered.

“Here,” the girl said firmly, “you are just another Alley Cat in my sewer. You have no rights.”

Kimie raised her left fist, angry at being told what to do. “Got some good lefts though!”

The girl, this *Queen*, rose to her feet, looming over Kimie from her brick platform. “Your unblemished mouth is in no position to question me. One word and I can fulfil the appetite of the sewers!”

Kimie was about to respond, then decided it was better to shut up.

“However,” the Queen continued, “since you are new to my realm, I will show you leniency. You will learn your place in time.”

Kimie tensed as another vague memory resurfaced. “You sound like my teacher.”

“A wise person indeed,” the Queen replied, “though ultimately you failed to be taught. No matter. We shall rectify that.”

“I’m not staying,” Kimie stated. “I’m just passing through. I’m looking for a way out.”

“You have no right to make demands!”

“And you’ve spent way too long with your head down the drain,” Kimie retorted. “You really better drop this royal crap and start thinking like a human again or you’re not gonna last long.”

A sharp blow struck Kimie across the face.

Kimie’s cheek burnt from the blow and she seethed, “That’s it, bin bag!”

She leapt in, pulling the girl off the platform. The two crashed to the ground, rolling around in the grime as the Queen clawed and tried to bite Kimie. Kimie pounded back, equally fiercely, until two Sewer Rats ran in and pulled her off. She kicked wildly for the Queen’s stomach and missed as she was hoisted away.

The young Queen hissed and stood up, wiping the grime from her mouth, then inhaled sharply and said, “You cannot leave.”

Kimie scowled. "I'd tell you to get stuffed but you already are."

The Queen observed her with a frown, as if contemplating what to say.

"Talk!" Kimie ordered. "Or in your case, squeak."

The Queen spoke curiously. "You are new here."

"Yeah?" Kimie replied. "So what?"

"You will not be allowed to leave," the Queen stated. "Even if you escape my realm, the System will not release you."

"I sort of picked that up when robo-Hookers came in and started *killing everybody*," Kimie pressed. "What I don't get is what that Orion guy, or whatever his name is, was playing at. If everything here's so covert, why send me out into the dead of night to lead the bad guys right to the club and—" She stopped as realisation hit. "Oh, I get it now! I totally get it! That bastard! That total, deadhead, sh—"

"You understand nothing!" the Queen snapped. "A traitor in the Epi-Centre sold it out to the System. We had to ascertain it was not you, hence the Into-Net security system. My subjects have since discovered that a signal was sent from the club to summon the Hookers there *before* you reached it. That much is clear."

Kimie wasn't won over. "So if you hate the System so much, why weren't you helping everyone in the club fight back? Not impressed so far. This is garbage."

The Queen's eyes lit up. "I love garbage!"

"You are garbage …"

"And proud of it. The EpiCentre was much too clean for our liking, and it is unfortunate that many had to die to make it look better. We serve the resistance by scouting the streets. We dare not enter the Orion Sentry's inn, for its powers fade rapidly and our presence there would only drain it further. You, being young and fresh, may have supplied the energy it needed to stay open for slightly longer, but would have only delayed the inevitable. The InnerCent is soon to fall."

Kimie was baffled. "So he turfs me out onto the street right into the thick of it and lets me walk into a bar where the bad guys stroll in and rip it up?"

"He was not to know that the EpiCentre would be attacked," the Queen said sternly. "It has also grown harder for him to get word to us, or else we'd have known of your coming." Her head rose. "He clearly believed you are important. He wanted you away from his inn to meet with the resistance factions, either above or below ground, and to fight rather than hide."

"Which isn't exactly what you're doing," Kimie pointed out.

The Queen stepped in close to her. "We are warriors. Do you wish to put that to the test?"

Kimie relented. "So what am I s'posed to do? If I can't go home do I cover my face in dirt and slum it with you guys?" She sighed. "I don't know what I'm meant to be doing. I don't think I have for the past couple of years from what I can remember but, hey, welcome to my life."

The Queen peered at her curiously. "You have fire in your heart, like another girl I once knew."

Kimie recalled her conversation with the Orion. "You mean Bluey?"

The Queen nodded. "Yes."

"I don't want to disappear like her. I know that much."

"Her fate has yet to be determined," the Queen stated. "You must aide us in our fight against the City, but not from here. We scurry about, assisting the resistance factions where we can, yet the one faction we all adhere to without question is a base outside the City—"

"In the forest?" Kimie concluded. "You want me to get geared up for jungle warfare?"

The Queen dismissed this. "The forest is out of bounds for all of us. There is a barrier that surrounds the Village of old."

"So people keep telling me," Kimie said.

"The Mountain is your only hope …" the Queen continued.

"Mountain?" Kimie cut in, confused. "What the hell …?" A thought struck her. "The girl in the club was talking about a big base. Is that it?"

"Only then—"

A piercing scream erupted from outside and a boy bolted into the throne room. "My Queen! Hookers!"

A hook burst through his leg, hoisting him backwards.

Kimie nearly gagged.

"This way!" the Queen ordered. She pulled Kimie up onto the brick platform, booted the so-called Throne away and kicked the wall behind it.

A click sounded and part of the wall swung inwards, revealing a tunnel.

"In there, child!" the Queen commanded, pushing Kimie ahead.

"We're the same age and I have a name …" Kimie retorted.

"As do I," came the hasty reply. "It is Yushera. Go to the end of the tunnel, turn right and run to the very end. Then go left, straight, and right again …"

"Hang on, what—?"

"There you will see a ladder which rises to a manhole. It will lead you to the streets. My people will find you. Eventually."

"That gives me great comfort," Kimie scoffed. "What about you?"

"My rats will not desert their sinking ship, nor will their Queen. Go!"

She shoved Kimie inside, then slammed the entrance shut, sealing her in. Kimie ran into the darkness and hadn't gone far when the Queen's deafening wail erupted behind her.

Shaken, she hurried on.

Chapter Five

The water in the sewers filled with blood.

Kimie shuddered and focused on the journey ahead. The glow in the walls had dimmed and there was less fluorescence to guide her along. She prayed it wouldn't get any darker. The last thing she needed was to be trapped in pitch-black sewers with a bunch of trigger-happy Hookers for company. Even worse, she was once again disorientated and had no idea where to go. Thankfully, a ladder appeared ahead and she made for it, wanting a quick exit. She climbed it, making a face at the slimy rungs, then reached the manhole cover at the top, cautiously pushed it open and peered out.

A cool stream of fresh air breezed over her face. The sewers hadn't been as bad as she'd expected, but she was glad to be out of them. She slid the lid away, emerged from the opening and found herself in a junkyard. Mounds of scrap towered over her and there were bits of twisted metal everywhere. How all this had come to be in the centre of an otherwise pristine City was beyond her.

The sound of the lone car revving through the City began again and she wondered who was driving it. Probably one of the CEO's City brats having fun, she thought, as it revved off into the night.

She observed the surrounding junk, which was damaged, broken and left to rot. She almost knew how it felt. Like the kids in the sewers, it was seen as an unprofitable embarrassment to be tucked away out of sight.

A whooshing noise came from overhead. She recalled it from the alleyway after leaving the EpiCentre, and before that too. The City was being surveyed from above, she figured, but she'd never seen from what.

Her foot hit a piece of metal. It rolled for a short way and hit a mound of junk slightly bigger than herself. There was an opening in the mound around eye height, along with an occasional glimmer of light every few seconds. Perhaps a faulty torch dying, she guessed.

She started to walk away, then something snagged her foot. She kicked it to the side and looked down. It was an old and tattered dog leash.

She recalled her talk with Orion.

"Bluey? Who's she?"

"The girl I was telling you about. That's what she called herself when she arrived, apparently after a dog she once had. She carried its leash around for luck, and used to lay all sorts of traps with it too."

She frowned, remembering Club-Girl's words as well.

"Last I heard she was running out of here for her hideaway about eight blocks up. A place in the streets that kept her down to earth, or so she said. She had a lot of knick-knacks there, like her trademark dog leash she used to help her out of scraps. That little hidey-hole was her safe haven after the Village went out of bounds for everyone."

Kimie turned to the junk mound and placed a hand on it. It was humming, as if alive. Curious, she peered inside. The light flickered momentarily, revealing nothing. She peered in further, waiting for it to return.

When it did, she gasped and recoiled.

Someone was in there.

It had been hard to see who. All she'd seen was the head of an adult whose eyes were closed, meaning it wasn't Bluey, and that they had to be a Hooker. She wondered if this was a station where the Hookers powered up, but even that didn't seem right. Why do it in a junkyard in the middle of nowhere and not a hi-tech lab? Besides, there was also the dog leash on the ground.

Orion's words returned to her. *"We're on System time."*

Kimie's thoughts churned. If System time was different to normal time, then there might be a chance, just a chance, that it was Bluey asleep in there. Orion had told her that Bluey had vanished six months ago, System time. For all Kimie knew, that could have been thirty years. Maybe that's how the City deals with threats, she thought, by downsizing them to the scrap heap where they'd lie trapped until they died, but that still made no sense. If this was Bluey, why not just kill her outright?

Summoning up her courage, Kimie reached in, brushed her fingers against the person's cheek and then pulled her hand back quickly. Their skin was warm, so they weren't a robot. Now things made even less sense. Why keep them alive like this? The person could tell her—if they were able to be woken. Yes, there was a chance that they might be a psycho who'd wake up and kill her, but Kimie was too curious to walk away.

She picked up a long metal pole, lodged it into the mound and shifted part of it. Large bits of junk tumbled to the ground with a loud clang, making the opening slightly bigger.

She peered inside again. She couldn't see the person's face in any great detail, yet knew they were a woman, though it was hard to see much of her. A small box with a screen flickering on and off every few moments, aimed at the woman's head, was humming softly. Kimie had no idea what the screen's symbols meant, for the codes were far too technical. The way the light flickered over the woman made it seem like it was keeping her dormant.

She reached in, grabbing the box. It was screwed in tightly. She stepped back, raised the pole and smacked the box hard. The thing barely budged. She smacked it again, harder this time. A screw came loose, the screen faded, and the box dangled on its side.

She raised the pole once more, ready to pry it away, when a hand suddenly clasped her shoulder, whirled her around and brought her face to face with a woman in white.

Kimie knew from the cold steel touch that the woman was a Hooker, even if she looked nothing like one, for she was dressed in a long white gown and had a red ribbon in her hair.

Kimie gulped, wide-eyed.

"Are you looking for help?" the Hooker asked, in a childlike voice.

"I can see you need some," Kimie replied shakily.

"You must be," the Hooker continued. "You shouldn't be out on a night like this. You're not meant to be here. That's when bad things happen to good people, like my sister." She grinned happily.

Kimie stared at her, horrified. "You're insane!"

"She's very sensitive," came the chirpy reply. "I always try to cheer her up when she's down here in the dumps. I was brought in as her saving grace, which is my name by the way. Grace." Her voice lowered. "Thing is, you hit our SORE Point."

"Sore point?" Kimie asked nervously.

The Hooker indicated the mound behind Kimie.

"Station of Recharging Embryos," she said simply, as if everything made sense.

Kimie frowned. The Hooker's touch had been mechanical. The dormant woman had felt human. What was a human being doing in a Station of Recharging Embryos?

"It's our energy cell," the Hooker explained, "and it's a little full right now, since it's carrying our baby."

Kimie swore under her breath, realising that Junk-Pile woman had to be on team evil, perhaps a kind of hybrid Hooker.

"My sister hates anyone trying to break in to steal her stuff," the Hooker said. "That's why she watches it day and night, at least until she got distracted by our Barbie Q's street party earlier. It wasn't easy to pull my sis away from it. Luckily, I had help from you."

"So where is she?" Kimie asked hesitantly.

The Hooker beamed. "Behind you!"

Kimie looked back and jumped.

A Hooker stood there, dressed in black, with her hair just as dark and her face gothic white.

"She's my twin," the first Hooker said. "We're opposites in the family. She's our DisGrace."

Kimie shuddered, wondering if she was about to end up in the SORE Point next to Junk-Pile woman.

She tried bolting around Grace. DisGrace reached out, throwing her against the SORE Point. Kimie winced as the two Hookers stepped in, raising their right hands.

Whirring drills emerged from their palms.

"Our daddy screwed us up," DisGrace said bitterly. "Now we do the same for others."

Kimie tried running again.

Grace clasped her remaining hand on Kimie's neck, pressing her up against the SORE Point. Kimie struggled wildly, averting her gaze as the whizzing bits of metal came for her throat. She flinched and then—

Crash!

A piece of junk flew from the SORE Point, straight into Grace's face, making her recoil.

Kimie broke free of the Hooker's grip and ran. Multiple crashes behind her made her stop and turn back. More junk was being bashed and kicked from the mound as Junk-Pile woman emerged.

DisGrace scowled, lunging at the newcomer with her drill.

Junk-Pile woman blocked the blow and kicked DisGrace with such force that the Hooker flew into the trash heap opposite. Grace's face hardened to the point where it almost seemed cute, then she ran in. Junk-Pile woman dodged the thrust from Grace's drill, pulled her in, whirled her around, grabbed her by the neck, severed her head in a shower of sparks, aimed it at DisGrace and hissed, "Kiss this!"

Grace's cold face smacked into DisGrace and rebounded.

Kimie grinned, impressed.

DisGrace's drill retracted and a cord flew out in its place, aimed at the woman's neck. The woman grabbed it with lightning reflexes and tugged fiercely. DisGrace flew in and was kicked in the chest before her legs were swept from under her. She clunked to the ground and another savage kick booted her in the head so hard that her scowling expression went flying high into the night in a trailing blaze of sparks.

Kimie's eyes lit up like that trail as she whispered, "Respect!"

She stepped in to get a better view of the woman, who seemed older than herself by at least a decade. The woman had a solid physique, short, spiky blonde hair, and wore a brown singlet over army pants and black boots. Kimie watched as she took a few staggering steps, then fell to her knees, coughing hard.

"That was awesome!" Kimie said, wide-eyed.

The woman kept coughing.

Kimie moved in. "I don't normally say this about anyone, but you are cool, lady!"

The woman panted heavily. "Shut up!" She examined her arm curiously, then leaned over, peering into a small metal dome on the ground. A distorted reflection of herself stared back up at her in the moonlight.

"Oh sh—!" she began, and touched her face. "What the hell? No, no, no, no!" She looked at the hanging box in the SORE Point and her eyes widened. "You bastard!"

She trembled, then saw what Kimie was standing on.

A dog leash.

"Move, ya scrag!" she snapped, pushing Kimie away. Her eyes welled with tears as she grabbed the leash and clasped it to her chest. Another glimpse of her face in the reflective dome made her shudder.

Despite the woman's age, Kimie observed, she held the presence of a child. A very bitter, angry and sad child. Therefore, it could only be one person. The way the woman had gone for the dog leash meant it was …

"Bluey?" she asked softly.

"No!" the woman scowled, stuffing the leash into the pocket of her army pants. "Not anymore. I hate that name. I'm nothing now."

"At least you're not a Hooker," Kimie said.

The woman looked up angrily. "Excuse me?"

"I heard Bluey was a kid."

"Stop saying that name."

"Sure," said Kimie. "Whatever you are, you're like a … mystical form of coolness."

"What the hell are you yapping about?"

"Maybe I can call you … Mysti Cool? Suits you."

The woman mulled this over. "Yeah, I like that, but Mysti's better."

"Mysti it is," Kimie confirmed. "So gimme some answers. What happened?"

The newly named Mysti rose to her feet. "Same thing as you. I got screwed. It's called life. I can see in your face that you suck at it too."

"So congrats, welcome to team loser," Kimie retorted. "You wanna be Captain?"

Mysti pointed at Grace's severed head. "You wanna end up like that?"

"I feel like it already. How'd you end up in a SORE Point? It wasn't just 'cause life screwed you over."

"No, someone else did," Mysti replied. "A spaced-out psycho sold me out."

"Could be anyone around here," Kimie said.

"Tell me about it. We need to move." She strode away.

Kimie ran to keep up. "Why? Where we going?"

"Anywhere," Mysti answered. "Those Hookers were guarding me. They're all on the same wavelength, so if one goes out of action, the others know about it, meaning their buddies are on their way." She stopped and winced. "Arrrgh! My damn back! Guess that happens when you get old and haven't moved in ages." She strode on again. "Couldn't have been in there too long. Couple of months maybe, going by the box's readings."

"Six months, System time," Kimie told her, "and don't ask me how long that is."

"Not long enough to get me to this age," Mysti said. "It's more like someone gave me a massive growth spurt."

"Out in the open and not in some lab?"

"Don't ask the bait, ask the Hooker."

"So you don't know?"

"Don't care either. It was a trap I fell for when I was having a really bad day. What's your story?"

"Not as good as yours," Kimie answered.

"Mine ain't good."

"Join the club. I'm Kimie."

"I don't want your name, I want to know what you're doing here."

"Same goes for me about you."

"I want out of this damn place."

"I want a whole new reality."

"Yeah, don't we all?" Mysti stopped and looked down at herself. "Look at this! What the hell am I? Big and ugly! Super strong for some reason, which is good, but the rest of me … bleuuurrrgh! Yuck, man!" She held her hands up, examining them. "I'm not even nice anymore. I've only just met you and I'm more of a cow than ever! I talk different! I feel funny! What is this?" She held her stomach.

"I'd probably feel the same if I'd shot up overnight," Kimie said, then looked around. "Is it overnight? I get confused here."

"*You're* confused?" Mysti asked, hurrying along. "I have to lie low! Nobody can see me! They'll freak out! I'm freaked out!"

"I've heard a lot of good things about you," Kimie said, following. "Seems the world went to hell after you left."

"And now I've rejoined it, leaving us both in a worse state." She stopped again, causing Kimie to nearly crash into her. "Or should that be State, in politics talk?" She shook her head, placed a hand on her temple and winced. "Okay, that's weird."

"That's not the only thing," noted Kimie. "What's up?"

Mysti frowned. "I hear giggling. Like a kid's laughing in my brain. It's freaky." She moved on again, with Kimie running after her. "It's gone now. Thank god."

"Could be a side effect from growing up in one hit," Kimie speculated. "You might be reacting 'cause you don't want to suddenly be a feral grown-up joining the political rat race. One second you're a kid, the next you're a—"

"Monster!" Mysti yelled, punching a junk pile and sending part of it clattering to the ground. "Why does it happen? Why do children have to grow up to be drinking, swearing, tattooed, pierced, sleeping around …?" She smacked the junk pile again. "Why can't we just stay in our perfect playground? Look at me! I'm everything I didn't want to become!"

"Guess what?" Kimie cried back. "Me too!"

Mysti gulped as the tears returned to her eyes. "I felt it coming on. As a kid, I mean. My body was changing. I saw the adults and how they acted and knew I didn't want to be like that, not with the Village falling and the City sweeping in. I never got why kid's dreams turn into adult nightmares."

"That's life," Kimie answered.

"That's garbage!" She picked up a brick, hurling it away. "Now I bet a new batch of kids has come along, leaving me old and useless!"

"You're only thirty-something—"

"Yesterday I was only twelve!"

"I know, and you were missed!"

"Bluey was missed! She was another person! Another life! Not me, nuh-uh, not me!"

"You're still pretty cool in a fight," Kimie pointed out.

"That's about all I can do," Mysti retorted. "Look at me! The whole world's changed and I'm a whole lot older with nothing to show for it. Where do I go? What do I do? How do I start from scratch in this crappy System?"

"I've been doing that since I got here," Kimie said. "There's an inn we could go to. The InnerCent—"

"No!" Mysti cut in. "No way! I'm *not* letting them see me like this!" She hit the side of her head. "And I wish that giggle in my brain would shut up. It's back again." She shook it off once more. "Hope it stays away this time." She looked ahead. "I think the main strip's this way."

She moved through an archway, onto the street.

Kimie followed, hearing only the City's mechanised hum. The place was still spotless, and as quiet as the grave. What's more, there were no natural elements. Not even the wind.

Mysti scowled. "Damn! The EconoMe's in full control now. Not people. It's exactly what I didn't want. None of us did. This ain't a city anymore. It's a living organism. With us in its cells."

An engine roar rose from a few streets away, growing louder.

"That damn car," Kimie said.

"What are you crapping on about now?" Mysti asked sourly.

"It's been shooting round the City all night," Kimie answered.

The roar grew louder.

Kimie stepped into an alleyway's shadows. Mysti stayed out in the open, defiant, as the vehicle screamed around the corner, with rock music blaring from its speakers, and fishtailed down the street.

Kimie was impressed by the car. A sleek machine of silver with flickering flames over its bonnet and tyres. Strangely, neither the alloy nor the rubber burned. She watched as it veered around another corner and out of sight.

Kimie returned to Mysti, her ears ringing from both the engine and the fading music. "That was random. At least I got to see it this time."

Mysti kicked a streetlamp and stormed down the street. "This place just gets worse and worse! You had to wake me up in hell, didn't you?"

"*I'm* the one who woke up in hell," Kimie corrected, following her. "What do you mean?"

"That!" she cried, pointing after the car. "Even he's been corrupted!"

"Who?"

"The freak driving that thing! Didn't you see who was behind the wheel?"

"Sorry, the flames distracted me while I was trying to stop myself from *getting smashed!*"

"*He* certainly was!" She picked up her pace. "Drunken idiot!"

Kimie ran after her in disbelief. "You're saying there's a drunk guy hooning around in a flaming car?"

"Damn straight."

"In a city where the economy's so in control that everyone's afraid to show their faces?"

"Totally."

"So why's he allowed to do—" She threw an arm up. "That?"

"As a warning for others, probably," came the reply. "He was the City's biggest science geek. A lab coat and glasses nerd, always wrapped up in his stupid gadgets. Loved to mix mechanics with music. Had a good ear for both, that's why they called him the Engine-Ear. He was the brains behind this place's tech and was repaid for it by being turned into its prisoner, just like me. Who'd you think made the trap I was in?"

Kimie frowned. "You mean, booze-formula-one winner?"

"Only he could have come up with something like that," Mysti said. "The City was paying him big bucks, 'specially after he made those Hookers for 'em. He was such a sad freak that all he wanted was a little—"

Kimie cringed. "Don't tell me …"

"—friendship," Mysti finished.

"Still sounds gross."

"Among other things. He joined the City to advocate for us. Bastard sold us out."

"Why?"

"'Cause the City corrupts. Does that to everything." She stopped, clenched her fists and seethed. "I need … something! To fight, to party, to sing, to dance, to smash someone! I want to shut this giggling in my head off—arrrgh!" She punched the wall, then looked over to an alley-way's shadows.

Kimie wondered what she was staring at, then saw a crouched figure peering out.

"You!" Mysti cried, pointing at it.

The figure ran. Mysti bolted after it, leapt in, grabbed their arms and pushed them back against the wall.

Kimie ran in to see it was a boy. A Sewer Rat.

He struggled and hissed.

Mysti held him tightly. "Where ya goin', huh?"

"He was probably following me," Kimie said. "I was with gutter Queen right before I met you."

"There's more, I can see it in his face." She tightened her grip. "Talk!"

He spoke with a voice that hadn't even broken. "The EpiCentre's down. Our battlelines are severed …"

"That means phone lines are out," Kimie told Mysti.

"I know," Mysti retorted, and shook the kid. "Go on!"

"We must let the other clubs know that the Hookers are hunting …" he began, then stopped, staring at her curiously. "I've seen you before."

"Yeah, I'm your worst nightmare," Mysti shot back.

"How's your Queen?" Kimie cut in quickly. "Last I saw she was about to be hooked, lined and sunk. What's the story?"

"She lives," the Sewer Rat answered. "She survived the onslaught against her realm and has regrouped with her people."

"Who's this?" Mysti pressed.

"Sewer Queen," Kimie replied. "Totally glories in it. Calls herself Yushera."

Mysti blinked. "You're kidding!"

Kimie shrugged. "Don't need to. This whole place is a joke."

"Sewer Queen, huh?" Mysti mused. "Man, she really got downsized. Can't believe she was voted most likely to succeed."

"Seriously?"

"Oh, yeah," Mysti said. "It's a big drop from Prom Queen to sewer one. That's her career gone to crap."

"Things are growing worse," the Sewer Rat continued. "The resistance is in danger of being annihilated, both in the City and the Mountain."

"What the hell's this Mountain?" Kimie asked, annoyed.

Mysti sighed wearily. "I remember hearing that someone wanted to make it into a big base or something, but right now I care as much about it as a smack in the head."

"You have to help us!" the Sewer Rat pleaded.

Mysti glanced around for Hookers, then said, "I don't *have* to do anything. I want out of this City. Got that, fleabag?"

"You won't be able to leave without weapons," he told her. "More Hookers than ever walk the streets, and the sky's filled with DeciMauls."

"What are these DeciMauls?" Kimie wondered, even more annoyed.

The boy ignored her. "You must get to the nearest club and warn them of what's coming."

"As long as we don't have to pay a high price to get in," Mysti said sourly.

"Or out again," Kimie added, thinking of the EpiCentre.

The boy continued. "Their only door charge is an alarm system which can fry intruders if needs be."

"Talk about overcharging," Kimie muttered.

"No money is asked for entering," he explained. "The City deals with economics, not the clubs. This one's called the New-Clear Club, for it is a weapon of both clarity and defiance, and was made to hit back hard." He glanced in its direction. "It's around the corner, halfway along the street, and down the stairs."

Kimie looked at Mysti. "It's the safest bet we've got."

Mysti relented. "Agreed." She cast the Sewer Rat aside. "Get lost."

She strode away.

Kimie started to head after her, then stopped and turned back to him.

"Thanks," she said. "I'm sorry about that but … thanks." She ran after Mysti, calling, "You know we really have to work on your attitude!"

"Yeah, like you've never heard that before!" came the glum reply.

Kimie stopped dead. She couldn't remember her parents, though vaguely recalled some arguments, and suddenly had an awful feeling of what she must have put them through. "Ouch! Ouch, ouch, ouch! Right,

I get it now." She took a breath, composed herself, and followed Mysti down the street again. "What's the deal with you, anyway? Why the big sad?"

"Like you care!"

Kimie took a moment to absorb this. She shook the awful feeling away and said, "Just chill, will you?"

"I can't!" Mysti cried, turning to face her. "I'm on fire! I got stuff raging in me! There's these thoughts and feelings and, goddammit, I want 'em out!" She kicked a bin over.

Kimie realised what was happening. "Oh! Okay, now it makes sense. Super growth kick."

Mysti was baffled. "No, that was crappy bin kick!"

Kimie inhaled sharply. "You've grown up too fast. Normally it happens bit by bit over a few years. You got everything in one big hit."

"Got my what?"

"Your … adult juices."

Mysti went green. "Oooh, yuck! Eeeeewww!" She made a face. "See, this is exactly what I didn't want! How do I get this crud outta me?"

"Well, the thing is … you don't."

"What?" Mysti wailed.

"Keep it down!" Kimie hissed. "Hookers, remember?"

"And Sewer Rats!" the boy called from the alleyway behind them.

Mysti picked up a can and hurled it at him. It hit the wall near his head, making him turn and run.

"No, this ain't right," she shuddered. "Can't I get to a doctor or something? Might help get this annoying laugh outta my head too."

"That might be a really, *really* good idea," Kimie said, "but right now you need to breathe."

"Breathe, hell, I need to party!" She strode away.

"What?" Kimie cried, running after her. "Oh god, no!" She bit her lip and muttered, "God, I'm dealing with a hormonally charged kid here. I am so sorry, Mum, whoever you are, I am so, so sorry!"

Now feeling like karma had kicked her straight in the guts, she ran on.

The New-Clear Club's double doors burst inwards and Mysti strode down its stairs with her head held high.

Kimie hurried after her. This place was much smaller than the EpiCentre, she noted, and seemed pretty casual. At least until a cry went up at the sight of Mysti and several people recoiled in fright as the music died.

"It's cool!" Kimie called. "She's not a Hooker!"

"Yeah, but what about you?" a guy asked her.

Kimie stared at him, aghast. "No, that's your mum's job, deadnuts!"

Mysti strode over to the bar. "Right, let's have some fun." She pushed a guy off his stool and sat on it. "Relax, man, I'm on your side." She caught sight of a good-looking guy seated at a nearby table. "You'll do."

She leapt out of her seat, grabbed his collar, hoisted him to his feet, pushed him against the wall and kissed him long and hard.

"Oh god!" Kimie cried, rushing in and grabbing her. "Cut it out!"

She pulled Mysti off him.

"It's okay, she doesn't have to stop," the man said dreamily.

"Yeah, she does!" Kimie countered firmly.

Mysti grinned, winking at him. "Catch ya! Ooh, yum, yum! That tasted nice. I like that. Gimme more!"

"You're over the limit already," Kimie warned. "Way over."

Mysti broke away from Kimie and moved to the bar.

Kimie sighed. "We're here for a reason, remember?"

"Sure are," Mysti agreed. She saw the drink bottles on the shelves behind the barman and said to him, "I want the strongest thing you got." She noticed his solid physique. "Ah, who am I kidding?"

She grabbed him by the back of the neck, pulled him over the bar and kissed him passionately.

"God!" Kimie cried, running in and pulling her away again. "Enough already!"

"Yum, yum," Mysti said, smirking. She picked up a silver bottle from the bar, opened it and took a swig. "I could get used to this joint. Damn, that juice was nice. It shut up the laughing crap in my head too." She kicked the jukebox. A blaring roar exploded and she punched the sky. "Rock and roll!"

She ramped the music to the max. The walls shook as she leapt into the middle of the room, jumping around and pounding her fists. Kimie ran in to hoist her out but was cast to one side.

Everyone else watched Mysti, bewildered. When they saw she wasn't a threat a few people found the courage to join her and soon there was a whole group partying on the floor.

Mysti grabbed another man, kissed him hard, cast him away, then pulled in yet another and kissed him as well. She'd barely discarded him when a well-built man pulled her off the floor. He motioned to a back room, leaned in and whispered in her ear.

Mysti frowned, confused, then her eyes widened and she punched him out cold, before leaping back onto the floor and jumping wildly to the music again.

Kimie took a seat at the bar and slumped over it, defeated and miserable, with her head on her arm, moaning, "And for all my teachers, however I may have treated you, I hope you have long and happy stress-free lives now that I've well and truly learnt my lesson. For whoever my mum and dad are, I promise *not* to give you hell again, and may I never *ever* have kids …"

An unopened bottle, looking like a soft drink, sat on the bar near her. She despondently sat up, opened it and sniffed. It didn't seem to have alcohol, so she took a sip. It tasted more like lemonade than anything else, but also had a slight tingle she couldn't identify. Not caring, she took another sip, then drank the whole thing.

Mysti yelled, punching the air repeatedly and pumping up the crowd. She grabbed another bottle, downed it, and went even wilder with the music. A massive leap sent her flying high over everyone, she dropped beneath them all and didn't resurface. The crowd kept dancing, caught in the moment, while she crawled through them, scampered up to Kimie, hoisted her out of her seat and pulled her behind a column a short way from the bar.

Kimie saw that Mysti's mood had suddenly changed. The woman was shaking, like she'd been scared half to death.

"What's up now?" Kimie asked. The world swirled from the effects of her drink. "Whoooa …!"

Mysti pressed herself up against the column and gave a rough nod, indicating the entrance.

Kimie peeked out and saw who'd come down the front steps.

The Dragonfly.

Kimie's heart glowed and she peered out a little more to see him.

"It's okay," she said. "He's a friend. You just got stung. He has a way of doing that."

Mysti pulled her back behind the column.

Kimie winced from the force of the tug. "Quit it!" Nausea overcame her and she placed a hand to her temple, feeling sick again.

Mysti trembled. "He makes me feel funny. Always did."

"You met him before?"

"I don't want to talk about it. This whole place is weird."

"I'm not surprised, after what you drank." She blinked dazedly, feeling the effects of her own drink. "Or what I have too."

Mysti shuddered. "I don't get it. That guy back there—" she indicated the one she'd knocked out by the bar, "—he wanted me to go upstairs and dance the horizontal hokey-pokey with him. I don't know what he meant."

Kimie giggled.

"What's so funny?" Mysti asked.

"Let me get to the Dragonfly," Kimie said. "He'll explain … explain …" The room spun faster than ever and her speech grew slurred. "Whoa! When did I hit the desert? There are spin-effects everywhere."

She dropped into a chair and passed out.

Mysti watched Kimie slump over a table. She shook her quickly.

"Kid! Hey kid!"

No response.

"Flippin' great!"

She hid once more as the Dragonfly walked past, oblivious to Kimie. Mysti peeked out and saw him approach the bar, lean over and speak to the barman. The two went out the back and, after a short time, the barman returned alone.

Mysti cautiously went up to the bar, peered out the back and saw nothing.

"What happed to buzzboy?" she asked the barman.

"He couldn't stay," came the reply. "He came to let us know there are Hookers in the area. We'll have to shut up shop."

Mysti nodded. "Can I get a drink first? A soft one this time?"

"I'm surprised you don't want anything stronger."

She pulled him in roughly and kissed him. "Forget it, I'm full." She pushed him away, licking her lips from the kiss. "Yum, yum."

A loud bang came from above, then the front door flew down the stairs, hitting the ground. A metal device swept in after it, striking a man who jolted wildly under the electrical impact, then dropped like a stone.

"No door charge for us," came a Hooker's smooth voice.

The music stopped and the bar went silent.

Dead silent.

Mysti tensed as metal footsteps descended.

Chapter Six

Kimie opened her eyes. A sharp pain from the hard floor seared her neck. Even worse, a deathly cold cheek was pressed up against hers, covered in blood.

She shuddered and pushed herself up, wiping the blood off her cheek. Her head pounded, knowing that the drink had knocked her clean out. She wasn't used to it, that much was obvious, but there was a higher chance it had been spiked.

She saw the room and her stomach heaved.

The club was littered with bodies. Severed heads, limbs and organs were splattered everywhere. She covered her mouth, rose shakily to her feet and stumbled through the trail of dismembered corpses towards the stairs. Her insides churned as she staggered up the steps, then burst out into the fresh night air, gasping for breath and feeling truly disgusting.

Things were spiralling. She didn't know how long she'd been out for but more people had died and all because she'd failed to warn them by drinking something she shouldn't have. That left two massacres in one night, with her in the middle of both and a severe motherload of guilt.

She started sobbing as the full impact of how screwed she was hit home. The world she'd come from was gone, along with her memories, replaced by this lunatic asylum in the guise of a city. She now understood why the kids here had retreated into the sewers and gloried in them so much. The odds of them rising above anything else in life were enormous and they'd simply descended into what they felt like: utter crap.

She emerged glumly onto the street. How much lower could she go, she wondered, before a complete meltdown?

A snarl came from around the corner, sounding like a large dog.

Very large.

She ducked behind a gleaming metal trashcan and peered up. After everything that had happened tonight, she wasn't taking any chances and expected the worst. She watched, hidden by the shadows, as a hairy figure stepped into the dim glow of a streetlamp. She gasped, horrified, as she stared at it in disbelief, then whispered, "Now … I am truly … insane!"

The biped was twice the size of her, with muscular biceps covered by thick, silver armour. Its head wasn't human, but that of a wolf, with a collar around its neck that beeped with a flashing light.

She inched away and hit the lid of the unblemished trashcan. It fell to the pavement, clattering loudly.

The beast grunted, looking in her direction.

She turned and bolted. The beast's hand rose, holding a large gun that charged with a high-pitched whine. Sensing what was coming, Kimie dived.

The laser blast ripped over her head, hitting the trashcan and sending it bursting into flames. She scrambled to the side as the beast fired again.

This shot only missed her by inches.

She scurried behind another trashcan. A gun blast sent it flying down the street and hitting the ground heavily.

She glanced around quickly. No more cover. She braced herself for the worst.

A roaring whine arose, but not from the gun. This was from an engine, and a serious blast of rock music.

The beast looked back to the incoming rush of light, heat and screeching tyres, before a heavy object rammed into it, sending it flying across the road and into a wall with a fierce thud. It slumped onto the pavement and was still.

Kimie rose to her feet.

The flaming car was before her. It reversed with an awkward jolt, bumping off the kerb and onto the road. An electronic door slid up, releasing a deafening roar of music, making her cover her ears. The car stopped and a man fell out, holding a silver flask. His face was pale, his hair long and his clothes dark. He tried to pick himself up but only succeeded in rolling over and laughing, as if in a haze.

The booming music sickened her and she moved over, peering into the car. The dashboard was lit up like a rocket ship and there was a piano-like keyboard where the steering wheel should have been. She smacked the controls with her fist. They were hot, making her wince. She ignored the pain and hit them again. Several beeps came from various instruments and the music died, bringing much-needed relief to her ringing ears.

The man on the ground took a swig from his flask, gave a drunken, slurring laugh and cried, "Whoa! Damn, I'm good!" He took another swig.

Kimie was aghast. "Holy crap! Didn't know you were this bad."

He giggled. "Worse."

She grimaced at the sight of him. "I hate drunks. Always did." She grabbed his flask and hurled it away.

He stared at her curiously. "Are you one of mine?"

"One of your what?" she retorted. "Delusions?"

He pinched her. She yelped and smacked his arm.

"You're not," he said with a groan. "Could have been, though."

"You're seriously off the planet." Realisation dawned. "Wait! Did you think I was a Hooker? Heard you made 'em."

He looked away glumly.

She indicated the City. "Did you do all this too? Is this craphole down to you?"

He shivered. "Where's my drink?"

"It is, right?" she concluded. "That's why you're drunk. You're trying to forget what you did."

His face fell. "I'm not the only one who's trying to forget. You ain't all here either, kid. You're filled with fractures. You're alone. Painfully so. Just like me."

Kimie tensed. "What the hell do you know about me?"

"I listen to your eyes, not your mouth," he replied. "They speak volumes. Way more than you know. I see a pattern of a human being with colours, textures and equations all going haywire 'cause of too many random elements from inside and out. You're wounded music, flooded by streaks of red and black, along with a big festering sore in your heart that oozes like a bloodied chakra. It's weeping now. Believe me, I know the feeling."

Kimie swallowed hard. His words had hit home, like he'd reached into her mind and pulled a curtain away from behind her eyes to reveal a hidden wound. She quivered, realising she had an affinity with him. They were both in immense pain, weighed down by guilt and shame from their pasts, which were invisible, but always there.

She shook her head. "I don't get it. One minute you're a rambling drunk, driving around in a flaming car, and the next you're a head shrink. What are you?"

His tone lowered. "Fragmented. Very, very fragmented."

"No," she disagreed, "you're just sensitive. You feel things deeply and probably overthink 'em too. When they don't make sense your brain hits overdrive and you vent your rage into your engine to slam it onto the world in a mechanical scream. You really are an Engine-Ear, huh?"

He looked sadly at the sky. "Not anymore. Now I'm just a Stargazer."

A snarl came from down the street. Two more beasts were approaching.

"I wish that's all *they* were," she said. "What are they?"

"Downsizers of the EconoMe," he replied. "They'll happily rip you apart. That's why we call 'em DeciMauls."

"Oh, so *that's* what they are," Kimie said, relieved that she could finally put a face to the name.

The Stargazer continued. "They patrol the skies but have to land at times to sniff out resistance factions. You stumbled onto a DeciMaul Point. If I hadn't shown up you'd be turned into fractions by now. Help me into the car."

"Why? So you can kill yourself?"

"So I can get us out of here," he answered. "Car has safety buffers that'll stop us crashing into things. We won't hit nothing, unless you wanna have some fun and turn 'em off?"

"How do I know you won't sell me out to the nearest Hooker?"

He shrugged. "Gotta take a chance, kid."

"So, what? You don't work for the City now?"

"Oh, I work for it," he told her. "Just not the way I used to."

She nodded. "Course not. You're a broken car wreck. That's what happens to anyone who crosses the System, right? You set the example."

"Yep. I'm the hazy grey area, babe."

"Yeah, but I think you're about to take a side since you just saved my butt from the wolf pack." She looked inside the car. "You're too wasted to drive. I could have a go though."

"You wouldn't know how," he said back. "These ol' legs don't work anymore so you'll have to help me in."

Kimie was astounded. "No legs and you wanna drive?"

"Don't need 'em for that. Now you wanna hurry up or you wanna wait till this place is really bitchin'?" He indicated the DeciMauls again.

They were getting too close for Kimie's liking. She placed his arm around her shoulder, grimaced at his alcoholic stench and lifted him to his feet, finding him surprisingly light. Once she'd moved him into the car he shifted over to the driver's side and she got in after him.

"Getting into a flaming car with a drunk driver," she muttered. "Mum'd be so proud!"

He hit a switch. The door started closing with a musical hum.

The DeciMauls fired. Kimie jumped as the blasts hit the door and the car jolted wildly, but there was no damage.

"Relax," the Stargazer said as the door locked into place. "Alloy's so thick that nothing gets in unless I say so. This thing's fast too. Makes me proud to be a *Ralloy* Car driver." He chuckled.

"Pretty slow shooters, aren't they?" Kimie quipped.

"Slow at everything," the Stargazer confirmed. "In mind and body, but you don't want to fight one up close. They'll tear you to shreds."

Kimie found the car's interior much warmer with the doors closed, and nowhere near as bad as she'd thought. The engine revved, sounding like a synthesiser, as hard rock blared from the speakers, making her jump again. Ignoring the heat, she struck at random controls on the dashboard to make it shut up. Finally, she succeeded.

"Grandma," the Stargazer said sourly, and flicked several switches.

Kimie lurched violently as the car reversed hard, even more so when it slammed into a DeciMaul, then spun around on the spot, smacking the other into a wall. She barely had time to refocus before the Stargazer hit the keyboard and the car revved down the street.

"Does this thing have an autopilot?" she asked sickly.

"Oh yeah," he replied. "Don't use it. I can drive this thing blind."

"No crap. Chuck on the autopilot."

"Forget it. We've got safety buffers, remember?"

"Not a good idea," Kimie warned.

"Chill, will ya?"

"Repeat, not a good idea."

"Where's my drink?"

"Back on the pavement."

"Gimme another."

"No way."

"I wasn't asking you, I was asking the car."

A hatch above him opened, dropping a flask into his lap. The car skidded fiercely as he undid the lid with one hand and took a swig.

Kimie cringed. "This just gets better and better!"

He offered her his drink. She smacked it away, then turned to look out the rear window. The streets were empty, with no sign of any more DeciMauls. Quickly, she turned back and asked, "Reckon you can get me out of the City, spaceman?"

"Oh, yeah," he said. "We won't get far, though. This whole place is growing rapidly and catches up with you wherever you go. Why do you think I'm still here?"

"You're not *all* here," Kimie pointed out. "I don't want to be skidding around in a drunken car party all night. The whole City's gonna be after us now."

He flicked a few more switches. "Uh, no. I've hacked into the City's network and used my sensory disruptors to stop it from tracking us. Little hobby of mine. It aint hard to make the car invisible to the sweeping CT scans, for a while anyway."

"CT scans?" Kimie asked.

"Stands for City's Tech," he answered. "It means the DeciMauls and

Hookers'll have to get up close to see us, and they *will* be on the lookout. It's a game that goes back and forth between them and me. They always adapt. Good thing is, I do too."

Kimie drew a sharp breath. "We need help."

He offered her his drink again. "This ain't bad, kid."

She smacked it away once more. "God, I've had enough drinks for one night. I woke up lying on the floor of a club earlier."

"Sounds great," he said glumly.

"It was feral. I passed out and the place was shot up by bad guys. Woke up with all these bodies around me, giving a whole new meaning to New-Clear Club. Never thought I'd say this, but I'm so glad that someone spiked my drink."

"There was no spiking," he told her. "You're new here, I can tell that much. The City's water—and god I hate that word—dulls people down. Those club drinks free the mind. If you swig a straight-out shot and you haven't had the City's water first, then bang! Messes with your head, leading to zonk central. Also slows your body so much that you look dead for a while, which is probably why you were left there. Your life signs weren't detected."

"I did drink something when I first got here," Kimie recalled. "At a place called the InnerCent."

"Good thing too," the Stargazer confirmed. "They'd have known what they were doing. Bet it put you to sleep right away, huh?"

She nodded. "Sure did."

"They'd have given you the right dose to help you out. If they hadn't, then that New-Clear Club shot would have put you out for nights on end, and considering how long the nights are here, that's a good thing. The resistance started pumping drug-free water into the City's main supply earlier tonight. Not enough for the City to detect, but pretty soon there'll be a lot of people round here waking up."

"So why'd you save me from the hell hound?" Kimie wondered. "Angry at the City, are you? What'd it do? Promise everything, deliver nothing, then screw you over? Got news for ya space brain, most cities do that."

He veered the car dangerously close to a wall, shooting around it.

"Thank god Mysti's not here," Kimie said sickly. "She'd smack your head in.”

“Who?”

“You probably knew her as Bluey.”

He swung the car to the left, sending it up on the pavement, hitting a bin, swerving past a lamp pole and zigzagging across the road.

“You trying to get us killed?” Kimie cried.

“Been trying for years!” he snapped. “Can’t quite get the hang of it. Too much heart.”

“Is it because I said—?”

“Shut up!” He swerved the car around a corner. It hit a wall, scraped along in a shower of sparks and sped away.

“Stop this damn thing!” Kimie yelled. “Now!”

A screech of brakes sent her lurching forward as the car came to a halt. The world swirled from the sudden stop, making her feel sick.

The Stargazer fell despairingly onto the keyboard, reaching for his flask.

Kimie was faster and pulled it away. She looked outside, then asked, “Why are the people in this place turning into such wrecks?”

“Why do children?” he countered sadly. He paused, before asking in a soft voice, “She’s back?”

Kimie sighed. “Well she was. I didn’t see her sprawled out in the club with everyone else, but then again, I was ready to chuck. If she’s alive, she’s a kid in a grown-up body, hell-raging against the world.”

“Just like …” the Stargazer began, then trailed away.

“I know,” Kimie finished. “You. It’s not living, is it?”

He stayed silent.

She gazed up at the sky. Clarity dawned, and she looked back at him in astonishment. “*That’s* why you saved me from being a dog’s breakfast just now. You thought I was *her*. I reminded you of Bluey.”

He sniffed.

“What happened?” she asked. “You okay to talk about it?”

He wiped his eyes, shuddered and sat up. “That kid was the most perfect colour ever, but even I saw she was fracturing. She wanted to leave the City before she lost her innocence and broke. She knew, like I do, that the System corrupts. It grows relentlessly to assimilate and destroy. I got suckered in by it and sold everyone out. Now we're screwed." He bit his lip. "How was she?"

Kimie wondered how to break it to him. "Confused and trying real hard to cope with her adult juices kicking in all at once."

The Stargazer choked back the tears. "She's alive. Kid's too smart to let anything happen to her, no matter what age. She's spent her whole life fighting, but she's still little Bluey underneath it all. A droplet in a raging ocean who's swimming against the tide." He snatched the flask from her, brought it to his lips, then stopped and threw it onto the back seat. "Better not do that if she's up and running."

"Good call," Kimie said. "How'd you get started on that stuff anyway?"

He sighed wearily. "Everyone has their price, kid. Like you, I never had any friends …"

"Hey …!" Kimie began, then huffed, thinking he was probably right. "Go on."

He continued. "Reality was so bad that I just wanted a never-ending party to forget it all, so I built my own buddy network. Electronically, that is."

Kimie knew what he was getting at. "The Hookers, right?"

"The Hookers," he confirmed. "It wasn't long before the System turned the mathematical tables on me and I got kicked out. Now the City sucks because of *moi*! I took away its innocence and all because I was lost to begin with. Just a star looking for home." He wiped his eyes. "It was me. All me. The Hookers, the City's Tech, what happened to the kid, all me." He quivered. "I was only following orders. B-B-Bluey was getting too good for the City. The big boss saw her potential and knew she'd be an economic bonus if we sped up her growth and made a few adjustments. The resistance had its Sentries, so the City needed *its* warrior. A visible one. Not like the covert operative they've got running around behind the scenes."

Kimie frowned. "Who's that?"

He shook his head. "Don't know. The big gun's being real cagey on that one. Can't hear nothin' about 'em when I patch into the City's network either."

"Makes sense," Kimie agreed. "Two clubs were taken down tonight, right before an attack on the City was about to kick off."

His brow furrowed in thought, then his face filled with dismay. "I created the SORE Point. B-B-Bluey was thrown inside and aged into super freak. Thing is, I rigged it so she couldn't be changed mentally. That's why she's a raging banshee right now. Once again, too much heart on my part." He shivered. "The shields I put around the SORE Point protected her big time. No one could get into it, she couldn't be removed, and *it* couldn't be picked up and taken anywhere either. I figured if she was left out in the open there'd be more of a chance that help would reach her sooner or later, and it paid off. The bad guys were stumped and you got there in the end."

"Hang on," Kimie said, "if you fixed it so that no one could get to her, how come I got in so easily and let her out?"

He shrugged. "That wasn't 'cause of me. When the City caught on that I was tampering with their vision of her, *and* when I started doing things to help out the people on the street every now and then, I lost everything and got thrown to the dogs. That's why I can't walk. It's not the drink. I'm kept here as an example of what happens when you cross the System." He sniffed again. "I'd have gone back to help the kid but she was guarded too well. The City's always watching me and I'm never out of sight for too long. I don't want to leave anyway. I have to make up for what I did. The most horrific thing anyone can do. I robbed a kid of their childhood. I—" His words trailed away and he slumped over the keyboard once more.

Kimie put her arm around him, rested her head on his shoulder and felt every inch of his pain. "Looks like we've both been screwed over. We're really lost, aren't we?"

He wiped his eyes and sat up, along with her. "Got that right. We're also targets since taking out those DeciMauls back there. We'll only be off the City's radar for a short time, so we can't sit here for long."

Kimie gazed at the gleaming towers above. "I want to know who the hell runs this place. It can't be a machine. There's gotta be someone up top pulling the strings."

The Stargazer nodded. "Yeah, there is."

"He got a name?" Kimie asked.

"Did once," came the reply. "It was forgotten long ago, like mine. He makes the rules round here. Likes to think he's the king of an economic empire, so he calls himself the Moneyarch. He's totally possessed by the System." He flinched at the memory. "He never should have become like this, only …"

"Only what?" Kimie pressed.

"He was ordinary once," the Stargazer continued, "like the rest of us, then he turned suddenly. It was way out of character. We never found out why."

Kimie tried to make sense of it all. "So Bluey grows up and goes nuts, you fall apart, the big boss becomes power-crazed and Yushera goes down the drain. God, it makes me sick! Everyone here's either screwing up the present, stuffing up the future, or crying about the past. Why can't you all just move on and do something useful?"

"Your mum tell you that?" he retorted.

"I—" She stopped as an icky feeling came over her, then shook it away. "You and Mysti are right, though. We'll blame the System for corrupting everyone. You'd better get us moving."

He played some notes on the keyboard. Their gentle harmonies resonated through her as the car headed off.

"Be good if we could fix this place up," Kimie said, watching the world go by. "With your brain, and my guts, we might make a real dent in this dump." She looked at him, seeing a glimmer of a smile. She knew what he was thinking. "Am I that much like Bluey?"

"Same colours," he noted.

She smiled back, then thought of the situation at hand. "You built the Hookers, so you must know how to throw a spanner in their works. It'd be a good start on Operation Meltdown anyway."

"I can't even get close to them now," he told her. "They're loyal to the Moneyarch and worship him like a god, even more so since he's reprogrammed their sect's drives."

"Shouldn't be too hard to turn 'em off," Kimie speculated. "I took a few out tonight with a microphone and speaker."

"I heard about that when I was listening in on things," he said. "That was pretty impressive and got the resistance talking over its hidden networks. The City might like to think it's perfect but that's an illusion. Once it kicked me out from the top job, its cronies tinkered with the Hookers, turning 'em nasty, but also creating a defect in their system that you found out about. Thing is, the Hookers adapt real easy and won't let that happen again. They want to stay as working girls."

Kimie bit her lip. "Be good if you could just, y'know, take me home."

"Love too, but can't," he replied. "Car was tampered with so it can only get as far as the City's borders before it conks out. I've fixed things a smidgen and can get you to the Mountain if you want."

"What's this Mountain I keep hearing about?"

The Stargazer paused, seemingly hesitant to speak. "Uh … yeah. There's help there. For you anyway."

"I'm guessing there's a bigger problem?"

"Yeah," he answered. "Gilwain."

"Who?"

"My scientific partner from a lifetime ago. Guy's talented but lacks restraint. Streaks of red run through him like magma veins and he has a temper that blows *a lot*!" He shuddered at the memory. "He's another enemy I made by selling out to the System. Now he's fled the City and made base camp in the Mountain. Once again, I only found out about him when I was hooning around, hacking into the resistance networks. He hates my guts for what I've done." He sighed. "Working in the Mountain would suit him down to the ground. Haven't seen him for a couple of hundred drinks. Don't want to either."

"Yeah, but I'm running out of options fast," Kimie warned. "Okay, so you've annoyed some people. Big deal. Fix the problem."

"That your mother talking again?"

Kimie clenched her fist tightly. That stung. She composed herself and said, "Then there's your old village on the outskirts of town …"

"Uh, no," he cut in. "Not even *I* can break into that one. The City's used its Freakquency to create a mist on the Village borders that stops anyone reaching it. Try and enter without the right code and it'll freeze your assets off. There's a high price to pay for going up against such a weapon that's been taxed to the hilt by the City. That's why it's called a

TaxonaMist."

Kimie blinked, astounded, and shook the term away.

He continued. "I might be able to dissolve it, given time. Thing is, the ol' Village has *its* barrier up too. Big clash going on there."

"Probably to stop itself from being stuffed by that taxidermist or whatever it's called," Kimie concluded. "What about calling for help from beyond the Mountain?"

The Stargazer dismissed her. "The City's Freakquency blocks any resistance transmissions going out that far and, believe me, various factions have tried. The City's remoteness, plus the fact that it controls who we talk to, makes it the biggest remote control of all."

Kimie was more baffled than ever.

"Can you take me to the Mountain?" she asked. "You won't have to stay. It's just straight in, drop me off and then come right back. Shouldn't be a problem if we work fast. Maybe you could find out what happened to Mysti too."

His face fell. "She won't want to talk to me."

"You only have to check if she's alive and then message me in the Mountain to tell me what's up. I'll get whoever's in there to do the rest. Who knows, if things work out, people might look at you differently. You might even see yourself in another way." She shrugged. "We gotta do something."

He considered his options, then said, "Fine. I'll do it, but that's it. Final gamble."

"Final gamble," Kimie agreed.

He keyed in some coordinates. "The odds are against us." He hit a switch, heard a low note and tensed. "'Specially now that ..."

"Now what?" Kimie pressed.

His reply was glum. "The InnerCent's fallen. Report just came in on the City's Freakquency."

Kimie shivered. "Can we do anything to help? I mean—"

"Nothing," he answered. "Looks like the City's gone all *Inn*cide on itself. That's a backblast."

"What about the guy who runs it?" she asked. "Orion, or whatever he's called. Is he okay?"

"I dread to think," came the sombre reply, "and with Mysti—or whatever her name is—either dead, captured or crazy, the Mountain's your only option."

He placed his hand on the keyboard and played. The car picked up speed, heading for the City's outskirts on a controlled course.

Kimie thought of Orion. "He trusted me. Thanks for doing the same."

"Sure," he replied. "Makes a difference, doesn't it?"

"Totally." She looked out the window and up at the towers. "We could use a bit more trust round here."

The Stargazer turned the car into a long street. "The City's become way too polished for me. I've always believed that you can't have the word 'trust' without a little 'rust', right?"

Kimie nodded. Now the Stargazer seemed so much more than a madman driving drunkenly around in a flaming car. He was almost … human. Flawed nonetheless, but that was humanity all over.

He grew more reflective. "Guess we really need to look beyond the superficial at what's underneath."

"You know that from experience?" Kimie asked.

"No," he answered. "I learnt it from watching you."

She brushed him off. "Liar."

He continued. "Tainted, battered and rusty from taking years of crap is one thing. Hiding serious decay by looking good for survival's sake, that's this place. Don't worry, kid. You ain't so bad."

"Compared to what I could be?" she replied, watching the pristine towers go by. "Nah, No way."

The car sped on, with both of them feeling a touch brighter.

Chapter Seven

The Ralloy Car was fast.

Kimie grimaced as the world flashed by. She felt sick, even more so when they'd shoot dangerously close to an object and veer away at the last second. She cringed and told the Stargazer to slow down. He said not to worry since the external stabilisers would stop them from hitting anything and the internal ones would stop them from flying forward even if they did.

Kimie found the car's synthesised tones soothing, to a point. They calmed her a little as she was driven out of the City, then the forest on its outskirts, before streaming across a long desert highway. Nothing seemed familiar in the slightest. This place, wherever it was, only made her confused, even more so when a mountain loomed in the distance.

The car picked up speed, morphing everything outside into one big blur, save for the Mountain which grew larger, as if rushing in to greet them. Kimie did her best to control her nausea and was more than grateful when they reached the Mountain in no time at all. The car veered up its rocky slope before stopping suddenly where the Mountain met the desert. The outside world solidified so fast that Kimie lurched onto the hot dashboard, feeling as sick as hell. The car door next to her slid open with a hum, thanks to her dashboard strike, and a blast of cold night air hit her.

Kimie made a face. "I think I'm gonna be sick."

"It's better with a drink," the Stargazer replied, and took a swig from his flask, having decided not to go with his earlier vow of abstinence after all.

Kimie shuddered. "I thought you said this thing had internal stabilisers. Why am I feeling so god-awful?"

"I changed the parking settings a smidge too fast," he answered, "but that's nothing. Next time I'll switch the gravity off and we'll have some *real* fun!"

She looked out of the car and back at the City, now only a blip on the horizon. Her hand moved to a cooler part of the dashboard to push herself out, then slipped and hit a button.

"No!" the Stargazer cried. "Not—"

A roof hatch opened and he shot up out of it, flying high into the air with his arms and legs flailing before thumping into the desert sands at the base of the rocky slope. He winced painfully, then rolled over with a groan.

Kimie giggled as he sat up, and called, "Serves ya right! Who puts an ejector seat in a car?"

He rubbed his head groggily. "Comes in handy if the flames ever get out of control. It happened once when the alloy wore down."

Kimie gulped and leapt from the vehicle, deciding the further away she was from this deathtrap, the better. Shivering in the cold, she descended the rocky slope to where he lay. She passed a boulder, then yelped as a hand suddenly reached out, wrapping over her mouth and pulling her back. A blade pressed against her throat, making her freeze.

The Stargazer reached into his pocket, pulled out a small device and hurled it at her. It zipped through the air, magnetising onto her attacker's metal armour. Kimie jolted, hit by an electrical surge, but not as much as her attacker. Their grip loosened and she broke away, stumbling down the slope and landing next to the Stargazer before looking back.

Standing behind her was a round-faced man with a moustache and beard, gripping an axe with a fine blade and carved handle, which, strangely, had buttons on its side. Not the decorative kind either, Kimie noticed. These were electronic. The most astonishing thing she found, was his speed and strength as opposed to his size, for he was a dwarf.

"Fantasy land central," she muttered.

The dwarf ripped the Stargazer's electrical device from his shoulder, cast it to one side and spoke gruffly. "Apologies, girl. Thought you were one of his. Should have known he never makes 'em so young."

Kimie threw an arm up. "Why does everyone around here think I'm a Hooker?"

The Stargazer scrambled through the sands, making desperately for his car.

The dwarf's hand rose sharply, pressing a button on his axe. A beep followed and the car door slammed and locked. He hit another button and the car reversed a little, out of the Stargazer's reach.

The Stargazer looked glumly at Kimie. "If you'd left me in the car I'd have seen him coming."

"No," the dwarf countered, walking down the slope towards him, "you wouldn't have. Your gadgets, like you, have stagnated, and the drunken state of you doesn't help either. Your wretched car stood out from miles off." He snorted. "Look at you, cowering there like a wounded animal! Pathetic! On your feet, train wreck! Stand and face me!"

The Stargazer's fingers clawed tightly at the sand and he quivered.

The dwarf ran down the slope, grabbed the Stargazer and hoisted him up, pressing him against a large rock.

Kimie leapt up, ready to rush him.

The dwarf sensed her movements.

"You stay out of this!" he snapped, pointing his axe at her. "He sold the City out and can pay up for it. He doesn't need a girl to step in and save him."

"From what?" she snapped back. "An ugly mushroom?"

He dropped the Stargazer, lunged in, whirled around, tripped her up and pointed his axe at her throat.

"Do you want to say that again?" he hissed.

"Go sit in a garden somewhere!" she retorted, with a strength she never knew she had.

He raised his weapon, ready to strike her with its handle. She rolled nimbly out of the way, grabbed a rock and hurled it at him. He deflected it with his axe and scowled as she grabbed another and rose to her feet. Gruffly, he reached to his belt, removed a sling with a metal sphere on each end, then dodged the rock before hurling the sling. Kimie winced as it bound her legs tightly and she crashed to the ground. She'd barely landed when he swept in, grabbed her cheeks roughly and growled, "I expected more from you. I thought you'd have a warrior's spirit. You insult me and waste my time!"

"Yeah, I should have known I wouldn't find any help here," Kimie shot back, struggling to kick the sling apart and failing. "You're as bad as the rest of them. No wonder Bluey wanted out."

The dwarf stopped dead. "What's that? What did you say?"

"That she's around," she replied.

"She's telling the truth," the Stargazer added wearily.

"If you think she was good at twelve, you should see her now," Kimie continued. "She's twenty years older and gone street commando. Changed her name to Mysti too."

"Older?" the dwarf speculated. He turned menacingly to the Stargazer. "How did she grow so old so fast?"

The Stargazer tensed guiltily. "Uh … yeah …"

"You used our tech, didn't you?" the dwarf snapped.

"She isn't as bad as she could have been," the Stargazer mumbled.

"You augmented a child! *A child!*"

"Yeah, keep fighting," Kimie said sourly. "The bad guys love that."

The Stargazer looked away.

The dwarf's axe beeped. He held it up, and to Kimie's bewilderment, a voice spoke from a speaker on its handle. She couldn't hear what it said, but there was no mistaking the dwarf's deathly cold tone that followed.

"Are they really? Thank you."

The Stargazer gulped. "Good news?"

The dwarf lowered his axe and descended the slope. "It seems," he began, as his shadow engulfed the Stargazer, "that your car's sensors are as fried as your brain. The City's preparing for a long-range strike against this very spot."

Kimie stared at the Stargazer in horror. "I thought they couldn't see us leave?"

The Stargazer slumped into the sand in despair.

"Yes," the dwarf concluded bitterly. "A trap. They wanted to see where you were going. Your stupidity led them right to us.”

Kimie’s heart sank. “Mother of sh—!”

“The Mountain can withstand such a blast,” the dwarf cut in. “Its mines are strong enough to hold out against the mightiest of strikes. That’s lucky for the resistance, but not for you, since I’m lacking a reason to let you two inside.”

“Up to you,” Kimie said, trying to overcome her shame at their monumental stuff-up. “We can tell you a hell of lot about what’s been happening in the City lately, but hey, if you know better …”

The dwarf loomed over her, raising his axe.

Kimie braced herself.

The axe swept down, she cried out, then felt the bonds on her legs sever.

“Very well,” the dwarf stated. “You, girl, made it this far, and you deserve respect for that.”

Kimie rubbed her ankles. “Thanks.”

She scrambled over to the Stargazer and helped him sit up.

“Yeah, baby, yeah,” the Stargazer muttered. “Just need a drink, that’s all. Just one drink …”

The dwarf’s face filled with rage. “He, though …”

Kimie pointed at the dwarf angrily. “He comes with us!” she bellowed with a death glare. “Okay, so he may be a drunk who helped the wrong people, screwed the City over and built the Hookers—”

“Not helping,” the Stargazer said grimly.

“ —But he knows his stuff, and if he can do that on a bad day then I’d sure as hell like to see him on a good one. We need him.”

The dwarf gripped his axe tighter.

“Hey, I got us here,” Kimie continued, “*and* I got Bluey out of her mess too, so I’m *way* more important than you think.”

She stopped in realisation and her heart glowed. She’d never thought much of herself before. Now, for the first time ever, she felt worth something.

The dwarf snorted. “You don’t know the risks involved.”

“You don’t know what you’ll miss out on,” Kimie quipped, with a growing sense of wisdom. “Try and see the bigger picture, huh?”

The dwarf relented. "You speak with the heart of a warrior, lass. So be it. He may enter, but I'm not happy about it."

The Stargazer looked at her sadly. "You don't have to stick up for me. I don't want to drag you down too."

"You've been through enough," Kimie said. "No more drinks, okay? You can lose the 'poor me' talk too."

"What's the point of—?" He stopped and sighed. "Yeah, sure."

"Good." She clasped his hand tightly.

He indicated the car with a nod. "Got a hoverchair in there if you really want to help."

"Sure," she answered.

He gazed deep into her eyes. "Sealing wax."

"What?" she asked.

"You. You're sealing wax. Thank you."

His words made her glow again. "I hope so," she said. "After all, this sealing wax plans to stick by you."

He pulled a device from his pocket, pressed a button, and his car boot hummed up.

The lift doors hissed open.

A blast of hot air hit Kimie in the face. She coughed as she followed the dwarf into the sweltering atmosphere of rock, fire and deafening drilling. Her eyes adjusted and she saw that high above, and far below, the Mountain had been hollowed out and carved into many paths where groups of people were now mining. Many scanned the walls with digital devices, while others used basic instruments, like hammers and chisels, to extract the rocks with precision and accuracy.

"Random," Kimie noted. "The City goes hell corrupt and you guys go old school. Way to rebel ..."

"Gilwain," the dwarf stated.

Kimie indicated the Stargazer, who was following in a humming hoverchair from his car. "Oh yeah. He told me that before."

The mountain rumbled and a cry went up. Kimie steadied herself on the Stargazer's chair as several rocks fell past them, plummeting into the pits below. Much to her relief, the tremors soon stopped.

A blip came from Gilwain's axe. He held it up, pressed a button, listened, then said, "Understood."

Kimie looked upwards. "That was a City blast, right?"

Gilwain lowered his axe and turned to her, doing his best to contain his anger. "A mere test to see how much damage they could do. Our shields held out, but word is that ground troops are on their way."

The Stargazer dismissed this. "Yeah, but you're prepared for such an attack, right? I mean, look at your tech here. You couldn't have pinched all this from the City. They'd know if so much had been stolen, and you didn't build it from scratch either. Now since the Village is out of bounds, and communications from further afield are blocked, I'm guessing there's another factor at work."

"Yeah," Kimie agreed. "What's the deal? We want answers."

"You're not in a place to make demands …" Gilwain retorted.

"Then we both lose," Kimie countered firmly. "You fill us in on what's been happening here, then we'll spill on what the City's been up to. So, you wanna wait for another missile strike or what?"

He was unmoved. "Be wary of your words, girl. I suspect it's why you're here in the first place."

Kimie shivered as a memory returned. One from *before* she'd arrived in the City. She'd been in a fight with another girl in her … *school?* Was that it? She rubbed her temple, swearing that there was a presence here helping her memories resurface.

"This way," Gilwain indicated.

She followed him along a rocky walkway. They traversed over the dusty paths, winding up and down along the many twists and turns until arriving at a large hatch in the wall. The dwarf pressed his axe against a sensor pad, there was a beep, and the hatch rolled open with a hiss.

A long metal tunnel lay inside. The three of them entered, and as the door rolled shut behind them, Kimie made a face. The place's smell brought up another vague memory of a hospital ward. Many rooms branched off from the main tunnel. The closest, she saw, had several people working over benches.

"In here," said Gilwain, leading them in.

They headed to a bench where a man was attaching a wire to a crystal.

Another man was nearby, examining a second crystal under a microscope.

"Well, glory be," the Stargazer said, hovering in. "You found more, huh?"

"Envious?" Gilwain asked.

"Not in the least."

"Somebody wanna tell me what the story is?" Kimie pressed.

Gilwain ignored her, picked up a crystal and held it to his ear. Kimie wondered if he really was nuts, even more so when he handed it to her and said, "Listen."

Kimie didn't like his tone and was about to tell him exactly which crevice to shove the crystal in when she felt it vibrating faintly. She raised it to her ear, and her eyes widened at the pure resonance inside it.

"It's beautiful," she whispered in awe.

"Totally," the Stargazer agreed. "When I first started working for the City, its digital transmissions were shaky. We found the interference coming from a mineral in the ground. The stuff was mined and became the City's dominant wavelength, the Freakquency."

"Set up by you," Gilwain said bitterly.

"By me," the Stargazer confirmed.

Kimie examined the crystal. "So this is it in its raw state?"

Gilwain nodded. "Indeed. We've modified its natural vibrations to shield our operation here, at least until you two showed our enemies exactly where to target. We were liaising with the City's resistance factions to place these crystals around the City. It worked, to a point. These minerals stopped the System from detecting you *and* have been used effectively by our defence networks."

"Makes sense," Kimie said. "They're what shielded the club's, right?"

"Totally," the Stargazer agreed.

"Talk about alternative rock ..." Kimie muttered.

Gilwain continued. We've been learning how to use them for attacks, and since the City now knows our location, we've no choice but to fight."

"You're not ready," the Stargazer pointed out. "What you've got here is a start, but you'll need help from here on in. Try and fight the City with what you've got and they'll just raise their TaxonaMists round the whole thing, stopping you from getting in. I can help you with that, and you gotta go with me on this 'cause any direct attack'll leave you slaughtered. If I could stop the City from detecting my car at times, *as well* as hacking into their Freakquency, *and* without any help from you, then I'm a real bonus, right?"

Gilwain went silent.

"Whatever's happened between us has gotta be ditched," the Stargazer pressed. "We gotta hit the City before it hits us. Whether you like it or not, you'll need my help to creep in and launch a counterattack."

"I have enough help," Gilwain retorted.

"I bet you do," the Stargazer said, leaning in. "Which leads me to my next point. Who's backing all this? You've got your stuff from further afield, meaning this isn't your game. You're a scientist, like me. Who's pulling your strings and how do you know you can trust 'em? Believe me, trust is a hard thing in this day and age."

"Yeah," Kimie agreed, "and if we're not, like, a million percent sure your boss is against the City, then our trust factor is zilch."

Gilwain frowned. "A million percent?" He looked at Kimie sternly. "There's still the issue of my trust in you."

"Who's behind all this?" Kimie pushed. "Show some guts and speak up. Who are they?"

"Sir!" a woman called. "Contact!"

Gilwain moved past Kimie and they all headed to the middle of the room where a woman stood by a table, holding a circular digital pad. She pressed a button, and Kimie stepped back as a large holoscreen appeared, bathed in static.

"We've broken through the City's Freakquency," the woman reported to Gilwain. "It won't be for long, but longer than our first attempt. There's a ninety-eight percent chance we won't be detected."

Gilwain's jaw tightened. "Not high enough for me."

"Big deal, they know where we are," Kimie scoffed.

"Yes, but I want to see what they're up to," he replied.

The Stargazer observed the image and said to Gilwain, "Well done. Hacking into the Freakquency isn't easy."

Kimie observed the circular pad the woman held. "Great toy. Like the shape too. Hey, since it looks like an eye, why not call it an EyePad?"

The Stargazer grinned. "Already is. Thought of it ages ago. Great minds think alike."

"Cool." She peered at the holoscreen as its Static cleared a little. "Where's this place?"

"The Moneyarch's office," the Stargazer answered darkly. "His tower ruins the scenery, not to mention our dreams, so we call it the Sky Scrapper."

The static cleared further. Kimie gasped at who was in a chair. "Orion!"

A figure walked towards him.

"Is that—?" she began.

"Barbie Q," the Stargazer cut in scornfully.

Gilwain's response was bitter. "Your pride and joy?"

Kimie peered closer.

The holoscreen crackled.

"Can we hear anything?" she asked.

Gilwain adjusted the volume. "I fear the worst."

They listened as voices grew.

Chapter Eight

The Orion Sentry hung his head, spitting away a trickle of blood from his mouth. His bloodied hair draped over his defiant face, which throbbed with big black bruises, as Barbie Q walked around him, running a cold steel hand across his neck. He sat, molecularly magnetised to a chair, as every inch of him rippled, care of its force, along with the Hooker's delicate torture techniques.

He scowled as she leaned down and whispered seductively into his ear, "Was it good for you too?" A slow saxophone melody played from the speaker in her neck. "You're the best I've ever had. You've gone the longest so far. So tell me ..." She moved in close. "Who's the girl?"

He averted his eyes.

"WHO IS SHE?" she boomed.

He jumped in shock.

She sat on his lap, crossed one long leg over the other, put her arms around his neck and purred, "I hate it when we don't communicate." She stroked his face, piercing his skin with a razor-sharp nail. "Now, we know *where* she is, but I want to know *who* she is. Come on, baby, you can tell me. You've got so much to gain by opening up to the Banking Sect-Whore!"

He stayed silent.

She grinned. "Oooh, I love it when you turn up the heat on your Barbie Q!" She leaned in, kissing his cheek. His flesh sizzled and he winced, fighting against the pain as wisps of steam rose. She removed her lips, leaving a big black mark.

"Our little girl's travelled all over the City," she continued, caressing his forehead. "From your inn to a club, to the sewers and beyond. She joined the wrong crowd, gave a very naughty girl a get-out-of-jail-free card from her SORE Point, and now's run off into the desert. Where did we go wrong?" She sighed, allowing the air to echo hollowly inside her. "It's a shame, 'cause I want to get to know this baby of ours. She's got so much potential." She smirked at his defiant expression. "You really are a sucker for punishment, aren't you? I can see that you love to suck at things and you know what? So do I!"

She opened her mouth wide, placing it over his. A hum ignited as a vacuum rose from her throat, sucking the air from his lungs. He sensed what she was doing. Depriving him of oxygen and making him delirious. She'd then listen to whatever he spilled.

Her voice spoke from the small speaker in her neck. *Tell me who she is. Who's she working for?"*

He did his best to recall his inn, and before that, the Village in the forest. It didn't last long. The air rapidly depleted from his lungs, making his memories fade. Bit by bit, they became fainter and fainter until—

"Enough!"

The command came from a figure in the doorway.

The music died and Barbie Q's head rose obediently.

Orion welcomed the rush of air back into his lungs as the world returned to focus.

"Playtime's over," the newcomer ordered. "Go!"

Barbie Q rose smoothly and turned to face the person who'd spoken. She glanced back at Orion, blew him a kiss and strode confidently from the room.

Orion watched wearily as the newcomer approached. The man was dressed in a black business suit, like any typical puppet of the System, and seemed as dull and as boring as it too. Just a face to be propped anywhere as a mouthpiece for the City—at first glance anyway. Orion didn't underestimate him for a second. He knew, that despite this man's appearance, he was one of a kind.

"A visit from the Moneyarch himself?" Orion asked croakily. "These must be desperate times."

The Moneyarch spoke coolly. "Not at all. The market's fallen in my favour. Whatever you like to think about yourself, everyone has their price."

Orion stayed defiant. "Only in an ugly System where they're blind to alternatives."

The Moneyarch ignored him and pressed on. "This new girl is someone I see as a rather impressive investment opportunity. I'm prepared to offer you a good deal for her."

"You wouldn't know the meaning of the word *good*," Orion retorted. "It's just an online term to you. You're afraid of her and anything else that's a threat to the survival of the System you suck from, and being its boss makes you the biggest sucker of all."

The Moneyarch gave a small laugh. "Yes, she has caused some minor disruptions, but nothing significant. The difference between you and the System, however, is that where you see threats, it sees opportunities. The girl may be an irritation but look at the results. We took out the Sewer Queen's base, we've rid ourselves of the EpiCentre and the New-Clear Club, *and* we now know all about our Mountain of resistance too. Defiant operations on this scale are too cohesive for the resistance factions, meaning they have to be financed by someone. So who's behind it? Who's *your* superior?"

"The same one you'll have to answer to," Orion countered. "Eventually."

The Moneyarch wasn't fazed. "Are you that determined to see what the System can do? Very well. I'll show you." He paused. "Bluey's back."

Orion's face dropped.

The Moneyarch was pleased with this reaction. "She's changed her name to Mysti. Mysti Cool actually, which I rather like. She's going through an identity crisis right now, which isn't surprising, since she was released from her SORE Point before we'd augmented her fully. We're on top of that."

Orion scowled. "You're pathetic. Not evil, just sad. What did you do? Give her the identity crisis you have?"

The Moneyarch clicked his head to one side, activating the COM link behind his ear. "Bring her in."

Orion tensed.

The Moneyarch clicked his head again, severing the signal. "I'll let you see her briefly, then I'm sending you downstairs to be interrogated further by my Hookers in their Wreck-Creation room. They'll get the answers we require from you, and you *will* tell the truth. You can't lie to us when you're hooked up to our *de-fib-drillator*. I have other matters to attend to."

He pressed a button on the wall.

A TaxonaMist shimmered over Orion, surrounding him. He still saw and heard everything in the room, but knew he was invisible and mute to everyone in it, making him feel like a ghost.

The office door opened and a muscular woman was thrown to the floor. The blood drained from Orion's face as he saw Bluey's presence in her eyes, albeit minimally. She was no longer proactive, he realised, but reactive, and ready to explode. It made sense that he'd been shielded from her sight too. Bluey, or Mysti, or whatever she called herself now, was still fighting the System and it couldn't sway her easily. There was no way the Moneyarch would want her to see a battered Sentry.

She wiped her bloodied lips as Barbie Q and another Hooker stepped into the room. Barbie Q was the Hooker that everyone in the City knew about, but he'd only ever seen the other one in digital images. A ruthless Hooker who rarely left the Sky Scrapper and sincerely believed that anyone, alive or dead, was merely a unit of information to be processed by the System. She was a research collector, known as the Info-Maniac.

The Moneyarch's hand moved to his desk, touching an EyePad's screen.

Orion heard a hum from behind him, then his chair tipped up and he fell backwards through a hatch in the wall, plummeting into the darkness and the sound of giggling Hookers below. His heart sank, now knowing that Barbie Q's sick interrogation of him was only the beginning.

He braced himself for the worst.

The TaxonaMist that had shrouded the Orion Sentry flickered and vanished, leaving a blank wall. Mysti was none the wiser about who'd been there and glared up at the Moneyarch through a bruised and blackened face. She seethed as her rage grew, then lunged at him.

Barbie Q pulled her back.

Mysti struggled wildly as the Hooker giggled.

"Girl-on-girl action!" Barbie Q mocked. "What do you say we go for it?"

"I'm gonna rip both your heads off!" Mysti hissed.

"That's not going to happen," the Moneyarch said smugly.

"I was talking to them!" Mysti snapped, indicating the Hookers. "Your sick face is gonna make an inwards nose dive!"

He addressed the Hookers, unfazed. "Still nothing?"

The Info-Maniac spoke. "Her neural barriers are too strong. We can't break her in."

"I'm still up for grabs on her body," Barbie Q purred.

"What about chemical inducement?" the Moneyarch pressed.

"She's resisted everything so far," the Info-Maniac replied. "Leaving us with one tough nutcase who's here physically, as Daddy made her, but not mentally, since he lost his nerve at the crucial point."

"A fighter not a lover," Barbie Q mused, looking over Mysti with a mischievous grin. "I'm happy either way."

The Moneyarch's jaw tightened, burning at the Stargazer's treachery. He addressed Mysti, not giving anything away. "No matter. We were led to the resistance's primary base. We might not be able to break through whatever force is protecting your old Village, but at least we've confirmed that it doesn't hold the heart of the resistance. That dwells in a mountain of opportunity instead."

"Which has also got protection against our big bangs," Barbie Q added.

The Moneyarch observed Mysti thoughtfully. "In any case, you're half-way to where we want you to be. Aren't you, Blue Cloud?"

Mysti flinched and averted her gaze, hating her old code name.

He pushed on. "It's what got you into your SORE Point in the first place, isn't it? You've achieved most of your potential, just not all. We'll fix that." He glanced at the Info-Maniac. "How long until you can ensure her complete subservience?"

Her reply was cool. "Daddy's the only one who can get into her head and fix what he tampered with."

"You can't do that on your own?" the Moneyarch asked.

"Yes, with time," the Info-Maniac said, "and as much fun as it is by myself, it's better when someone's there to give you a helping hand. Her neural programming's impressive."

Mysti gave the Moneyarch a death stare. "Step outside the building, man! Just you and me. Let's see how tough you are without your cash!" She kicked a chair over and felt Barbie Q's grip tighten. "You took away everything I had, numbnuts! You stole the life of a child. No System can protect you from that!"

The Moneyarch was unmoved. "You're failing to see the alternatives. We could offer you so much."

"I'd rather have dirt," she scowled, and indicated the Hookers. "You already have the trash for it!"

He stayed calm. "I have other ways into your head. There are always market forces pulling us in every direction and you, my dear, are a very great investment opportunity. You're far more special than you think."

"So are you," Mysti jeered. "The amount of people out there gunning for you is incredible."

His fingers flickered across the EyePad. A hovering holoscreen activated over it, showing a layout of Mysti's body. "Look at these details and tell me otherwise. Your heart beats four times faster than anyone else's. Your hormones are twice as strong and your muscles have increased tenfold. Don't tell me the System hasn't improved you."

"I didn't ask for this!" she shot back.

"That's the beauty of economics," the Moneyarch said. "It can provide whatever we desire, *with* the right financial backing." He stepped in. "Little girls are becoming regular thorns in our sides these days. It's getting to be a pattern. Almost as if there's an instigator behind it all." He paused. "The Mountain may give us some answers. If you won't help us, you can watch it go up in flames." He addressed Barbie Q. "Prepare to fire."

"I'm fired up already," Barbie Q said. She threw Mysti into the Info-Maniac's clutches before moving to the EyePad on the desk.

Mysti tensed, then flinched. She shut her eyes tightly and held a hand to her temple, clearly in pain.

The Moneyarch motioned for Barbie Q to stop.

"More trouble?" he asked Mysti.

She winced. "Laughter. Can hear it all the time, even when I was in that damn prison. It's like a kid's knocking on a door in my head. She won't go away."

The Moneyarch frowned. "A new mystery. No doubt my people can fix that too."

Mysti cringed as the child's giggling grew louder in her mind.

"I can end your pain completely," the Moneyarch continued, "if you'll submit to the System. You can prevent so many casualties, simply by siding with us."

Mysti shuddered, torn between his offer and the child's mirth.

"Come on, girl," he pressed. "Show me who you really are!"

She bubbled with rage, simmering like an angry volcano with sick, festering lava ready to erupt. She wanted to unleash it on this suckhole before her, who stood grinning like a hyena. She clawed at her temples. Who to trust? The annoying kid in her brain, or the feral pig in the suit who had the resources to shut the kid up? Then there was the Mountain base. If she didn't work with the Moneyarch, people would die. If she perished, they'd endure a living hell. Who to listen to? Who to—?

She shifted awkwardly and an object tapped against her leg. The one thing she'd always trusted.

A dog leash, half-hanging from her pocket.

Choice made.

"Fire!" the Moneyarch ordered.

Barbie Q reached for the EyePad.

Mysti broke free of the Info-Maniac and swiped the EyePad from Barbie Q, sending it clattering to the ground. She crushed it under her foot, then shouldered the Hooker into a sensor pad, making a hatch in the wall hiss open. The Info-Maniac lunged for Mysti, who let loose with a savage kick, booting her hard and sending her plummeting into the darkness.

Mysti turned to Barbie Q, dodged a blow, slammed her into a wall, leapt at the Moneyarch, wrapped her dog leash around his neck and glared at him. Unfazed, he stared back at her, and she froze as a red glow filled his pupils and he spoke in a voice that wasn't his. *"You ARE the System!"*

She quivered, trying to resist his stare but finding it hypnotic. His eyes grew wider, swamping her. Part of her felt the urge to dive right in and go with it, to uncover the real secret of this useless puppet in a suit and find out what lay at the ugly root of all this, yet she also sensed herself dissolving into his gaze. The world faded and she drowned into—

Her fist tightened defiantly around Bluey's leash.

She blinked and the world solidified, allowing her to focus. There was a higher power to believe in, she concluded, and it came from the only real friends she'd ever had.

Her dog and herself.

That was all she needed.

She released the leash from the Moneyarch's neck, furiously struck him in the face, then threw him onto his desk. Barbie Q dived in, striking hard and hurling her across the room. She steadied herself against the wall as the world swirled and the laughing kid in her head returned.

Barbie Q raised her arm, letting loose with a hook.

Mysti dodged the hook and grabbed an ornamental vase from a podium. The hook hit the window, weakening it, then retracted into Barbie Q's socket.

Mysti hurled the vase at her. The hit was square on and Barbie Q's head clanged loudly. The vase fell to the floor and, to Mysti's astonishment, didn't break.

Barbie Q laughed gleefully as she leapt at Mysti and was booted into the wall in return. She bounced back easily before being kicked into the wall again and struck in the face.

The Moneyarch stepped aside, watching Mysti lash out with savage blows at Barbie Q. The Hooker blocked them all, giggling the whole time, then grabbed Mysti's wrists, leaned in and said, "Give us a kiss!"

A roaring vacuum came from inside her.

Mysti headbutted her into the wall. Barbie Q's head hit it with a clang and rebounded to headbutt her in return. Mysti seethed and tried wrenching herself free, but the Hooker was too strong.

There was only one option left. She trusted herself enough to know that she was too valuable for the Moneyarch to waste her. That meant only one thing. A leap of faith.

"Here goes nothing," she hissed. "Which was pretty much my whole life anyway!"

Still in Barbie Q's grasp, she propelled them to the window. The Hooker not only went with her but happily picked up speed. Together, they leapt into the air, hurtling themselves through the already weakened glass which shattered under the impact as they flew into the open sky high above the City.

The cold night winds swept around them as they fell towards the shimmering TaxonaMist surrounding the building's peak. Mysti had learnt, since being taken prisoner, that the TaxonaMist's strength could be adjusted and was currently set at minimum. Energy weapons couldn't penetrate it, yet it was permeable enough to allow various objects to pass through. She had an idea of which ones. They were buzzing closer and weren't the only things she heard. The kid's laughter was still in her head, and Barbie Q's insane giggles were rising as they spiralled out of the TaxonaMist. The Hooker kept her gaze fixed on Mysti, as if searching for something. Mysti glared back, refusing to play mind games, all while trusting that she wouldn't be allowed to die.

Her hunch paid off.

Barbie Q's arm rose and her hook fired up, rippling through the energy shield and hooking itself into the Moneyarch's office where it thudded into the wall tightly, bringing them to a sudden stop. They swung at the building, hit it hard, bounced off it, twirled around and dangled from the line as Barbie Q squealed with delight.

Mysti struggled free of her grip and let herself drop backwards into the open air, out of the Hooker's reach. She stretched her arms wide, feeling calm, as the wind embraced her, knowing that she was too valuable for the System to release. If her gamble paid off, great. If she died, she'd lose nothing, but dying was the last thing she wanted and always had been. The laughter in her mind ceased as she clasped her dog leash ever tighter. All she needed was faith in a dog. One simple dog to—

Whoosh!

A heavy object slammed into her and she found herself being carried through the air by the very thing she'd prayed for.

A DeciMaul riding a hoverboard. Or, as the machine was formally called due to its roving abilities, along with the canine features of the beast riding it, a Roverboard. She'd sensed that the Sky Scrapper's shield was at its lowest setting to allow these spawns of bitches in and out, and her plan to nab one by diving out the window had paid off.

The DeciMaul snarled as the Roverboard ascended.

Nearby, Barbie Q's cord retracted into her hand as she too rose.

Mysti struggled wildly, wrenched a blaster from the DeciMaul's holster, pressed it against the beast's side and fired. The DeciMaul jolted, its strength lapsed and it dropped into the clouds below. Even worse, the dog leash she'd always treasured, the one thing that meant so much to her, also fell from her hand, spiralling into the night.

The Roverboard flailed, making her swear under her breath. She quickly placed her feet into its magnetic holds, using its foot controls to steady it. It was tricky. She wobbled violently, having never used one of these things before, and prayed that it wouldn't be taken over by the City's Freakquency. Finally, she managed to work it properly and steered it through the air, glancing down to see the DeciMaul she'd shot slam into an empty police car, crushing it.

Several more Roverboards, ridden by DeciMauls and Hookers, swept around the side of the building. A Hooker flew up to Barbie Q, who detached from her line, dropped behind her and snuggled in comfortably before they both picked up speed.

Mysti navigated her Roverboard up to the Sky Scrapper's smashed window and fired at the Moneyarch. He stood motionless, having increased the TaxonaMist's strength over the window, and watched as her shots were deflected.

With no other choice, she turned and fled, swishing skilfully from side to side, surfing the wind currents high above the City streets whilst dodging the laser blasts from the DeciMauls and Hookers. Her face hardened, fuelled with anger, as she soared to a building's peak and crashed through a billboard of the Moneyarch's face. She yearned to destroy this whole damn City, to burn it to the ground in a raging inferno, but to do that she needed to strike a very big target.

A whirring noise came from ahead as a helicopter rounded a tower's corner, piloted by a Hooker.

It aimed its cannons and fired.

Mysti veered upwards. A blast caught the end of her Roverboard, blowing it in half. She plummetted in a cloud of smoke as another shot flew over her shoulder, hitting the tower's side and sending masses of rubble spiralling down after her.

She tensed as the rubble swept in.

***

The holoscreen faded.

"What the hell?" Kimie cried. "Get it back!"

The City's various camera feeds had shown her the sky battle, only cutting out when Mysti had fallen, making it impossible to tell if she'd survived or not.

The woman tapped the EyePad and fiddled with a wire on its back. "We can't. There's a Freakquency spike."

Kimie wrenched the EyePad from her, ready to have a go with the wire. Its spark zapped her hand and she yelped, dropping it.

She moved to reach for it, then saw that the Stargazer was shaking more than ever. He'd been quivering for a while, triggered by the sight of Mysti. Now he looked sickened to what was left of his stomach.

"What have I done?" he whispered. He smacked the bench. "I need a drink! Get me a drink! Just one damn—!"

Kimie knelt and clasped his hands; driven by a sympathy she never knew she'd had. "No you don't. Colours, remember? Think of happy colours. Everything you need is inside you. Not outside. Inside."

She'd never said anything like that in her life and had no idea where the words came from, yet they were truer than anything that had come out of her mouth in a long time.

He trembled. "It all turns to crud! Whatever I touch turns to crud!"

"Exactly!" Gilwain agreed.

Kimie grabbed the EyePad from the floor and hurled it at the dwarf. He dodged it, letting it smash into the wall.

"Breathe," she told the Stargazer. "Come on, we can make things better, just the two of us. Us against the world." She stopped, frowning at a vague memory of those words as she'd sat on a bus, long before this madness had started. She shook it off and continued, "We have a choice. I

106

need you. Mysti does too."

"I ..." he began.

"You're worth something," she pressed. "Not because of what you can do, but *who* you are. You're valuable. Your skills'll all come back. Trust me!"

He stared at her, entranced, then his breaths slowed and he whispered, "Sealing wax."

"Sealing wax," Kimie agreed. "That's me. Like the name. Could use it."

He swallowed hard. "Thank you."

She leaned in and hugged him. He hugged her back and she felt strange, like this was the first time in her life that she'd ever helped anybody.

Gilwain cut in. "An attack's imminent. I doubt they'll wait to get Mysti, or whatever she's called now, back before launching a full-blown assault."

Kimie rose, indicating the space where the holoscreen had been. "Can't you fix that so we can find out where she's gone?"

He submitted, albeit hesitantly. "Yes, but not soon enough. Because of you two, our enemies know our location. Their missiles can't penetrate our Mountain shields so they'll be launching ground troops next."

The Stargazer blinked as his mind cleared from the anguish of seeing Mysti. He inhaled sharply and addressed Gilwain. "The ol' Moneyarch had a point. It's strange how mystery girls keep popping up round our old Village. That the work of your employer too?"

Gilwain didn't respond.

"Which is who?" Kimie pressed. "We could sure use your boss's help right about now."

Gilwain shook his head. "No. They were clear about that. They're out of range for the moment and we can only reach them through encoded transmissions."

"Any sign of 'em showing up any time soon?"

"They've been delayed by other work."

"What could be more important than this?" Kimie asked in disbelief.

"They must be powerful," the Stargazer speculated.

"So powerful they run," Kimie scoffed. "A mother of a crisis goes down and the big boss is nowhere in sight. Typical manager!" She huffed, annoyed. "We can't just sit here waiting for your boss from inhuman resources to show up. I also know you've got bigger secrets. You haven't been skulking around in the dark all this time doing squat, am I right?"

Gilwain flinched.

Her spirit rose. "Oh, I so know I am. Go on, what's the story down here?"

The dwarf tensed.

"You wanna blow first, or you wanna wait for more missiles?" Kimie pushed. "Yeah, that'd really please your boss."

"This base isn't hidden anymore," the Stargazer pointed out to Gilwain, "and there's nowhere to run to out there, only desert." He paused as realisation dawned. "You know, I think you don't want to fight 'cause this operation's in trouble and you're too proud to admit it."

"Yeah," Kimie agreed. "What are you working on? Spill."

Gilwain fumed and then, to Kimie's astonishment, relented. "You speak the truth. It seems we have no other option. Our operation must be brought forward, even if our boss is out of contact and our weapons aren't ready."

"What weapons?" the Stargazer asked.

The dwarf hesitated, then submitted. "Come, I will show you."

"Thank you," the Stargazer said gratefully, "and that's from all the resistance factions."

"Yeah," Kimie added. "Thanks."

Gilwain nodded. "Time is short. This way."

He led them to the door.

Kimie and the Stargazer followed Gilwain into the Mountain's ash-stricken tunnels, then the three of them entered a lift. When they emerged, they were in a cave deep underground. To Kimie's bewilderment, there were several more dwarves, each with their ears pressed up against the cave wall, like they were expecting something to happen.

Kimie was baffled by the sight of the dwarves, and said curiously to Gilwain, "Don't tell me there really are seven of you."

"Sssh!" a dwarf hissed.

Gilwain moved in close to Kimie and whispered, "Yes, they are my immediate family, now shut it!"

"Why?" she asked. "What's down here?"

Part of the far wall creaked. A cry went up from the dwarves and they ran over to it excitedly, leaned in, and listened again.

"Can this get any sadder?" Kimie wondered.

Another dwarf waved his hand at her, whilst listening to the rocks intensely. "Sssh!"

"That's it!" Kimie cried, throwing an arm up. "This is way too weird for me. I'm outta here!"

"Yes!" a dwarf called. "Take her away! She's impeding our progress."

The other dwarves agreed, waving her away crossly.

"Get a life, ya kids' toy!" Kimie shot back.

The Stargazer buried his face in his hands. "Oh no!"

The dwarves ran at her.

Kimie tensed, ready to defend herself. She raised an arm, brushing it past the wall. The rocks flickered, glowed and then hummed with a gentle resonance.

The dwarves stopped in their tracks.

Kimie glanced down at the wall. "Okay, what's that?"

The dwarves gazed at her, astounded.

Her nervousness grew. "What?"

The Stargazer spoke. "That's what they were all looking for."

A dwarf approached the glow, peering at it curiously. "How did she …?"

"What's the deal?" Kimie cut in.

The glow faded, along with the resonance.

Kimie jumped as the dwarf grabbed her hand and placed it on the wall. To her astonishment, the rocks glowed again, now with a much louder hum.

"It likes you," the dwarf said.

Kimie was confused. "The wall likes me?"

"It's what's inside it," he replied.

He came in close to her, stood as high as he could and brought his face up to hers.

She grimaced and backed up against the wall, brightening it further as he spoke.

"There are crystals in these walls. They serve as nests to the insects here. The insects lay their eggs in the crystals, and when the eggs hatch, the newborns sing for a time before the family moves on. Once they're gone, the crystals hum slowly fades away. We're trying to find the crystals with the insects still in them. Creatures that we now call, ResonAnts."

Kimie stared at the wall's dimming glow. "That's what you're going to use to fight the City? Bugs and rocks?"

"Precisely," another dwarf confirmed. "The sonic vibrations, when harnessed properly, can aide us, and you're going to help locate them."

"Hang on ..." Kimie began.

"We've no time to argue," Gilwain cut in firmly. "The City's soon to attack, so there's no telling how long we have to prepare. You need to find as many crystals as possible for us to work on."

The Stargazer looked at Gilwain. "I can help you modify the biotech layout. I'll need a couple of bags of nitro, some quartz and a pinch of sodium. These babies'll be ready before you can blink."

Kimie shook her head. "So all I get here is that you need my help to find bugs in the walls to fight the bad guys with. Fine, I can do that if you two—" she motioned to Gilwain and the Stargazer, "—promise to play nice."

Gilwain sighed and nodded.

The Stargazer held Kimie's hand. His grip seemed a lot warmer now. "Good stuff, Sealing Wax."

"Thanks," she said back, holding his hand equally tightly. "Same goes. We got this."

"Yeah," he agreed. "We got it."

She grinned and touched the wall again. It flared brightly and her grin grew greater than ever. "Oh, we have so got this!"

The Stargazer and Gilwain left for the labs, conferring about the enhanced ratios of trigonometric, hieroglyphical harmonies. Kimie stayed with the scientists, scanning for the ResonAnts in the walls. It took her a while to get used to their technology, but soon she was extracting the crystals with delicacy and precision, all while hearing the squealing noises from within.

It was hot in the mine and she worked for ages, growing sweaty and covered in ash. Luckily, the City fired no further missiles, nor did any attack come. Finally, and much to her relief, she was summoned back to the sterile labs, and when she entered she was not a happy girl. Yes, she'd enjoyed extracting the crystals from the walls, but the conditions she'd worked in had been horrific. Now, looking dishevelled and seriously annoyed, she found Gilwain and the Stargazer absorbed in their work.

"If we relay the temporal conversion field—" Gilwain began.

"Followed by a multi-loop feedback circuit—" the Stargazer added.

"Cross-referenced with a phenolomic indicator—"

"Corresponding with the fluctual dynamics—"

"We should have—"

"Water!" Kimie cried, grabbing Gilwain's shoulders and pulling him up to her. "*I need water!*"

Gilwain was unimpressed by her lack of resilience. "If you must."

He motioned to a scientist, who placed a jug of water before her.

She released Gilwain and downed the whole thing in one go. When finished, she wiped her mouth, then her face, and said wearily, "Don't ever do that to me again."

"Don't ever mention our height, then," Gilwain muttered.

The Stargazer grabbed an EyePad. "Here we go. Get ready to rock and roll!"

"You got something?" Kimie asked.

"Oh yeah, kid," he replied, activating a sequence. "The ResonAnts crystals plus big guns equals—"

The hatch to the next room rolled open and a well-built man emerged, carrying a massive gun with a ResonAnts crystal attached. The weapon hummed, sounding like synthesised music which was also—

"Pure rock," the Stargazer announced.

Kimie observed the man curiously. "Is he …?"

"A scientist," Gilwain confirmed. "A Tech with a military background."

The Stargazer indicated the weapon's gem. "We've given him a telepathic link to his gun's ResonAnts crystal. That makes him a Symbiotech."

Kimie was too curious about the newcomer to appreciate the term. "So the crystal adds power to the gun?"

"More than that," the Stargazer said proudly.

The Symbiotech raised his hand, waving it past the weapon. An electric guitar's resounding bellow erupted as the gun powered up.

"Okay," Kimie stated, "that's cool."

More Symbiotechs emerged from the doorway, all carrying guns that hummed in unison.

Kimie was more than impressed. "Awesome!"

Gilwain saw a terminal screen's readout. "And only just in time. The City's launched ground troops."

"Game on!" the Stargazer said.

Kimie gazed at the Symbiotechs in awe. "Looks like the hills really are alive with the sound of music." She grinned. "Let's rock!"

Chapter Nine

Kimie nestled into the Ralloy Car's passenger seat and watched the Stargazer activate his keyboard. They were back in the desert, facing the City, with the Stargazer gloating that his car's automated defence shields had protected his car from being wiped out by the City's test missiles.

A humming ResonAnts crystal sat on the dashboard, attached to a small screen by colourful wires. The screen flickered, showing an image of a military buildup heading across the desert for the Mountain. They were still some way off but getting closer by the moment.

"How are we getting to the City through all that?" Kimie wondered.

The Stargazer tapped the dashboard. "This baby's got a couple of surprises tucked away."

She tensed. "I still don't like the idea of setting ourselves up as targets while your mountain buddies launch a covert attack."

"Relax," he told her, "you're with me, remember?"

"Yeah, driven by a drunken space cadet into an ambush. Why didn't I set off with them instead?"

"'Cause we got on so well," he answered.

She drew a sharp breath. "Can't argue with that, spaceman. What's the genius attack plan that you two were babbling about?"

He keyed in a sequence of coordinates. "The City's TaxonaMist now shields it completely, kinda like a security shell on its nest egg. It's all thanks to the Info-Maniac, who's been screwing around with things as usual. The shell's tough and stops any form of attack."

"Which is what we're doing," Kimie pointed out. "Openly."

"Yep," he confirmed. "We're doing a full-frontal spectacle."

"You have *no* idea how disgusting that sounds."

He hit a switch. "Gilwain and his team created a network of tunnels leading into the City a while back. The plan's to creep up through the sewers. They also loaded the tunnels with modified ResonAnts crystals to shield themselves. That's why the rodent kids can live in 'em undetected, or they'd have been fumigated long ago. Our job's to bring down the City's shields and then cut out its digital networks to stop the bad guys from talking to each other."

"Not asking for much, is it?" Kimie muttered.

He tapped the crystal on the dashboard. "I can do that with the help of this thing. When we've done our job, Gilwain and the Symbiotechs can enter the City covertly through the sewers. We've already contacted the resistance factions, including the Sewer Queen. They're moving the civilians into her territory with the City none the wiser. Gilwain's lot'll start getting 'em outta town. When they're all gone, his army'll attack the Sky Scrapper."

"There was a traitor in the clubs, remember?" Kimie pointed out. "How do we know we're not being sucked into something?"

"We don't," he replied. "There's secrets on both sides. We just have to do what we can because—"

"It's the right thing. I know."

"Sure is," he confirmed. "Taxes are so high and everyone's so broke that no one can afford cars or anything else. There's not even a news system, which is fine by the City. The last thing it wants is to broadcast any of this 'cause democracy's bad for business. The most recent cutbacks to feather the nests of the big boys up top means no emergency services either, so even the hospitals are empty."

Kimie sighed. "Why do we have to be the open target here?"

"'Cause it's fun. Hold tight."

He hit several keys, igniting the car's fiery jets. Kimie's stomach heaved as the car shot ahead, making her feel like a human cannonball.

"I hate this crap!" she wailed, going greener by the moment.

"Whoops!" the Stargazer called over the noise. "Forgot the internal stabilisers!"

He hit a button.

The pressure around Kimie eased, along with most of her nausea. A loud whine erupted as two wings sprouted from the car's sides and she braced herself, knowing what was coming next. With a searing roar of its thrusters, the car lifted into the air, soaring over the desert.

Kimie forgot about her nausea, thinking this was way cool. The thought of the army up ahead brought her back to reality and she asked, "We're just gonna rush headlong into battle?"

"Totally," the Stargazer answered simply.

"Care to fill me in on what you got planned?"

"What you don't know can't—forget it."

The Ralloy Car blurred through the sky, sweeping over a large sector of the desert in mere moments. It wasn't long before the City's attack force appeared, coming way too soon for Kimie's liking.

A warning light flashed on the dashboard.

"We've been targeted!" the Stargazer called happily.

Kimie was astounded. "That's a good thing?"

"Oh, yeah, watch this!"

She yelped as the car turned upside down, spinning wildly with bellowing synthesised rock music.

Furious blasts flared up from the army, flashing at the swirling vehicle. The car predicted their trajectories, rolling over in mid-air as it evaded them all, and leaving Kimie somewhere between complete and utter fear and hurling big time.

The firing ceased abruptly, then several DeciMauls on Roverboards swept in. Their gunfire bored into the car with little effect, before a few of them were rammed into the sky. The rest veered away.

Kimie looked ahead, seeing the City encased in a dark halo.

"Shield looks tough," she noted.

"Yep," the Stargazer agreed. "It's a bad Freakquency." He played the keyboard lightly, releasing a soft melody. "Always keep a spare set of keys …"

The DeciMauls surged in again, firing relentlessly. The car shook under the impact as its melody rose.

The City's halo flickered wildly, then dropped altogether.

"Hell, yeah!" the Stargazer cried.

He let loose with a powerful burst of the car's thrusters and sped in.

"Don't get so excited!" Kimie called. "We're going straight into hell, remember?"

"Been there for years," he quipped.

"So the City's turned into a free-for-all?"

"Yep. Its Freakquency's down. Defences and communication are out, except for—"

"That never sounds good—"

"—the Sky Scrapper," he finished. "It's still too high there. I can't break it."

"But that's where we wanna go."

"Relax, there's another plan, then another one after that should worse come to worst."

Kimie cringed. "Oh, crappy day!"

The controls beeped rapidly.

Kimie shuddered. "Do I wanna know what that is?"

"No," the Stargazer answered. "Incoming!"

"What—?"

He rolled the car over again, veering to the side. The edge of a shell clipped its front wheel and exploded, making Kimie lurch sickeningly. Thankfully, the car's alloy held firm.

The Stargazer turned a dial. "Surf's up! With sonic waves!"

Kimie recalled her trick in the EpiCentre with the microphone and the speaker. "Aren't the Hookers ready for that now?"

"You got about five seconds to think up a better idea."

He worked the keyboard quickly.

Kimie grumbled under her breath as they entered the City limits. The Sky Scrapper was in sight, surrounded by its defence shield.

The Stargazer worked furiously, trying to bypass it.

Kimie saw his frustration. "Problem?"

"Can't break the TaxonaMist," he answered.

"Your music's not working?"

"The Moneyarch's is stronger. It's formed a tough shell."

"What's he using?"

"Heavy metal."

Clank!

Clank!

The car jolted violently.

"Looks like we've been Hookered," the Stargazer said grimly.

Kimie gulped at the sight of a long metal line attached to the car door. She looked down. Barbie Q was on the other end, having left her Rover-board to explode into a building behind her. Her line retracted rapidly into her hand as she ascended.

Kimie glanced over to the Stargazer's window, saw another line, and knew that a second Hooker was ascending too.

"Ballop!" the Stargazer said, in what Kimie assumed was a curse. "New and improved Hookers."

"Made of the same stuff as your car?" Kimie asked. "They can hook on when the big guns can't hurt us, so I'm guessing yes?"

"Their alloy's been strengthened," he replied. "God knows with what, but they'd probably call it tough love."

"'Cause Hookers are the toughest lovers there are, right?"

"Your heart's not the first thing they'll break."

He steered the car towards a bridge.

Tap, tap, tap!

Kimie yelped. Barbie Q was at the window, having appeared with surprising speed. Another Hooker was on the Stargazer's side. Despite this, he was unfazed.

"There's an easy way to get unhooked," he said coolly "We just need to distract 'em first."

He hit a control and the windows lowered with a hum.

Kimie was aghast. "What the crap are you doing?"

Barbie Q reached in for her.

Smack!

The edge of the bridge hit Barbie Q hard, sending her flying off the car.

The second Hooker opened her mouth, revealing a flicker of flames, ready to erupt.

The Stargazer swung the car to the right, veering by a building and smacking her away.

"Score against the ho-bots!" Kimie called over the wind.

He put the windows up, cutting off the gale.

"VolcanHo," he corrected. "That's her name. She was an old flame. The clingy type too. See?" He indicated a screen, showing the Hookers again dangling from his car by their lines. "You gotta get outta here."

"Forget it," Kimie retorted. "Can't leave anyway."

"You got no choice, kid."

The car descended.

Kimie saw Barbie Q rising to the car again and knew that the VolcanHo was doing the same. She gulped as they reached it in no time, climbed on swiftly, then ducked as it swooped under another bridge.

"Good luck," the Stargazer said.

"Get stuffed," Kimie shot back. "I'm not going anywhere."

"I used to think the same thing until I found you," he replied. "Trust me on this one, Sealing Wax. Or should that be Ceiling Wax?"

"What the—?"

He hit a button. A seat belt came out of nowhere, strapping itself around her waist and almost squeezing the air out of her. She winced as the roof hatch swung open, hitting Barbie Q in the face.

Kimie's seat shook as the chair bellowed with rock music. A thruster blast shot her high, the world blurred and the cold night wind engulfed her as she was ejected past a skyscraper. Darkness, sickness, anger and terror all warped into one as her seat flew through a cloud, blaring with an air guitar.

The chair reached its peak, her stomach caught up a moment later, then both she and it started descending. The full view of just how high she actually was shook her and she gasped in shock. Thankfully, a chair setting activated and it steered her downwards.

She inhaled sharply. "Anti-grav tech. Way cool." She thought back to the Stargazer's final words and muttered, "Ceiling wax, god you're a kno—"

A burst of DeciMaul fire shot past her, making her jump.

Her seat whined, as if sensing her thoughts, and propelled her through the sky, dodging the blasts.

Somehow, she spotted the Stargazer's car shooting in for the Sky Scrapper. It too, had a halo, just like the building's, only not as dark. She knew what he was up to—breaking through the Sky Scrapper's shield with the only option left. Brute force.

"No, ya tool!" she cried, flooded with dread.

The car rushed in.

Another wave of DeciMaul blasts shot past her. The chair veered round the side of a building, leaving her unable to see what happened next. A distant explosion compensated for that. She shuddered as the shock of the blast hit home, like the car had slammed into her instead.

She held back her tears—there wasn't time to cry with gunfire sweeping in. The Stargazer had brought down the tower's barrier by finally thinking of others. He'd thrown his life away but it was too little too late—he could have done so much more.

The chair descended smoothly as she hoped, and prayed, that the dwarf and his lot were doing better than she was.

Gilwain stood, holding his enormous jeep's window tightly, as his driver led the military convoy through the sewers. The vehicle, broad and strong enough to carry a fair amount of passengers for the imminent evacuation, had been built to fit through the sewers perfectly. Several jeeps were behind him, driven by Mountain personnel and carrying Symbiotechs. Getting into the City had been easy once its barrier had dropped. It was dealing with the refugees that Gilwain found to be a headache. Up ahead, a large group of them, along with Alley Cats and Sewer Rats, were running in.

He leapt off his vehicle, hurried to a ladder, ascended a few rungs and held on as the crowd swept past. The first wave of civilians clambered on the lead vehicle. The next lot went on the one behind it, and the jeeps soon filled rapidly. When they were all full, the rear ones reversed through the sewers.

Gilwain climbed his ladder. Nearby, a few Symbiotechs were climbing another. They seemed eager for battle, he noted. Too eager. He'd planned to have everyone evacuated in a smooth, orderly fashion before the attack commenced. Now he knew that wouldn't be possible. His army was as keen to rush into the City as its people were to leave it. There was no other option but to start the assault, he concluded. He'd just have to ensure that no civilians up top were harmed.

His blood boiled with the heat of battle as he rose through a manhole and into the street above. A short distance away, another manhole cover shot up high before dropping heavily onto the pavement. A Symbiotech emerged from below, followed by two others, only to be greeted by fierce blasts from DeciMauls on Roverboards. The Symbiotechs raised their guns in an electric burst of rock music and fired back, sending multi-coloured waves streaming into the beasts and hurling them to the ground as husks of burning dog hair.

A hand reached out from the shadows, grabbed a Symbiotech's shoulder and whirled him around to face a Hooker.

"Naughty, naughty," she warned. "How 'bout a kiss?"

She pulled him in close, pressed her lips on his, opened her mouth, and a tongue-like dagger squelched out the back of his head, making him slump. Gleefully, she threw him aside as her tongue retracted and she licked her lips.

"I've had better."

Gilwain bellowed with a warrior's cry and ran in, swinging his blade into the Hooker's metal stomach, striking it with a heavy clang, and pressing a button on the axe's handle, releasing an electrical surge. The Hooker jolted awkwardly, before a ResonAnts gun blast sent her flying straight through a shop window. Furious shots from the other Symbiotechs illuminated the night, sending DeciMauls and Hookers flying.

A Hooker ducked a Symbiotech's wavering blast, leapt at him, smacked his gun away, grabbed his face in her hands and sucked the life out of him. He fell to the ground as she jumped onto another Symbiotech, doing the same.

Two more Hookers ran past, giggling and holding hands as they eagerly entered the battle. They released their grips, somersaulted high in the air, flew over a blast and landed on a Symbiotech, with one on his back, the other on his front.

He growled as his gun was smacked away. Picking up strength, he hurled himself straight at a brick wall, slamming the Hooker on his front into it with a resounding clang. She laughed as he whirled around and smacked himself backwards into a window, thumping the Hooker there against it. Like the first, she too held on firmly and giggled.

"We need to strengthen our relationship," she whispered.

Their chests expanded to a dangerous level, engulfing his head and ready to mash it. He kicked at his gun on the ground in a desperate attempt to release the crystal, to no avail. He kicked a few more times, and the crystal came loose, erupting with a blinding light that flared high, along with a piercing squeal. The Hookers' grips weakened as he grabbed their hands, aimed them at each other and …

Thuk!

Thuk!

Their hooks ran right through their metal craniums, bursting out the other side as their heads exploded in a mesh of sparks. He pushed them off him, grabbed his gun, reattached the ResonAnts crystal, and sealed off its blazing effects.

A buzz came from behind him and he turned swiftly, dodging another Hooker's line. She screamed like a banshee and ripped a postal box from the ground, hurling it at him. He dodged that too, ran in and kicked her straight into his people's blasts. She writhed wildly in the shots, then slumped to the ground.

There was only one Hooker left now. She cowered in terror as the Symbiotechs loomed in, surrounding her.

"No, Daddy, no! I'll be a good girl, I promise!"

Her head was severed by a blast, flew high and smacked a DeciMaul on a Roverboard in the face. More shots sent both the beast and his Roverboard into a flaming plummet.

A Symbiotech walked over to a fallen Roverboard lying between two others. He stepped on it, before his comrades mounted the remaining ones. Whirrs rose as all three ascended, soaring high into the night whilst evading the shots from the approaching DeciMauls.

Another whine caught their attention. A human one, this time from Kimie who raced past them on the Ralloy Car's ejection seat, with several

DeciMauls hot on her tail.

"Coming through!" she called.

A Symbiotech fired. Kimie jumped as the shot skimmed past her head, hit a DeciMaul, zigzagged off two more and hit another. All fell from their Roverboards.

"Thanks, man!" Kimie quipped, swooping away.

The Symbiotechs ignored her and continued their ascent, picking up speed as they glided over the City.

Finally, they reached what they were looking for: the central power station.

They fired, sending ResonAnts blasts streaking from their guns in long lines of fury, pummelling the building.

The Moneyarch watched from the Sky Scrapper as, bit by bit, large sections of the City fell into darkness. Finally, the only things left to see were the explosions, the laser fire and the full moon. He sneered as the night breeze wafted in through his broken window, courtesy of Mysti, and embraced him in its smoky touch.

The Sky Scrapper's shield was gone. That was thanks to the traitor who now called himself the Stargazer. Long ago, the treacherous wretch, then known as the Engine-Ear, had created the shield in a drunken state from a device called the GenEarator. He'd now rammed his car into that machine, knowing exactly where to target. Thankfully, the tower's shield had been strong, leaving minimal damage to the building. It also left it defenceless, save for a small forcefield emanating from the Moneyarch's EyePad on his desk. Regrettably, the EyePad's range was limited, confined to the building's interior.

A few DeciMauls on Roverboards flew past his shattered window. He seethed. They were no longer under his command, now that the City's Freakquency had fallen, and were free to do what they wished. The Hookers were the same, leaving everyone to run amok. Still, he'd be safe in his tower, for the moment. His EyePad kept everyone here under his control.

His face hardened as three Symbiotechs on Roverboards fired at the City's bank in the distance, sending it up in a rip-roaring explosion that billowed high into the night.

His head rose. They'd hit him right where it hurts by blowing up the bank. To him, it was the worst kind of …

"Bankruption!" he hissed.

Kimie too, saw the flaming bank as her chair hit the ground. In the distance, three Symbiotechs on Roverboards were hovering over its remains.

She unbuckled her belt and stood up, shaking from both the chair's rapid descent and the surrounding chaos. Dread rippled through her. The attack was meant to be on the Sky Scrapper, not going off like fireworks all over the City, putting lives at risk. She watched as a group of DeciMauls swooped in for the Symbiotechs and were gunned down ruthlessly. Their burning bodies plummeted as the Symbiotechs turned and fired on the City, letting loose. An apartment block went up. The hospital went next, then the community hall imploded. She dived for cover as a crackling wave of gunfire flew past her and she scampered behind a flaming bin and peered around it.

For the first time since leaving the New-Clear Club, she saw people. Not dwarves or DeciMauls or Hookers or anything freakishly weird, but ordinary people. Men, women, children, the elderly. They were fleeing from the burning buildings and running to whatever safety they could find. Weren't they all meant to be in the sewers, she wondered. There should have been an underground army guiding them to the Mountain.

Further bursts of gunfire rained down, turning the landscape into a searing Armageddon. An apartment window shattered and a child's wail erupted inside, along with the piercing crackles of growing flames.

"This is wrong, this is so wrong," Kimie whispered.

The child's wails grew louder. She watched as two people ran into the building, then re-emerged with a family. She was glad they were out. Really glad. If no one had been here she'd have been forced to try and save the family herself, which could have turned out nasty for everyone.

Four more Symbiotechs appeared down the street and fired. The survivors ducked, letting the blasts fly over their heads, then fled.

"Talk about a population explosion," Kimie said shakily.

Her thoughts turned to Gilwain. The little runt had betrayed them.

He'd used the Stargazer to get into the City. Now everyone here, good or bad, was a Symbiotech target.

Her lips pursed and she murmured, "You are so dead."

Gilwain too, gazed in fury upon the Symbiotechs, both in the sky and on the streets. He pulled out a device—a failsafe mechanism to deactivate their guns—and stabbed his thumb on a button.

Nothing.

He tried again.

Still nothing.

"Betrayal!" he hissed.

He threw the device to the ground, crushing it under his foot. Clutching his axe tightly, he ran down the street, vowing to take on the Moneyarch himself. His blood boiled as he headed for the Sky Scrapper, still some way off.

A gun blast streamed in from above, blowing into a car and sending it sky high. The DeciMaul who'd fired leapt off a Roverboard, lunging at him with a savage roar.

Gilwain ducked a swiping claw and swung his axe heavily, thudding it into the beast's chest and hitting the button on its handle. An electrical surge rippled through the DeciMaul, making it jolt awkwardly before dropping to the street.

Another DeciMaul landed and sprang.

The dwarf struck fiercely, smacking its gun away. The beast swiped back, striking Gilwain's axe into a wall.

Gilwain dived. He hit the ground, grabbed the DeciMaul's fallen gun, rolled onto his back and then—

Bang!

The beast's head exploded in a blinding flash and its body fell backwards, crashing to the ground.

Gilwain rose and went over to his axe. He picked it up, placed it into the strap on his back, clutched the DeciMaul's gun tightly and ran into the night.

Kimie ran through the burning streets.

People were fleeing, but they were too far away for her to join up with and only focused on each other. She couldn't see any bodies—thankfully—yet knew she'd come across them sooner or later. The relentless gunfire and buildings blowing to high heaven told her that.

A woman cried hysterically in a doorway. Kimie headed for her, then yelped as a figure reached out from an alleyway, pulling her into it.

"Hey …!" she snapped, ready to bust their head in.

"Fancy meeting you here, Glow Worm," came the smooth reply.

The sight of the Dragonfly's face made time stop and she forgot everything as the chaos faded around her.

Doorway-woman's cries brought her back to reality. She looked out of the alley and saw her run into a man's arms before they both fled.

"Get down!" the Dragonfly ordered. He pulled her behind a dumpster as a blast exploded metres away. The DeciMaul who'd fired from a Roverboard snarled and soared away, pursuing greater prey.

"You okay?" the Dragonfly asked her.

She smacked his hand away. "What do you think? That I'm gonna be singing and dancing when all hell breaks loose 'cause someone screwed us over?"

"I heard Bluey's back," he said, concerned.

"Man, are you in for a surprise. She's called Mysti now."

They watched as a Hooker's cord swept in for a man on the street. He dodged it and bolted as the Hooker followed. Kimie moved to help but was held fast by the Dragonfly.

"Get off me!" she snapped.

"You're not going anywhere," he warned.

"I gotta help him!"

"With what? Hairbands?"

"With the guts you don't have!"

He held her tightly as they saw the fleeing man run past an alleyway. Another man emerged, holding a DeciMaul's gun, and fired at the Hooker who dodged the blast. The two men fled, with her in hot pursuit.

Kimie shuddered. "God, I wish I'd stayed home."

"And miss out on huddling up with a gorgeous guy like me?" he quipped.

She looked at him and her heart sparked, feeling an urge. A drive. A desire. The next thing she knew she was moving her hand to the back of his head to bring him in closer.

He stopped her. "Maybe if you were a little older, kid."

"What if I let you?" she asked, almost pleading.

"No deal," he responded, then turned away and stopped.

She tensed, her insides a bubbling flurry.

"Things are easing off now," he noted. "There's less firing."

Kimie blinked, amazed that she hadn't noticed. Flames still flickered in the streets and there were minor explosions in the distance, but things were somewhat quieter.

"Less people too," she observed, then frowned. "No bodies either, which is weird. You'd think after an attack like this there'd be some kind of sick urban sprawl."

"Worry about it later," he told her. "Come on, we'd better leave while we can."

He moved to go. She pulled him back.

"We don't have to leave just yet," she said softly.

"Yeah," he countered firmly. "We do."

He crept to the edge of the alley and cautiously peered out.

"Hey!" Kimie called.

He turned back.

She grabbed his face and kissed him. He didn't give into it and pulled away.

"Sorry," she said simply. "Just taking a chance."

"You're not sorry," he stated.

"You're right," she agreed. "Why didn't you kiss back?"

"You know why," he answered.

"Do you have to be so damn honourable?"

He indicated the surrounding chaos. "Look what happens when you're not. Still, you got lucky with that kiss, kid. Well done."

She shrugged.

"Just don't do it again," he warned, and headed away.

She sighed sadly and followed him. "You shouldn't be called the Dragonfly. You're HeartbreaKing!"

Chapter Ten

Several Symbiotechs on Roverboards soared over a smouldering pile of rubble, focussed on targets ahead. They glided over an empty square and had barely gone when the rubble shifted and a hand emerged. Slowly, and painfully, the Stargazer pulled himself out of the burning debris and fell gasping onto the road.

"That's some strong Ralloy," he murmured, thinking of his car. Its final power reserves had created an energy shield, protecting him from the crash and the building's pummelling rubble, and he was grateful for it. He rolled wearily onto his back and patted his pockets desperately, searching for his flask.

Another object caught his attention, lying in the rubble beside him.

A dog leash.

He shut his eyes tightly, knowing the leash well. He'd studied Bluey's love of it when he'd created the SORE Point to trap her. He trembled, then grabbed it, knowing it might come in handy. He quickly stuffed it into his shirt before searching for his flask again.

"Looking for this?"

Two long, smooth legs stepped in front of him.

His head slumped in despair. "Ballop!"

Barbie Q loomed before him, now with only half a face. The other half was a grotesque metal skeleton, thanks to her slamming into a bridge while on top of his Ralloy Car. Her stringy, burnt hair fell over her hideous features as she held up his flask with one hand and pulled him clean from the rubble with the other.

He wailed in agony.

She threw the flask over her shoulder, sending it high into the night, then dropped him heavily onto the road and rolled him onto his back. He cringed as she slid on top of him, lying flat and pushing him into the hot ground with her even hotter metal body.

"Hiiiiiiii-eeeee, Daddy," she purred. "Been a long time, hasn't it?"

"Not long enough," he croaked, averting his gaze.

"Oh, don't be like that," she said, with a macabre grin. "Remember the times we had? They were such fun, weren't they? Whatever you wanted, I always did." Her grin widened. "Always."

He quivered. "I've never forgiven myself for it."

She ran a cold metal finger along his blackened cheek. "You were my first real love. I always left you with sweet dreams."

He shivered. "What do you want? You got something to do, do it." Realisation dawned. "Oh, that's it. You're no longer under the City's control but can't leave it. Too many enemies. You need my help to get out."

She hummed softly.

He shut his eyes, recalling the tune well. "Stop it!"

She spoke tenderly. "They all say that."

"Code 137, deactivate!"

She smirked. "Emergency cut-out switch was the first thing to go after you walked out on us, Daddy. Since then I've had *improvements* in places you wouldn't believe."

He opened his eyes in horror. "You're a freak!"

She giggled. "Created by one. I've waited on you, now it's your turn to wait on me ..."

"Cut it out!"

Her eyebrows rose. "Really?"

"No, no, no ..."

She snickered. "You're funny, Daddy." Her monstrous face loomed closer. "Here's your chance to fix things, and in more ways than one. First, I need hair and makeup. Very important. I look like death warmed up."

Her skeletal eye glowered maniacally. "That's what happens when someone throws a banger on the Barbie Q. Luckily I don't get hurt that easily. I'm made of strong stuff." She chuckled. "Then we'll sort out that naughty lot from the Mountain who keep shooting at me. I can tell you had a hand in their creation. I want one in their downfall. A strong one. With my fingerprints all over it."

"I didn't make 'em do this," he said shakily. "I checked their backgrounds when I hacked into the Mountain systems just before the attack. The dwarf's security codes were so basic he may as well have left everything open." He blinked, still bewildered by how easy it had been to break in. "The Symbiotechs were scientists whose passion was learning. The crystals on their guns hold life forms that aren't evolved enough to have an agenda either. It's more likely that someone's manipulated the psychic link between the scientists and the crystals so they could shoot up the City. That level of manipulation takes skill way beyond me."

"There's also our precious Mysti Cool," Barbie Q reminded him. "She puts up a pretty good fight. We could use her."

His heart pounded. "She's alive?"

She silkily touched the warm debris on his skin. "Oooh, you're hot when you tremble. Last we saw she'd survived a sky attack and was running from a hotel, making for the sewers. Wanna find her?"

He frowned, then realised what she was getting at. "Oh, you don't want to run from the City at all. You've got free will now, so you're going for a takeover bid and need me to get rid of your rivals first." He drew a sharp breath. "I knew I should have left you as a dishwasher."

Her chest whirred as her metal grew hotter.

"I'm getting angry," she warned. "You know what that means, don't you?" The heat grew as she moved her head closer to his and whispered, "My silicon's overheating."

He shut his eyes again. The burning was intense, leaving him no choice but to agree.

"You win," he said glumly. "I'll do it."

Her temper, and her body, cooled. "Great! It's a date."

He opened his eyes and nodded reluctantly. "Yeah. A date."

"Goody!"

She rolled off him eagerly, stood up and reached down.

He groaned as he was picked up, hoisted over her shoulder and carried along the street. Gloomily, he glanced at the surrounding chaos, then at himself, and sighed.

"Carried through a burning Babylon by the closest thing to a whore," he said wearily. "Definitely the Apocalypse!"

Gilwain stopped in an empty laneway.

The Sky Scrapper was close. There were only a few blocks to go, but the path wasn't getting any easier. Enormous mounds of rubble were ahead and the long road around them led straight into gunfire. Going it alone was getting him nowhere.

He crouched behind a fallen gargoyle, raised his axe and activated its COM link, planning to let those in the Mountain know of the Symbiotechs' treachery. He hoped—and prayed—that no further betrayal had taken place back in the big base.

All he heard was static.

He increased the signal strength and got the same result.

He scowled. The City had no power, so there shouldn't be any digital interference. He twisted another dial and frowned curiously. The static was coming from deep below the City, from another source. Strangely, he couldn't get a fix on it.

He pulled a device from his pocket and activated it. A screen appeared, showing a desert highway, relayed by a Mountain observation camera on a separate wavelength. He zeroed the camera in and saw a Rolls Royce driving rapidly towards the City. His face dropped. Now he knew he was in trouble. His boss was on their way, and right after he'd gone against their orders by attacking the City too soon.

"Burn this damn beard!" he hissed.

He shut the image off, pocketed the device, rose and moved on, doing his best to forge a path to the Sky Scrapper. There was still a mission to complete and the more he could achieve before his boss arrived, the better. If not, he'd have a lot of explaining to do.

So would the new girl, he vowed, if he ever caught up with her.

Kimie and the Dragonfly splashed through an alleyway's puddles, trudging over masses of junk, gunk and DeciMaul corpses. The firing had ceased between the Symbiotechs and DeciMauls, but there were still screams and distant explosions. Even worse, buildings were crumbling, gas pipes were blowing, and the City itself seemed against them, ready to unleash its dying wrath.

Kimie stopped and peered over the ground. "Should be a manhole round here somewhere. That'll take us to the Sewer Queen, if she's alive."

The Dragonfly indicated a burning fire station up ahead. "Good call. When that thing goes up we'll need cover. I'd like to meet Yushera too. Heard a lot about her."

They saw a manhole cover and approached it.

A cat's hiss spat from behind them. They turned to see a figure crouching in the shadows.

Kimie knew exactly who it was. "Alley-Money, thank god!" She blinked, confused. "Why've I got a sudden memory of my mum saying that?"

"Do not lift the lid!" Alley-Money ordered, pointing at it. "A detonator lies underneath."

"Can you get us in another way?" the Dragonfly asked.

"The Labyrinth of the Underworld will not ensure your safety," Alley-Money replied. "Several royal paths were destroyed. Its foundations are unstable."

Kimie frowned. "Isn't there an evacuation happening?"

"As we speak," Alley-Money confirmed. "My people have guided many City survivors to our Mountain allies in the sewers. The bellies of the metal beasts are full …"

"You mean whatever their driving?" Kimie interjected.

Alley-Money nodded, " … and they now retreat from the City. They may not have time to return for those who remain, so my kind are guiding them out on foot. Our Queen is not with them. She refuses to leave."

Kimie grimaced. "A kingdom of crap? What is it with you guys?" She shook her head. "Shouldn't there have been, like, a more organised way of getting everyone out?"

"Yes," Alley-Money said, "but the attack started earlier than expected.

Our allies were too eager to taste the blood of battle."

Crash!

A trashcan hit the ground and rolled over. Kimie tensed as a Symbiotech rounded the corner. He was sleeker than the others, and moved fluidly, meaning he could run. She caught sight of a fallen DeciMaul's gun on the ground and went for it, but the Dragonfly got there first, grabbing the weapon. She yelped as Alley-Money wrapped a slimy cord around her stomach, pulling her back. Despite this, Kimie was only focussed on the Dragonfly.

"You can't throw your life away you tool!" she cried desperately as she was hoisted away. The cord dug deeper into her belly. "Let me go, ya fleabag!"

The Symbiotech's weapon charged with a whine.

So did the Dragonfly's.

The Symbiotech fired.

The Dragonfly ducked the blast and fired back. The Symbiotech dodged the shot and fired again, blowing a hole in the wall behind the Dragonfly and sending a mass of rubble plummeting, half-burying him.

Kimie froze, then screamed.

A fierce hoist from Alley-Money brought her around the alleyway's corner.

"Move!" the Alley Cat ordered, pulling her along.

Kimie swore as tears formed in her eyes. Her only thoughts were on saving the Dragonfly, if he wasn't dead already, but that would prove impossible now.

Alley-Money pulled her to a manhole cover, took both ends of the cord in one hand, reached down, and pressed a button on the cover. The explosive trap beeped and deactivated, she pulled the cover away, threw Kimie in and leapt after her.

Kimie dropped heavily, landing on concrete. She nearly gagged when she saw that the sewer water was filled with blood and large chunks of DeciMaul hair, having drained in from the streets above.

Alley-Money hoisted her up. "Hurry!"

Kimie was about to tell her to shove it when several bangs, crashes and laser blasts came from above, before a figure dropped, landing upright in the sewers. She hoped like hell it was the Dragonfly.

No such luck. It was Gilwain.

She pulled away from Alley-Money, making for a ladder by the open manhole.

The dwarf raised his axe, blocking her path.

"It's not safe!" he said fiercely.

"I know," she retorted, "and the Dragonfly's up there! Move!"

He stayed put.

"It is too dangerous," Alley-Money warned. "My people will fetch him."

Her head rose, letting loose with a high-pitched squeal. Similar squeals returned from nearby, then two Alley Cats scampered out of the shadows, climbed the ladder and moved cautiously into the street above.

Kimie started to follow.

The dwarf's furious glare stopped her. He spoke in a dangerously low voice. "Tell me, girl, why have the Symbiotechs suddenly turned on us? Did you sell us out?" He raised his axe's steel tip to her chin. "Answer!"

Kimie matched his glare. "I thought *you* sold *us* out. Shouldn't you have an off switch for your army?"

"It was bypassed," he revealed, and searched her gaze. When he found nothing, he raised his head, concluding, "The drunken Stargazer then. He is the traitor!"

"Wrong again," Kimie countered. "Your plan might've been hacked too, did you think of that?" Her thoughts returned to the Dragonfly. It was like he'd possessed her. "We don't have time for this."

"Exactly," Gilwain confirmed. "Events have turned. Badly. My superior is on their way to the City."

Kimie was bewildered. "*Now* they show up? Oh, that's perfect manager material."

Heavy footsteps rose from behind Gilwain, making him turn. Two large shadows loomed on the wall. Symbiotechs, Kimie determined, who must have come through the other manhole.

Gilwain pushed her away. "Go!"

Kimie ran with Alley-Money.

Gilwain tensed for battle. His axe charged with an electronic whine then—

Bang!

He recoiled as the sewer wall suddenly blew in.

Kimie and Alley-Money dropped to the ground as the Symbiotechs were engulfed and buried. When the debris settled, Kimie looked up, peering through the haze at the wall's large opening. Another tunnel was visible behind it, and a figure stood in its centre, holding a smoking ResonAnts gun.

Gilwain stared through the smoke in disbelief, as did Alley-Money.

Kimie grinned at their silhouette, knowing exactly who they were. "Hell, yeah!"

The dwarf spoke, stunned: "Bluey?"

The response was fierce. "*Don't* call me that! It's Mysti now. Who the hell are you?"

He was taken aback. "You don't remember?"

"Don't care either."

She strode over and held out her hand to Kimie who grabbed it. Kimie's hand was nearly crushed as she was pulled up, hard. She ignored the pain and came in, hugging Mysti tightly.

"Get off me," the older woman grimaced, shifting uncomfortably and breaking away.

"Good to see you're okay," Kimie said. "God knows how. Your Roverboard dive seemed pretty full-on."

Mysti was baffled. "You're spying on me now?" She scowled at Gilwain. "You hacked into the system, right? Explains a lot."

He dismissed this. "How did you find us?"

Mysti pulled a slimy flashing device off her gun. "This thing. Found it in the sewers."

Alley-Money was in awe. "A Royal Treasure!"

"What is it?" Kimie wondered. "A tracking device?"

"Just lying around too," Mysti replied. "The Sewer Queen must have dropped it when she went scurrying off somewhere. I used it to home in on your energy signature. You sure as hell stood out, kid."

Kimie was grateful. "Good thing you knew how to use it."

Mysti made a face at its stench. "Gave it to her a while back as a Prom

Queen present. If this is it now, I'd hate to see her."

"She has cherished it," Alley-Money said. "As she has done with your memory."

Mysti indicated the sewers. "I'm so pleased I can live up to it by turning into street trash!"

"Yeah, she wouldn't really have a problem with that," Kimie pointed out.

Mysti ignored her. "Mind you, some of it's useful, like this thing." She patted the gun, then glared at Gilwain. "And some of it's not. This your war, genius?"

His response was firm. "Not at all."

"No, we were just leading your army into it," Kimie muttered.

"They're called Symbiotechs," Gilwain explained. "They've formed an agenda and turned against us. It seems they were tampered with."

"Weird," Mysti said. "They're going after everything. Good guys and bad. The EconoMe's down and the Moneyarch's losing cash by the second. He's hiding in his ugly tower, the wimp."

"Which is the best place to find answers," Gilwain pressed.

"He's got a point," Kimie agreed. "We should head there. We'll check on the Dragonfly on the way."

Mysti shuddered and strode past them. "Nuh-uh! I'm savin' my butt and gettin' outta Dodge." She grabbed Alley-Money, pushing her ahead. "Hey, sewer scum, lead! These damn tunnels give me a headache."

Kimie followed her with the others. "Lead where?"

Mysti spoke firmly. "I'll get you to Yushera and her ferals. They've regrouped, or so I hear. Might as well, since you lot can't take care of yourselves. I haven't seen the Prom Queen in ages, so it'll be a fright for both of us. Once you're there, I'm off."

"Where to?"

Gilwain's head rose in realisation. "She's scared from her talk with the Moneyarch. Her inner child's terrified."

Mysti stopped in her tracks and turned to him. "Oh, I remember you. Gilwain, right? Hardly recognised you with all that face fuzz. Good move. Hides your ugliness."

"As does yours," he retorted.

Kimie giggled.

Mysti raised her fist, then stopped. "No, that was a good comeback. I respect it."

"Thank you," he said.

She smacked his shoulder lightly. "Do it again and I'll kill you." She turned and strode on again.

"Yeah, but you're still frightened of yourself," Kimie pointed out. "Don't blame ya. The System took away your childhood and turned you into a supersized killing machine, while the Starman let you keep your heart, splitting you right down the middle. Having it happen when all hell's breaking loose in a random blitz bonanza's only gonna screw with your head even more. You don't know whether you want to run, fight or help people."

She jumped as Mysti grabbed her cheeks, lifted her head and brought her in close.

"I feel it every time!" Mysti hissed. "The excitement! The rush! When I jump into battle I don't ever want to stop, and it's not just that."

She pushed Kimie away.

Kimie rubbed her face sorely.

"When I see a guy," Mysti continued, "a good-looking one I mean, I don't know if I wanna kill him or smother him to death with kisses. It's like I wanna yell, I wanna scream, I wanna fight, I wanna run, I wanna kiss forever! I get so worried that everyone'll be burned by my passion before I burn myself up. This is more than I can handle!" She smacked the wall.

Kimie nodded. "At least you've got a conscience."

Mysti shook her head. "I only hurt people. I need to find a place where everyone's safe from me."

"A hidey-hole where you can only hurt yourself, you mean?"

"That coming from an expert?"

Kimie shut up, feeling awkward. Mysti had triggered a strange feeling. Not so much a memory, but an echo of one.

Mysti headed down the tunnel. "I am so out of this dump."

Kimie inhaled sharply.

Sensing her thoughts, Gilwain said, "As much as I want to get to the Sky Scrapper, she is our best option. For now."

Kimie sighed, annoyed at being led further away from the Dragonfly. She raised her head and called to Mysti, "If you're so much of an animal, why are you making sure we're safe, huh? Shouldn't you be running by now?"

Mysti smacked the wall again and moved on.

Kimie followed, satisfied that she'd got one up on her.

"We have a new player."

The words rolled off the Info-Maniac's spiked metal tongue as she stood in the Moneyarch's office. Unlike the rest of the City, which lay shrouded in darkness, his office was dimly lit, and she, as opposed to the Hookers in the streets, still served the System. Being kicked into the Wreck-Creation room by Mysti had kept her under the City's commands.

The Moneyarch gazed out into the darkness, knowing that their new player was making the ultimate power strike.

"Their arrival doesn't surprise me," he said. "They've done our work for us by breaking our enemies into even greater factions, leaving them scattered, like the homeless and broken. Mind you, the City needed an overhaul. Now we can implement our strategies for a profitable upgrade." He paused. "So who's the real brains behind this strike on our City?"

The Info-Maniac flicked a switch. A holoscreen activated, showing a Rolls Royce driving through the City streets for the Sky Scrapper.

"Whoever that is," she answered. "If we zero in on this part ..." She did so. "You'll see there's no driver. The car seems to be activated by voice command, with our friend in the back. We can't make out who they are, but it appears they're coming to talk with us. I hope it's dirty."

The Moneyarch considered the possibilities.

"Clearly," he began, "anyone who can do this to our City has my respect. We have a great opportunity to learn from them but mustn't allow any leverage. Such an advantage in this volatile market would only lead to a catastrophic downturn." His voice lowered. "Arrange for the blood-red carpet treatment."

The Info-Maniac grinned. "Absolutely!"

She left the room eagerly.

The Moneyarch frowned, gazing into the image curiously.

The Stargazer watched glumly from a hoverchair as Barbie Q raised a bubbling test tube of green liquid, tapping it. The laboratory's remains were heavily battered, but various chemicals and electronics remained, as well as a terminal, which they'd linked to a giant battery. In the middle of the lab stood an enormous cylinder of green goo that was larger than both of them. Thick, heavy cables connected it to the terminal.

Barbie Q mixed the contents of two test tubes into a phial, then turned to the terminal, keying in a long sequence of numbers. "Nearly there. In a few minutes, we'll have made a baby. Congrats. You did beautifully!"

The Stargazer grimaced. Her words sickened him. So did her face, even if it wasn't as bad as it had been. It was repaired, but blackened on one side. At least he wasn't tied up while she worked, and he was grateful for that. He was fully aware that tying people up was her favourite thing to do, but since he couldn't run, and was needed to work on various calculations, she'd let him off the hook.

She threw her phial into the top of the cylinder, watching as it landed in the goo. "The binary sequence please, Daddy?"

He sighed wearily. "Point five, one, gamma, two."

"Thank you." She typed the sequence in, becoming absorbed in her work.

He reached into his pocket and pulled out Bluey's old dog leash. The Hooker turned to grab another phial and he tossed the leash into the cylinder. It landed silently, sinking into the thick concoction where the fumes stopped her sensors from detecting anything. He watched her turn to the test tubes on the far table, then he leaned over, entering a command into the terminal so she wouldn't see any changes to the cylinder. When it was done, he began working on a few circuits on his lap.

"The finishing touch," he murmured, "for a new *leash* of life!"

"Our enemies are close, my Queen!"

Queen Yushera turned to the Alley Cat who'd spoken. Nearby, the medical staff, known as the War Vets, attended to the wounded Alley Cats and Sewer Rats amidst the wildly flickering torches circling the underground Veterinary Chamber. Trickles of dust fell with the City's tremors, leaving Yushera certain that the whole City would go up sooner rather than later. Her Alley-Cat's report of the Symbiotechs closing in didn't help matters either.

"Their location?" Yushera asked.

"The Arches of Maltasia," came the reply. "Our people are doing their best to deter them but cannot do so for long. We must leave at once."

Yushera's resolve was firm. "A Queen does not desert her subjects, wounded or otherwise."

"My Queen, you can do nothing more for us," the Alley Cat pleaded. "You are a Queen and we are merely cats and rats."

"It is not the species, Alissia, but the dignity with which they live. You so-called cats and rats hold greater respect than the Moneyarch in his sky realm, and that's what separates us from him. No, we stay!"

"My Queen—"

The chamber door burst open and Mysti strode in with Kimie, Gilwain and Alley-Money in tow.

Yushera gazed at Mysti wide-eyed, and whispered, "Is it you? Could it be?"

Mysti scoffed at the sight of her. "Well, you've certainly come down in the world. Prom Queen to this? We are so screwed!"

The Sewer Queen stepped in. "Your eyes reveal your truth. It is you!"

Mysti shifted uncomfortably. "Can see something in yours too. Ugh!"

Yushera continued. "The sacred child of old lies within you. She glimmers in the shadows of the underworld …"

Mysti tensed.

"Speaking of light," Kimie interjected, "shouldn't it have been morning, like, ages ago?"

Yushera spoke gravely. "Ever since the City's ascension, there has been only night."

"Literally," Gilwain added. "The City made up its own laws when it came to power, including scientific ones. Look." He indicated a rusty clock on the wall. It said 11:59.

Kimie was confused. "That's not right. It was around midnight when I got here."

"It was around midnight when I *left*," Mysti stated. "As Bluey."

Yushera's head rose. "When the City's heart fell, time went with it."

"I don't get it," Kimie said, baffled. "All I want, all I've ever wanted since waking up in this nightmare, is to go home."

"Me too," Mysti agreed glumly. "I just can't remember where it is."

Kimie blinked, feeling the same, though wouldn't admit it.

Mysti swallowed hard. "Well, uh, you're safe now, that's what counts. I'd better split. Catch ya round, huh?" She turned to leave.

"You cannot go!" Yushera ordered.

"Damn right I can!" Mysti retorted, heading off.

"The City will not let you," Yushera called. "It is too powerful."

"We'll see about that!" Mysti snapped, turning back. "The City's shot to hell, we've got some real bad company on its way, and I'm stuck in the sewers with rats, cats, dimwits, ferals and failures! I'm grabbing a truck from up top and splitting."

"Yeah, forget about living," Kimie shot back. "Not to mention helping people. There's still a whole heap of 'em up top."

Mysti backed away. "You call this living? Sorry guys, you're on your own. I'm gone."

She turned and ran from the chamber.

Kimie moved to follow her.

Yushera nodded to Alley-Money who stepped in, blocking Kimie's path. Kimie tried moving around her. Alley-Money wouldn't let her.

"Move!" Kimie ordered.

Alley-Money stayed put.

Kimie tensed, annoyed. "Why don't you think for yourself instead of listening to your cult leader?"

Yushera kept her cool. "You must forget Bluey. She cannot go far. Like you, she will have no choice but to return."

"What do you mean 'like me'?"

"Neither of you have fully awoken yet."

"And you have?" Kimie cried, throwing an arm up, indicating the rumbling sewers. "You're not exactly leading the charge for a wake-up call."

Two Alley Cats ran into the chamber. Kimie recognised them from earlier. They'd been sent to the surface by Alley-Money to find the Dragonfly.

Yushera addressed them. "You have news from above?"

"Where's the Dragonfly?" Kimie cut in.

An Alley Cat spoke to Yushera. "We scoured the whole area. There was no sign of him."

"What are you, blind?" Kimie asked in disbelief. "A whole stack of stuff fell on him."

"We searched where he had fallen," came the reply. "Footsteps in the ash led away from the debris. They stopped halfway down the street."

Kimie was astounded. "So what, he woke up, pulled himself out of the rubble and vanished into thin air? Get after him!"

Yushera cat-spat at her.

Kimie jumped. "I hate it when she does that."

"Find him," Yushera said firmly to the Alley Cats. "On *my* orders!"

The Alley Cats turned and ran.

The device in Gilwain's pocket beeped. He pulled it out, activating its screen.

Kimie stepped in and looked, seeing an image of a Rolls Royce. "What's up?"

He drew a heavy breath. "I hacked into the Sky Scrapper's network earlier. Now I can see what they can. It seems—" he paused, "—my superior has entered the City."

"Who is this person?" Yushera demanded.

"His employer," Kimie answered. "The one who set things up for our Mountain of an operation. Of course, we didn't *exactly* follow their orders to stay there—"

"We went dead against them," Gilwain interjected. "Now things have gone belly up and we're about to be held to account."

"Well, your boss did go AWOL," Kimie pointed out.

"When they do, it's usually for good reason."

Kimie watched the screen. "Where are they headed?"

"For the Sky Scrapper," Gilwain replied.

Kimie thought this over. "Maybe they want to negotiate with the big boss."

"Impossible!" he scoffed.

"Not if they've sold us out."

He dismissed the mere suggestion. "They could also be coming to speak on our behalf. I must reach them and explain our botch-up of an attack. They need to know about Bluey too."

He made for the exit.

Kimie ran after him. "I'm coming along then. They may have a way of fixing this."

Yushera spoke up. "Alley-Money, show them to the surface. Keep them safe."

Alley-Money ran in front of them, leading the way.

"Do not approach the one in the car!" Yushera called after Kimie. "We know not of their intentions. They could be allies with the City. Observe only from a distance."

Kimie nodded. "Yeah. Sure."

She followed the others out of the chamber.

Chapter Eleven

Kimie and Gilwain scampered past a decimated telephone box and ducked behind a dumpster. They were across the street from the Sky Scrapper, and it was just the two of them now. Alley-Money had returned to her Queen to assist with the wounded and Kimie hadn't blamed her for preferring the sewers. The City was a bomb site, scarred beyond recognition, with burning debris penetrating the battered skyline. Strangely, the Mountain's Symbiotechs weren't attacking the City tower. Instead, they'd formed two lines before its entrance, like they were welcoming a royal procession.

Kimie watched them curiously and said to Gilwain, "I know you don't want to hear it, but I think your boss has sold out."

"No," Gilwain replied dismissively. "She would never do that."

"She?"

A dim glow illuminated the street corner, growing steadily brighter as the Rolls Royce approached the building.

Kimie peered at the car. "Is that thing driving itself?"

"Yes," Gilwain answered. "It obeys her command."

"So it does all the work while she sits back and is carried to glory? God, I hate managers!"

The car came to a smooth halt before the Symbiotechs. The door opened automatically and a black high-heeled boot stepped out.

"Is that—?" Kimie began.

"Yes," Gilwain stated. "It's her."

The figure rose smartly.

Kimie's heart missed a beat. There, before her, was a familiar blonde woman wearing sunglasses and a long dark trenchcoat. Kimie shuddered, recalling horrible fragments of a memory. "*That's* your boss?"

"Yes," came the reply. "We know her by her codename of Platinum. Is she familiar to you?"

Kimie was speechless. She could only watch in astonishment as the woman strode coolly between the lines of Symbiotechs without a care in the world. Her high-heeled boots took her smoothly across the ash-stricken pavement as she adjusted her sunglasses and placed her hands in her coat pockets, not even flinching when a Hooker in the building above let loose with a bazooka shell, blowing the Rolls Royce to kingdom come. The woman kept the same pace, breezing through her royal guard, who turned, firing at the Hooker in retaliation.

Several DeciMauls on Roverboards soared overhead, shooting at her, her people, *and* the Hooker. The blonde woman ignored the blasts, striding calmly on and letting her Symbiotechs do the fighting for her. Then, to Kimie's astonishment, the woman suddenly stopped, pulled out a phone and answered it, seemingly oblivious to the shots flying by. Kimie watched, baffled, as the woman spoke for a moment, then switched her phone off, pocketed it and strode on amidst the barrage of gunfire.

"She's insane!" Kimie whispered. She knew she'd met the woman before, she just couldn't think where. Her face was familiar, her presence even more so, leaving Kimie hesitant to cross her again.

More DeciMauls swooped in on their Roverboards, turning the battle into a bloody brawl as fierce laser blasts filled the ravaged streets.

Platinum strode up to the building's entrance, tried the door and found it locked.

She huffed, annoyed. "I had a reservation for one." She keyed in a sequence on its control pad and its screen flashed.

"*Access denied.*"

She knew the Sky Scrapper's power reserves were falling. She'd scanned its energy levels from her car on the way.

She pulled a card from her pocket, held it over the sensor pad and keyed in the sequence again. A blue light flickered over it and then faded.

The door slid open.

She pocketed the card, satisfied, and entered the building, ignoring another sweeping shot over her shoulder.

Kimie yelped as a nearby bin went up in flames.

Gilwain grabbed her hand. "Time to go, lass. It's too dangerous to follow her. Move!"

"Not gonna argue," Kimie said back. They turned and ran down an alleyway. "Ms Peroxide mightn't be freaked by this crap, but I sure am."

"That's what makes her dangerous," he warned.

Platinum strode through the tower's foyer, approaching a lift. It *dinged* as the door opened and a DeciMaul emerged, still under the control of the building's dying power.

"Right on time," she quipped.

The beast aimed its gun at her.

"Don't be rude," she stated.

She snatched the weapon away, throwing it over her shoulder.

The beast lashed out with a heavy blow. She stepped to the side, evading it, then entered the lift, pressed her card up against a sensor pad and turned to face the DeciMaul as the lift doors closed.

"Bye-bye," she said.

The lift shot upwards.

The Moneyarch saw the doors to his private lift open.

Platinum strode coolly out of it and into his office, her hands tucked in her coat pockets. The wind grew from his smashed window, filtering through the localised energy shield and billowing around her.

She stopped before him. "Not impressed with the service so far. Place needs brightening up too. It's boring central in here."

The Moneyarch was unfazed. "Whatever picture you paint on life's canvas, nothing exists without supply and demand in the basic struggle for survival."

She indicated outside. "You're doing a great job. Just look at your City burn. Political economic theory always backfires for the few up top, leaving the frustrated masses below to erupt with front fire. See what happens when things come from an unbalanced mind that burns the candle at both ends?"

He wasn't intimidated. "Talk all you like, but you've actually done my job for me. The City was long overdue for a stocktake. Now, I seem to have the disadvantage—"

"…Always," she cut in.

"Ms—" he pressed.

"Platinum." She held up her Platinum Card. "I have access to everywhere, care of a Higher Power." She pocketed it. "Mind you, the card's only what you are. A *tool* for something bigger. It also let me in on your personal secrets. Don't know why you hate your real name. It's so much better than Moneyarch. That's sterile, and you know what? Hiding behind mountains of cash isn't going to protect you from yourself. Once upon a time, believe it or not, you were a much-loved baby, like the rest of us. So go on, what's turned you into its plaything?"

His gaze darkened and he moved slowly around her. She did the same, leaving them to circle each other.

He spoke darkly. "You can talk about spiritual freedom all you like, but you can't escape economics."

Her head rose. "You had so much, didn't you? You had it all and you just sat on your assets, letting the City suck your butt into a power vacuum to root you into itself. It took away *who* you were by converting you into its product. A machine, or at least an attempt of one."

She noticed a vase on his shelf and frowned. Curious, she brushed her hand over it, sensing its energy, which aroused her interest even more.

He ignored this. "So where do you intend to place your masterstroke?" He paused. "Oh, I see! Your winning streak is our new girl. Or girls, I should say. Bluey was the first and when she failed, you brought in her replacement to get the resistance up and running again. You succeeded, to a point. The resistance is up. The City has them running." He smiled smugly. "No doubt you also liaised with the Orion Sentry. That's why he cast our latest girl into the streets. It was on your orders. You wanted to cause one big distraction so you could get to me." His anger rose. "You instigated *everything*!"

To his surprise, Platinum agreed. "Absolutely. Systems are boring and this place needed to liven up. Both my girls made that happen."

"You must be getting desperate," he noted. "The Orion Sentry failed. Bluey did too, and there's no sign of your second girl. They did your groundwork for you, which begs the question, why didn't you enter the City and free Bluey from her SORE Point long ago? Nothing would stop you if you're as tough as you'd have me believe."

"Did it from afar," she answered simply. "Believe it or not, there are things out there far stronger and much uglier than you are. Luckily I can multitask. Used a few contacts to take down the barrier around Bluey's prison, then got New-Girl into the City and manoeuvred her to it. I also left the Stargazer's old notes for that Mountain dwarf to find so he could start building his army. It was only a matter of prodding them all to get the focus off themselves and help others. They did the rest and did it well. All worked out great in the end, bringing out the best in everyone. It also helps to have friends in high places. Some in lower ones too, but at least they have hearts of gold, and not the kind you deal in. You and I might pull the strings from behind the scenes, but the difference is, I trust everyone around me. Completely." Her voice lowered. "Do you? Middleman?"

His face hardened. "I think it's time you met my Info-Maniac." He activated the EyePad on his desk and spoke. "Get in here, please. I have someone I want you to hook up with."

The only response was static.

He tried again.

Still nothing.

"*I* think," Platinum began, "that it'll just be the two of us from now on. I've used my little card to send your dogs and bitches out into the street to run free. I knew it was only them in the building and no one else. Humans would only bring humanity to the place and don't think low enough for you. That leaves us. The big players, duelling it out—the way it should be."

She grabbed the EyePad from his desk, hitting a button. The window's energy shield shimmered and vanished, leaving them open to attack.

The pad's screen caught her attention. She hit another button, zeroed in on an image and saw a mutilated corpse in a pool of blood.

"So," she whispered in a dangerously low voice. "You've killed the Orion Sentry!"

The Moneyarch was satisfied he'd struck a nerve. "So your Platinum Card does have limitations. It didn't find out about him when you entered the building, did it?" He smirked. "He simply wasn't profitable any longer and your arrival here signed his death warrant. I couldn't have you, or anyone else, using him. If part of your mission in coming here was to save him, you've failed."

She placed the EyePad on the desk as her jet-black sunglasses bored into him. "And if part of your mission was to get in my head, you've just scored a massive rebound. I want the codes for the powerhouse that runs this City. You've got it stashed away underground. The Nuclear Fusion GenEarator. It's time to spark things up."

He was unmoved. "That's hypocritical, especially after seeing your re-action to the Orion Sentry's fate. You get angry over his death and then want to see the City go up in one big firework just for the sake of it?"

"Yeah," she answered simply. "The spectacle will be awesome, won't it?"

Thick clouds of smoke wafted through the window.

"Presumably," he continued, "you'll leave something standing at the end of it all? Blowing up the City won't gain you anything in the long term."

"Doesn't matter," she replied coolly. "It's not your game. Never was." She brought her face right up to his. "I want the codes."

"No deal."

"I knew you'd say that." She stepped back and leaned on his desk. "You know, you really need more passion in your life—if only to hit a release valve for that overflow of garbage swirling in your brain. Bet there's a lot of anger from your childhood too, thanks to your family and what they did to you as a kid."

His gaze shifted momentarily.

She knew she was getting through to him. "Come on, take it out on me! Smack me, shoot me, stab me, pull my hair out, kick me in the head so hard that I cry blood on your floor. Feel something, *anything*, against ol' Mummy and Daddy! I'm right here, waiting to get the punishment *they* should have had!" She raised her hands. "Look, I'll sit right here, like this, and won't even fight back. I don't pack guns, so this is your call. See where it takes you. I'm all yours."

He paused, observing her, then spoke, not giving anything away. "There is another option. You see, the City has granted me a gift for my service, and I've been *allowed* a deeper insight into its workings. What's more, I have permission to share that revelation with others."

Platinum grinned. "Oooh! So now we've determined that wherever the System comes from it sure aint facts and figures, or logic for that matter. No, it's gotta be hate or greed or something in the dark tone I'd say, leaving us with a monster of a problem that has you as its false *profit*."

He wasn't swayed by her argument and stayed formal. "I think you'll find, my dear, that your concept of humanity is somewhat limited. Life is nothing but systems. They're all like animals, competing for survival and striving for supremacy. Like any kingdom, the strongest become dominant, it's just a matter of which system works best. Whether you like it or not, we're all slaves, if not to this system, then another. I'd much rather be in the toughest, and I'll do whatever it takes to stay there. You'll soon come to realise that we're all players in a greater game."

"You have no idea," Platinum agreed. "No, seriously, you don't."

He ignored her. "A game I'll show you." He paused. "I'm going to reveal the truth of what the System truly is."

"You think I'd be here if I was afraid?" she countered. "Go on, let's see it."

"You leave me no choice."

He grabbed her jaw. His touch was burning, but she stayed cool against the pain, watching as his eyeballs flickered, transforming into red orbs. A distant roar erupted in their linked minds, spawning from inside him, and she saw the extent of his suffering. Now she understood the ugliness that possessed him. The stinking, rotten core of what he'd become, but it was also clear that he was only a festering scab on a much greater disease. A rampant, conscious sickness that had grown to cover the whole of this reality.

His eyes widened and he held her jaw tighter as his inner fires grew and the beast's roar bellowed. Only then did she realise, that it was a wolf.

Strangely, she didn't flinch. Instead, she remained as cool as ever and quipped, "Oh, please. We all know life's a bitch."

His face dropped.

She smacked his hand away and rose from the desk, feeling the hideous presence fade in her mind. "You really need to start listening to a Higher Power."

He glared back at her, then retreated.

She stepped in. "Why do you put so much effort into helping what's killing you? You're only a bug on the back of a sick beast. Let's prod it. Bring it out into the open." Her voice rose. "Give me the codes for the Nuclear Fusion GenEarator."

Still possessed by his inner hellhound, his hand moved protectively to his throat, going for a golden chain.

She lashed out, grabbing that chain from his neck, ripping it off and turning away. A small circuit hung on the end.

He lunged for it.

She stepped to the side, evading him. Her shoulder hit a shelf, sending its vase clattering to the ground. Strangely, it didn't break. Even more strangely, the Moneyarch tripped over it, falling headfirst out the window and spiralling into the night.

She peered out to see a DeciMaul on a Roverboard sweeping in for him, then a fierce explosion from the building's window sent a giant fireball spewing out, engulfing the Moneyarch and forcing the beast to recoil. His flaming corpse flailed wildly and plummeted, splattering into a burning pylon far below.

Platinum watched the DeciMaul soar away. She wondered just where in Sky Scrapper the explosion had come from. She hadn't sensed any flames on her way up in the lift. It was like a gas pipe had spontaneously blown and got him, which seemed anything but random.

The vase on the floor also interested her. She knelt down, reached for it, then retracted her hand quickly. The thing was alive, confirming her suspicions.

She took off her long coat, wrapped her hands in it, picked up the vase and placed it on the shelf with the utmost respect. Once the vase was steady, she put her coat back on and then examined the chain she'd ripped from the Moneyarch's neck. She nodded, satisfied, before taking the EyePad from the desk, plugging the chain's circuit into its side, keying in a sequence and then hearing the pad whine. Moments later, the whole City shook as a deep rumbling rose from below it. She keyed in another sequence, activating a bar graph on the screen, and addressed the entity she'd seen in the Moneyarch's mind.

"Nothing like a little exorcise to start the day …"

She pressed a button.

"We've gotta leave now!"

Kimie ran past two Alley Cats who were carrying a wounded Sewer Rat through the Veterinary Chamber's archway. Another blast from above shook the walls. She grimaced as a trickle of dirt fell on her, then hurried with Gilwain up to Queen Yushera.

"You found no help?" the Queen asked.

Kimie spoke quickly. "There's a crazy lady up there I really didn't want to see again. She's either totally nuts or has sold us out. Blonde with sunglasses. Calls herself Platinum."

"Blonde?" Yushera said, unimpressed. "Clearly she does not know the glory of the sewers."

Kimie pulled a face. "Now you're talking sh—"

The sewers shook again, much louder this time, along with an engine whine.

Yushera gazed at the roof. "The City's belly rumbles with hunger."

"Meaning what?" Kimie asked warily.

Gilwain spoke gravely. "Its Nuclear Fusion GenEarator's been set to overload, going into meltdown."

Kimie tensed. "So either your blonde boss is corrupt or she really, *really* sucks at her job. What's a nuclear fusion … whatever?"

"The City's power source," Gilwain replied. "It was set up by—"

Kimie sighed wearily. "I know …"

"The Stargazer," she and Gilwain finished together.

Gilwain addressed Yushera. "We've no choice but to leave, your Majesty."

The Sewer Queen was dismissive. "It is unlikely we will get far before the City consumes us all."

"We have to try," he pressed. "Even if it's on foot. We can't wait for our Mountain transport to return."

Yushera nodded. "Many wounded have already been evacuated. I will organise for the last to be moved."

She issued the orders to her subjects. One by one, the injured were raised on stretchers made of torn rags and removed from the Veterinary Chamber. Soon it was empty, leaving Yushera as the last of her kind. She gave a final look around, then said to Kimie, "My kingdom is no more. All that remains are the crown jewels in the royal safe." She indicated it on the floor.

Kimie was bewildered. "What, a crappy old suitcase? What've you got in there? Rusty cans?"

"The first that were here when my kingdom was founded," Yushera answered proudly. "Be sure to carry it gently."

"Sure," Kimie replied. She picked it up and dumped it in the startled Queen's arms. "There you go."

Yushera scowled. "How dare you treat nobility with such disdain!"

"You're not nobility, you're *knob*ility," Kimie quipped. "You should ditch that junk 'cause we already have enough crap to deal with. You're one of us now, which for you is a big step up, and don't even think of chucking another hissy fit 'cause I'll hiss right back! Move!"

She turned and strode from the chamber with Gilwain, glancing back briefly to see if Yushera was following.

Still scowling, Yushera stomped after them, carrying her suitcase under her arm and vowing bitterly, "I will not be treated like a peasant girl! I will not, I will not, I will not …!"

The tin cans rattled inside.

"Got her!"

The Stargazer pressed a button on his EyePad. He was once again in his hoverchair and floating by a closed manhole in the street. His chair was more than a little damaged after Barbie Q had retrieved it from his burnt-out husk of a car. The chair still worked, albeit shakily, and he watched as she picked up the manhole cover and hurled it high into the night, smashing it through a hospital window.

He analysed the EyePad's tracking sensors, verifying the coordinates below. "Target's close. Thank the stars she's got a unique blood type we can scan for. Makes her a bloody miracle."

"Totally," the Hooker agreed. "Let's throw down our little Mysti Cool present, shall we?" She kicked the heavy sack beside them into the sewer. "Bon voyage, baby!"

She turned to the Stargazer with a smirk, then felt a device ram into her neck. Its piercing whine sent a rush of electricity surging into her circuits and she jolted wildly, gazing at the Stargazer in disbelief. He watched coldly as all the screws in her head, propelled by sonic waves, whirled into her cranium with crunches and clicks, penetrating her electronic brain and digging in hard.

"Daddy," she whispered. "You've … you've …" Her voice morphed into a low, drawling monotone. "… screwed me over …"

Her eyes rolled up and she slumped to the ground in a smoking heap.

The Stargazer pocketed the crude device he'd created in the busted-up laboratory and leaned down over her. "Your system was long overdue for an upgrade. I'm gonna make sure it gets one."

Mysti ran through the sewers in long, athletic strides. The air was heating up and she knew things were bad. The distant explosions were growing. Probably as a forerunner to a big mother of a blast that would blow the whole City, she figured. That suited her fine. Burning her past meant far more than saving it. What lay behind her could stay as one big blank for all she cared.

She approached a corner. A figure stepped out, bringing her to a skidding halt. She raised her gun, pumping it hard. The weapon whined as she aimed it at the small person in the shadows. Nearby, lay a crumpled empty sack.

She moved closer. This was no Alley Cat, she realised. What's more, the figure's silhouette was hauntingly familiar.

"Hell, no …!" she whispered in horror.

The figure stepped in.

Mysti shuddered, her worst fears confirmed.

Standing there was a twelve-year-old girl. Her hair hung in a long, clean ponytail that draped halfway down her back, hanging behind her spotless clothes. She wore a blue top, jeans and sneakers, all brand new and un-blemished, much like the girl herself.

Mysti clutched her gun tightly, her muscular arms grimy and covered in ash and her face as ravaged as the world above. She gazed at the girl in shock as the full impact of who she was hit home. The girl was her as a youth. Bluey. Pristine and as perfect as ever.

Laughter rose in Mysti's head again, though nowhere near as bad this time. It was soothing rather than painful. This kid's presence had eased it, she knew that much. Still, she was as sceptical as hell.

"Oh, you bastards!" she scowled. "Had to make a robo-kid version of me, didn't you?" She scanned the sewers for signs of anyone else. "Now we've all sunk to a new low." She looked her over. "A basic model but a good one, alright. What are you? A Hooker in progress?"

The girl indicated the gun. "Go on. Fire that sucker. Kill who you used to be. You're an expert at hurting yourself, aren't you?"

"You're a f—"

"Friend?" the girl cut in. "Uh, yeah?"

"I've had enough of this crud …"

"So shoot," the girl prompted. "That's what we're about, aren't we? Hurting people. No, that's not right. Oh yeah, it's *helping* people! You know what that means? You're people, right? You're gonna help everyone but yourself, is that it?" She raised her arms as if facing a firing squad. "You wanna kill yourself? Go right ahead."

"Smart-mouth thing to say to the one with the gun!" Mysti retorted.

The girl was unfazed. "Maybe I got more guts than you. You see me running?"

"Maybe you should!" Mysti shot back. "Forget about what's up top. Welcome to real life, kid! It's not innocent. Everyone I ever knew either left, died or went feral. Look at me, huh. Bred to be a killing machine! I bet the bad guys sent you to finish me off."

"That was the plan" the girl confirmed. "My body was meant to go the same way as yours but was turned back at the last second, care of an old buddy with too much heart. A static system can't crush every rising spark. A new girl to the City woke him up, he woke me, and now it's my turn, with this." She pulled an object from her pocket and threw it at Mysti, who caught it.

A dog leash.

Mysti glanced at the girl. She was her younger self to the bone. The way she'd spoken brought up memories that Mysti had long since forgotten. She shivered, feeling like she'd gone from being a cheeky fun-loving child to all grey and … Mysti.

"If you could only see the future, kid—" Mysti began.

"If you could only see yours," the girl cut in. "You never used to let any waves drag you under. They'd all pass, was your motto."

Mysti flinched. "Until they get too big, swamping you into hell. Talk like that gets you nowhere. Everything I tried to stop didn't work." She glanced upwards. "It's going to hell up there and you know why? Because that's nature. It decays and dies! There's a City burning above us and its people are getting slaughtered. We can't go anywhere and never could. The kids here dropped into the sewers. The InnerCent fell. The City's science freak sold us out and became a drunk-driving psycho. Hookers and animals are running amok in the streets, and the ol' forest Village is sealed off. Where's your big dream gone, huh? Where?"

"Untouched," the girl replied resolutely. "The City only sees the day-to-day mechanics of its survival. Its hunger's never satisfied. It only wants you as an addicted consumer that it can suck in and feed off. You're *not* a slobbering animal. You have depth. No matter how strong a system is, there's one thing it can never fight. Time. Things always change and there's *always* a bigger picture."

Mysti quivered as the girl's words hit home. "You're smart, kid. Real smart."

"You're even smarter," the girl said firmly.

Mysti got ready to retort when a savage pain rippled through her stomach. She cringed and dropped to her knees, clutching it.

The girl frowned. "Problem?"

Mysti shivered, feeling like everything was slipping away. "My stomach hurts." She tensed in pain. "Probably 'cause I never stopped beating myself up for not being good enough."

"Makes you human," the girl said.

Mysti listened as the child's laughter in her head faded away. She knew now that it had never been taunting her. She'd only made it scary by burying it deeper and hiding it. The one presence that had always been there to remind her of who she truly was.

She spoke softly. "It's like I've had a knife in me for so long and I've ignored it. I've trudged on instead of pulling it out. Now I can see it and know what I've done to myself. I'm an idiot!"

She whimpered, feeling her chest burn, like an inner poison was seeping out from a gaping wound. She let loose with long, drawn-out groans, feeling every inch of the horror that she'd held onto for so long pour out from her very soul. She wanted to rage against the overwhelming guilt but it was too intense and she doubled over. Just when she thought she was going to pass out, there came a sudden release.

Reality returned as, bit by bit, the world came into focus, a touch brighter this time. She felt like a dark veil had risen from behind her eyes, revealing a captivating light below, shining a path to a future full of possibilities.

She shuddered and spoke softly. "Thanks, kid."

The girl shrugged. "If you don't help yourself, nobody else will."

Overwhelmed by the outpouring of her inner glow, Mysti rose, embracing the girl and hugging her tightly, weeping out the anguish that had been shackled for so long. The girl hugged her back, just as tightly, as the dog leash hung between them. Mysti held on for dear life, exorcising her soul as the anguish streamed out from her until finally, there was no more.

Her turmoil released, she clutched the child's shoulders gratefully, then moved back in astonishment. She wiped her eyes, sniffed and spoke in realisation. "You're not a robot."

"Good to see you're not either," came the reply.

Mysti squeezed her arm warmly. "No, what I mean is, you're real."

"So are you," the girl said. "More than you think."

"But how are you—?" Mysti stopped, feeling the dog leash in her hand.

"Oh, I get it. You're a clone from the City's science geek, right?" She swallowed hard. "He's sure redeemed himself for this one."

"Hey, you did the redeeming," the girl corrected. "You—"

She suddenly wailed and dropped.

Mysti grabbed her in mid-fall and held her up, shaken. "What's up with you?"

The girl tensed. "We have the same problem. Can't stay kids forever."

Mysti pursed her lips and lowered her gently to the ground. "The loser only gave you a limited lifespan, didn't he? That sucks. You can't just fall and die in some god-awful sewer."

"No," came the soft reply. "I'm gonna lie down in your heart … and stay there."

Mysti choked back tears. "Screw that. I'm gonna find that spaced-brain freak and—"

"No time," the girl cut in. "It's time to move on. You gotta look forward, as a grown-up, but one with a child's heart."

Mysti nodded. "You did a real good job, kid."

"So did you, lady."

"I'm proud to have been you."

The girl gave a little smile. "And I would have loved to have grown into you. You're pretty cool." Her eyes closed, then opened again. "Huh?"

Mysti smiled back, with tears of gratitude. "Uh-huh."

"Yuh-huh," they said together, and each made a fist that tapped the other's lightly.

The girl's head rolled to the side as her presence faded. Mysti felt her body lighten as it crumbled into snow-white flakes that wafted into the air to drift along the tunnel. She sniffed sadly. The Stargazer had done a good job, she thought, but must have had limited time or he'd have made the clone's lifespan longer. Still, she was grateful for his work.

The sudden rumbling of the sewers returned her to the present. Her instincts told her to run as she sensed the apocalyptic chaos above growing ever closer. Her brain, and her heart, told her to stay and kick the hell out of the crap tsunami sweeping in.

She grabbed her gun, rose, and strode back through the sewers the way she'd come, no longer concerned for herself, but for others.

"I should have listened to myself long ago," she said firmly.

Now energised with the light of the heavens, she ran headlong into the darkness, ready to confront the worst.

Chapter Twelve

Kimie steadied herself against the shaking wall of the sewer tunnel, praying she'd reach safety soon. That's if the tunnel didn't sicken, scare or crush her to death first. She followed the Sewer Queen, Alley-Money and Gilwain around a corner, then bumped into Yushera, who'd stopped in her tracks.

The others also halted.

"What's up?" Kimie asked.

Yushera indicated ahead with a nod. Kimie followed her gaze. A figure was running towards them, holding a gun.

Alley-Money hissed.

Gilwain raised his axe, fearing the worst.

Yushera, however, stepped forward, peering into the shadows. "No. All is well."

Gilwain lowered his axe. "Indeed. That's no Symbiotech, it's—"

"Mysti!" Kimie called in sudden realisation. She could see her clearly now. The woman was filled with a glowing presence, like her inner shell-demon had cracked open to reveal a heavenly fire.

"You're going the wrong way!" Mysti called back, motioning in the direction they'd come from. "And believe me, I know the feeling!"

"What—?" Kimie began, then yelped as Mysti ran up, pulled her in and embraced her in a hug. Kimie blinked, surprised, then was pushed back, felt a hand on her shoulder and saw Mysti staring straight at her, as if gazing into her soul.

"You okay, kid?" Mysti asked, with genuine concern.

Kimie was confused. "No. You're a freak. What happened?"

"I woke up," came the reply. "Same as you will."

Kimie agreed. "Yeah, I'd so like that. Somewhere far away from this hellhole."

Yushera gazed upon Mysti in awe. "Is it you? Could it be?"

Mysti laughed, genuinely. "Real deal!"

Yushera gave a delighted squeal, resembling a cat's cry. Forgetting all about royal protocol, she swept in and hugged her tightly. Mysti hugged her back, before turning and embracing Alley-Money and then Gilwain.

"I knew you'd come back for us, lass," Gilwain said happily.

Mysti grinned. "Thanks. It's good to be back. I've missed so much, and in more ways than one."

Kimie could hardly believe what she was seeing. Mysti was no longer reacting to things. Yes, she was showing real emotions, only now she was in full control.

"What happened?" Kimie asked her.

"Do you not see?" Yushera prompted.

"Of course she wouldn't," Gilwain replied. "She's new to the City. She wasn't around in the time of the Village. In the days when we had—" he motioned to Mysti, "—a champion!"

"Yep," Mysti agreed, "I'm Bluey again. Well, sort of. Older and rougher around the edges, but still me. Still wanna be called Mysti though." She nudged Kimie. "Thanks for the name, kid. Love it."

Kimie smiled. "Good to see you've sorted yourself out. I thought you'd flipped your lid."

Mysti peered at her.

Kimie shifted awkwardly. "Or maybe I have. What now?"

Mysti frowned curiously. "You're just like her. Me, I mean. What I might have turned out like if I hadn't hit the SORE Point. You know, like an in between version of Bluey and me. You've got potential."

Kimie nodded. "Thanks. I don't get any of this, but thanks. So does this mean you're a goody-two-shoes again?"

Mysti smacked her arm lightly. "Got the best of both worlds now. I won't tip back into the ol' Mysti hurricane again, except on the bad guys."

"Why the sudden flip?" Kimie asked.

A mechanical whirring came from ahead and a large shape rounded the corner.

Yushera and Alley-Money hissed suspiciously. Gilwain raised his axe, Mysti tensed, and they all watched as the Stargazer appeared on a jolting, shaking hoverchair. A deactivated Barbie Q lay on his lap, her arm dangling on one side of him and her legs on the other.

"Don't mention it," the Stargazer said.

Kimie ran in and hugged him tightly over the lifeless Hooker. "For a guy who rammed his car into the top end of a City tower, you look pretty good." She looked at Barbie Q's limp figure. "At least you got yourself off the hook with her."

"She can still come in handy," he replied. "If I can patch into her neural network and get her on our side, we can use her to hack into all the other Hookers and have 'em working for us. Maybe even do the same with the DeciMauls. Just have to modify a couple of signals to rope 'em in."

Mysti approached him. Kimie moved back and watched her lean down and embrace him in a warm hug. He returned the hug, genuinely.

Mysti spoke softly. "You're such a loser."

"Nah," he countered. "We just got overwhelmed by life and sunk. Seems the only way we can go now, is up." He indicated the roof.

Mysti sniffed. "Thanks for bringing my fun spark back."

"Thanks for bringing *me* back," he corrected.

She rose. "Just wish I could whip up a mini-Starman clone for you."

"Don't you dare!"

She stepped away, allowing Yushera to move in. The Sewer Queen bowed with awe and reverence and indicated Barbie Q on his lap. "It seems we have much to thank you for."

"Yeah," Kimie added. "One ho-bot as evidence. At least we know he's on our side. He's not the big bad here. It's probably that blonde lady upstairs."

"Who?" Mysti asked.

The tunnel rumbled again.

Yushera retreated from the Stargazer.

Kimie continued. "She's called Platinum. We saw her go into the Sky Scrapper. The City started going belly-up after that." She indicated Gilwain. "She's *his* boss."

Gilwain looked away.

Mysti shook her head, confused. "Okay, now I officially have *no* idea of what's going on round here." She addressed Gilwain. "You wanna explain it?"

He shifted uncomfortably. "My superior's been out of touch for some time. We have yet to learn her intentions."

"That better be soon," Kimie said, watching a trickle of dust fall past her, "but it's best to hear her out first. People aren't always what they seem. Isn't that right, space man?" She patted the Stargazer's shoulder.

He gave a small smile. "Looks like we got a team now."

"Am I in charge?" Yushera blurted out.

"No," Mysti answered.

"But I am Queen!"

"Not of me," Mysti said firmly. "I'm no pussy."

"But—"

"No!" Mysti cut in. "We got bigger problems."

"Not to me," Yushera muttered.

The sewers rumbled louder.

Kimie looked at the Stargazer. "Can you change the setting on that nuke?"

"'Course I can," the Stargazer replied. "There's a small station on the City's outskirts. I set it up ages ago during my own little power struggle. It's one way I wanted to make things right after throwing Bluey into her SORE Point and another reason why I became dog food when the City found out about it." He flinched at the memory. "It's also the only place where I can use my old codes to stop hell going up. The City's had full control of the station up till now, but with everything in freefall, we may be able to get into it and activate an alternative energy source I was working on."

Gilwain glowered at him. "And you didn't think of heading there when we were planning our attack?"

The Stargazer dismissed this. "The City's shield's around it were too heavy at the time, but now we've got an apocalyptic chance to put things right. We don't know the full story with our blonde lady yet, but our priority's to save this place. If the City ignites, we won't have time to run. The blast'll be so big that half the Mountain'll go with it."

"Dead right," Mysti told him. "You're our only hope."

Gilwain stamped his foot.

"Along with you," Mysti added.

He pursed his lips, clearly not satisfied.

"You two," she continued, "need to reach that power station and work on getting those dogs and robowhores off our backs."

"Indeed," Gilwain agreed. "Only I don't trust his pickled brain when it comes to work as delicate as this and I *will* be double-checking his calculations."

"Yeah, but who's going to keep you two in line?" Mysti pressed.

Yushera stepped forward. "I shall. You forget that I am Queen, and they will have no choice but to obey royalty, even if you do not."

"You just wanna throw your weight around," Mysti said.

Yushera's lips curled up, ready for a hiss.

"Hang on," Kimie cut in. "What are the rest of us going to do?"

"Get answers," Mysti replied. "I want to know what's happening in the Sky Scrapper and who stuffed our attack plan. Could be the blonde lady, could be the City, or could be something else. I'll head to the centre of the storm while giving you guys—" she indicated the Stargazer, Gilwain and Yushera, "—a big distraction."

The Stargazer raised Barbie Q's limp arm. "We'll be using this one and her bosom buddies to help us out too, remember?"

"Good," Mysti said. "I've got a plan."

"You have?" Kimie asked.

"Kinda," Mysti retracted. "More like an idea. Doesn't matter, we'll work on it as we go along."

"Sounds like my life," Kimie muttered.

"As long as it excludes civilian casualties," the Stargazer warned.

"We have found none so far," Yushera stated.

"None?" Kimie asked, surprised. "Whoa, wait! Not any? Are you serious? You do know 'bout all the damage up there?"

Yushera was resolute. "I have heard of no deaths, which makes things curiouser." She addressed Alley-Money. "You will continue our work in guiding the civilians out of the City. It is no longer safe for anyone."

Alley-Money nodded. "My Queen."

"Excellent," Yushera said. "I shall depart on my quest."

"*Your* quest?" Kimie asked baffled.

The Stargazer prodded her to keep quiet, then said to Mysti, "Oh, and one more thing. If you attack the Sky Scrapper head-on, they'll call out their Army Reserve Bank on you."

Mysti sighed. "Let me guess. You created it, right?"

"Uh … yeah," he mumbled, shame-facedly. "They're called Centurions. You'll need help getting past them, and that's where one of my other toys comes in handy. It's in storage right now. Never got the chance to use it."

The sewers rumbled louder than ever, sending greater dust trickles falling.

"Explain on the way," Mysti ordered. "We've got to work fast."

She turned and strode through the sewers, glancing at a stream of sewer water, then at the manhole cover ahead. Her face hardened as she said, "Time to stop taking so much crap and move on up in the world!"

Kimie and Mysti were the first to part company from the others and ascended to the City streets. Alley-Money went the opposite way, travelling deep into the sewers to aid the Alley Cats and Sewer Rats with the evacuation. Yushera, Gilwain and the Stargazer stayed behind, allowing the Stargazer to work on Barbie Q. When the Hooker's relay signals were modified and she was under their control, they sent her to the surface to find and convert as many Hookers and DeciMauls as possible.

Once she was gone, Yushera led Gilwain and the Stargazer out of the sewers and into an open area on the City's outskirts. There, they found a small fenced-off building surrounded by several empty construction vehicles. The fence had been damaged from the City's battering, allowing Gilwain to pull part of it up while Yushera lowered her head and ran underneath. Once she was in, he pulled out a laser cutter from his pocket and sliced a section of wire away, allowing the Stargazer to enter on his hoverchair. When they were all through, they made their way across the grass to the battered building ahead.

"Looks like this place was about to be upgraded," the Stargazer noted. "Could use it too."

Yushera wasn't convinced. "It is satisfactory already. I tried claiming it for our kingdom to give the City some culture. My people and I were evicted."

"Makes sense," the Stargazer agreed.

She hissed loudly.

"That they'd want to evict you," he corrected quickly. "Bastards!"

She nodded, satisfied.

They approached the building's door. It was locked, heavily battered, and covered in small holes and crevices. A damaged sensor pad dangled from its side. Thankfully, it was still active.

The Stargazer raised his hand to it. "I got this." He started working, then stopped. "You'd think this place'd have some traps, or at least be guarded."

A snarl came from behind them.

"Ah," he said, dismayed. "Thought so."

They turned to see a DeciMaul on the grass.

Yushera was annoyed. "Has not the metal woman won this animal to our cause?"

The Stargazer indicated the beast's collar. It was inactive. "Seems our beauty hasn't got to this beast yet. Relax. My little signal should do the trick."

He pressed a button on his chair. A whine arose and the DeciMaul's collar flickered rapidly. The creature jolted wildly and, much to Gilwain's fury, became enraged.

"Or not," the Stargazer cringed. "Collar must be damaged."

Gilwain got ready to explode.

The Stargazer pressed another button just as the DeciMaul fired. An energy dome activated, shielding them and deflecting the blast.

Gilwain looked at the door's sensor pad. The very shield that protected them was impossible to reach through, thereby cutting them off from the door. He glared at the Stargazer. "Somehow I think you'd be much safer out there."

"You're alive, aren't you?" the Stargazer retorted.

"Barely!"

"You got that right!"

"Enough!" Yushera cut in. "I shall resolve this matter."

She opened her mouth, letting loose with several squeaks. A rat scurried out from a pile of debris, approaching the flickering dome. She squeaked at it. It stopped and squeaked back. She nodded. The rat turned and ran into a small hole in the building's side.

More laser blasts hit the shield. The barrier fizzled and dropped, just as the building's door whirred open, care of the rat.

The Stargazer reversed rapidly through the entrance. Yushera followed. Gilwain was ready to do the same when the DeciMaul fired again. He dived to the ground as the blast flew over his head, hitting the wall.

Rip!

Gilwain looked back to see Yushera holding a metal panel that she'd ripped off a circuit board. She tossed it to him as he rose. He caught it and turned, holding it like a shield before the DeciMaul.

The beast let off another shot. The blast flickered in, hit the panel, rebounded and struck the DeciMaul square in the chest. The beast groaned and thumped to the floor, dead.

Gilwain turned and entered the building to see the Stargazer activating a terminal's power reserves. He dropped the panel and said to Yushera, "Just as well you knew about the reflective properties of Mangun Alloy."

"I did not," she replied simply. "I was hoping you'd use it to strike our enemy."

A distant explosion sent rumbling shockwaves throughout the building. Gilwain and Yushera looked outside to see a small mushroom cloud billowing high into the night.

The terminal flickered to life. The Stargazer analysed its readings and said worriedly, "Not good."

Gilwain joined him. "We haven't much time."

"Ain't much power either," the Stargazer pointed out.

Gilwain saw a reading. "It doesn't matter. We're too late!"

The Stargazer's face fell. "Damn! There goes the City!"

Several enormous cracks split through the City Square as streaks of lava rippled along the streets like gold-blooded veins, uprooting numerous roads. Dollops of magma flew high into the night before splattering hard onto the devastated landscape. More eruptions followed as the City's Nuclear Fusion GenEarator, far below the surface, grew into a penultimate cry.

Platinum saw it all from the broken window of the Moneyarch's office. She looked at the EyePad she held. The countdown was almost complete.

Four … three … two …

The City's rumbling ceased abruptly as everything powered down.

She gazed up again at the savaged landscape, hearing the crackling flames in the distance and feeling traces of their hot wisps across her face. Things had stabilised—and not by her doing.

A dark presence entered her mind, then came a snarl.

"The System accounts to no one!"

She grinned, satisfied. "Smoked you out at last, have I? About time."

Yushera too, felt the City's rumbling cease, and said to the Stargazer, "You have succeeded?"

"He's incapable of success—" Gilwain muttered.

"We're alive," the Stargazer retorted. "Be grateful."

"You call this living?"

"Ah, go to hell!"

"With you here, I'm already there!"

"At least we're not burning. The City's GenEarator's on hold."

Yushera frowned. "By our doing?"

"No," the Stargazer answered. "It's still active but hovering right at a critical point. I can't identify the energy holding it there."

"Is it the work of my subjects?" Yushera asked, referring to Kimie and Mysti.

"We'll find out later," the Stargazer replied. "We've got a better chance of deactivating the GenEarator now, but it may be too late. Going by these readings, I think our labour market's just given birth to something new." He flicked several switches. "Can't see what it is, but it's sick as hell!"

"*Auto alert! Auto alert! Errors detected!*"

The automated voice came from Platinum's EyePad.

She addressed the shadowy presence in her head. "So you're not ready to talk shop yet? Fine. Soon you won't have a choice."

The pad spoke. "*Auto-defence grid initiated. System reserves online.*"

"Go ahead," she said simply. "Play it your way first. Learn the hard way."

She hit a button. An image appeared, showing the Sky Scrapper's roof. A red mist billowed out from a doorway at its peak, sending the EyePad's reading's spiking.

"And there we go," she stated. "So you're what's made the City toxic, turning us all into a state of toxi*City*!"

She put the EyePad down and strode from the room, making for the stairwell.

A few blocks away, a lone survivor staggered onto the street, looking ahead. His injuries were minimal. Good karma for smacking people away from a blast and taking a partial hit for them, he reasoned. Of course, they'd then fled and he didn't blame them, leaving him alone in a ravaged street.

Two Symbiotechs at the end of the street brought him to a standstill. They raised their guns, then stopped when a whine came from a decimated bank nearby. He ducked for cover, peered out, and watched as several platforms rose loudly from below the ground, bringing newcomers from the building's depths. They had human forms but were encompassed by dark halos and made solely of gold coins.

The Symbiotechs fired. The golden figures dodged the shots effortlessly and bounded in, striking the guns from their hands. A Symbiotech punched hard, sending a few dollars flying from a golden being's mouth. The being struck back with an equally hard blow, then grabbed the Symbiotech's face and hissed, "*Investment opportunity! Incorporate!*"

The Symbiotech groaned as an energy crackle rippled through his body, then he slumped to the ground. Another golden being sent the second Symbiotech toppling over the first, before both their necks were clasped and their bodies glowed, morphing into piles of golden coins. The beings tightened their fists and the coins surged up their arms, absorbing into their bodies whilst making them grow larger and stronger.

"Ten-point five percent profit," one reported mechanically.

"Ten-point six seven percent profit," the other added. *"Profits must be increased."*

The others joined them. *"Profits, profits, profits …"*

They ran into the streets, supported by the financial backing of their corporate bodies and moving as one in search of targets.

The hidden man rose, turned and hobbled away. He'd barely got anywhere when his foot caught on a fallen girder and he lurched to the ground with a cry.

The golden beings bounded in.

Along with the incoming roar of an engine.

An explosive crash burst through the night as a garage's metal door smashed open and a vehicle sailed out.

A monster truck.

It landed heavily, skidded hard, revved loudly, and violently turned to crush the attackers in a single swoop, sending their coins splattering to the ground by the thousands.

The man watched as the truck reversed before him, the door opened and a woman behind the wheel called, "You up for an EconoMe drive? We're gonna slash the budget, big time!"

He rose and climbed to the running board. The woman reached down, grabbed his arm, pulled him up with her enormous strength and hoisted him into the vehicle where he clambered into the backseat.

Mysti resumed her place behind the wheel and revved the engine. Kimie cried out in joy from beside her and punched the roof, feeling freer than ever. As the truck roared down the street she turned to the man and asked, "You okay?"

He looked out the back window at what was behind them. "No. Check that out."

The golden coins that the truck had crushed were reforming in a blur. Kimie watched as they reverted to their humanoid forms and then sprinted down the street after them, fast enough to catch up.

"Oh," Kimie realised. "So they're the Army Reserve Bank, right?"

Mysti seethed. "That creep has so much to answer for."

"What are they?" the man asked.

"Centurions," Mysti answered. "All cents but no sense."

"*Profits* of doom," Kimie muttered.

The man leaned forward, indicating the truck. "Where'd you get this thing?"

Mysti revved the engine into a higher gear. "From the same guy who made the crud we just drove over. It'll get us to the Sky Scrapper."

Kimie was confused. "Why wasn't the Stargazer hooning around the City in this thing? He'd have loved it."

"The System wasn't stupid enough to let him," Mysti replied. "This baby's a war machine. Suits us."

"Let me get this straight," the man said. "You're not heading *out* of town?"

"What am I, a wimp?" Mysti scoffed. "The System can throw whatever it likes at us." She opened the door and climbed out onto the enormous running board. "Somebody drive."

Kimie made a mad grab for the wheel as the truck veered off the road. She steadied it quickly and shifted into the driver's seat. The thing was easier to drive than expected.

"Back seat behind the cushions!" Mysti called in. "I checked before. Seems our space freak pinched a couple of beauties from the Sky Scrapper."

Kimie got the truck onto the road again.

The man pulled a cushion away, found a hatch, opened it, and removed an automatic pulse rifle.

Mysti grinned. "Sweet as hell!" She leaned in around Kimie, displacing her awkwardly, then kissed the man hard and fast before moving back and licking her lips. "Yum, yum." She indicated ahead with a nod. "Building!"

Kimie jerked the wheel to the right, narrowly missing a building's corner.

Mysti shifted further out onto the board, looped an arm through a side handle and raised the weapon.

"Hey!" Kimie called to the man. "Where's mine?"

"You want a kiss too?" he asked, baffled.

"No, you tool, a gun!"

He handed her one.

Kimie clutched it happily. "Party-pocalypse! Take the wheel!"

He climbed into the front seat and they swapped sides. He steadied the vehicle and she moved outside, stood on the opposing running board to Mysti, and also looped her arm through a handle whilst raising her gun.

The Centurions swept in, their limbs a blur. The closest leapt high and landed in the trailer, only to be caught by Mysti's heavy burst of automatic fire.

Kimie let loose with her own gun, finding the weapon smooth and easy to use. Her shots were direct and a Centurion jolted wildly as masses of coins flew from its body.

"Whoa!" Kimie called over the truck's roof to Mysti. "Check out the strength of the dollar!"

A Centurion picked up a spiked piece of debris from the ground and hurled it at the truck's rear tyre. The debris rebounded, deflected by the tyre's thick material.

Mysti was impressed. "Looks like the star freak thought of everything." She leapt into the trailer and saw where the truck was going. "Tough spot!"

She held on tightly and Kimie did the same.

The truck drove up a steep slope of debris, flew in the air and crashed down on three parked cars before bouncing over them.

"God, I hope that was my principal's car," Kimie quipped, then wondered why she'd said that. Her memory of him was vague, but her loathing wasn't.

A Centurion hung off the trailer's rear, having been pounded by Mysti's shots. Mysti booted its head hard, sending it flying.

"Way to start a bankroll!" Kimie called.

"I call it retrench warfare!" Mysti called back.

Kimie blasted another Centurion, splattering its coins everywhere.

"Yeah, and I've just started the ex-change rate!"

A Centurion landed in the trailer, only to be greeted by a kick in the head from Mysti who sent several coins spraying from its mouth. Undeterred, it kicked back, booting her against the trailer's side. She swore as the gun flew from her hands, then regained her balance, pulled the dog leash from her pocket, wrapped it around her fist and struck the Centurion fiercely. She lashed out again, but her blow was blocked, her cheeks were grabbed and she was pulled in close to the Centurion who hissed, *"Prime investment opportunity!"*

Its eyes glowed.

A shot from Kimie hit the Centurion's shoulder, distracting it. Mysti grabbed its head, smacked it down hard on the trailer's side, brought it up again and delivered a prime uppercut with her dog-leash fist. The Centurion hurtled high, flailing off the trailer as another of its kind leapt on. She whirled around, dealing a solid punch to its head before her double jump kick sent it flying off the truck.

Kimie saw two pursuing Centurions break away from the others and head up the steps of a radio station. She wondered what they were up to, but the truck's sudden jolt made her look ahead. They were rapidly approaching a construction site where a giant magnet hung from a crane's cable.

Mysti banged the truck's roof. "Left! Go left!"

Kimie relayed Mysti's instructions to the driver to make sure he'd heard.

Mysti kicked another Centurion off the truck and sent a second one spiralling after it. Two more leapt on. Mysti drove a kick at one. It grabbed her foot, she fell with a cry, then used her other to break free from its grasp.

"Get off me, ya deadweight loss!" She rose and called to Kimie, "Back soon, kid!"

"Hey, what——?"

Mysti stuffed the dog leash in her pocket, climbed onto the truck's roof, jumped up, hung from the magnet, aimed it at the Centurions and hissed, "Let's freeze your bony assets!"

The Centurions jerked awkwardly, flew up, clamped onto the magnet and hung helplessly as the truck passed under them. They struggled fiercely, morphing into a bubbling mass of coins that fought to break free.

Mysti dropped from it, landing smoothly on the ground. "Guess the almighty dollar isn't so strong after all."

More Centurions swept in.

She turned and ran into the construction site.

The Stargazer studied his readings. "Oooh, the System really hates us. Check out the negative feedback we're getting."

Gilwain saw the spiking signals on the Stargazer's screen.

"Explain!" Yushera ordered.

The Stargazer entered a sequence. "I detected a few bad boys entering a local radio station and it's just started transmitting. Means the City's trying to get back in business."

"Can we stop it?" she asked.

He initiated a command. "No. I can hold it off, but not for long. Ground troops are needed on this one and—oh!" He changed the screen's image and zeroed in. "Seems we've already got help. Take a look at this."

Yushera moved beside him and they all watched as the monster truck raced past a camera, with Kimie on its side.

Yushera's head rose. "She will need assistance."

"Totally," the Stargazer concurred. "Time to call in the cats and rats, your Majesty. I can fix things so you can talk to your people."

"I do not talk, I command," she corrected.

The Stargazer and Gilwain spoke instinctively. "Agreed."

She glared at them.

They gulped and quickly got to work.

The Centurions circled the monster truck.

The vehicle swung around hard, crushing two of them. The third evaded the impact by leaping high.

Kimie blasted it in mid-air. "This is crap!" She threw the gun on the passenger seat, reached into the back, scrambled around, pulled out another weapon and grinned at the sight of it. "Drool overload!"

A flamethrower.

She rose, strapped it over her shoulder and charged it.

A Centurion closed in.

Her finger tightened on the trigger as she hissed, "You're liquidated!"

A rush of flames engulfed it.

The closet Centurions recoiled, veering away. A few changed tactics and swept around the truck's side, ready to leap into the trailer. Kimie got a couple but knew she'd soon be swamped.

Up ahead, sat another truck with a cement mixer on its back. Her instincts kicked in at the sight of this abandoned vehicle, along with a desperate plan. It was a long shot but there was no time to think, just act.

"I hope that thing's full," she muttered, then called, "Head for the truck!"

The man swung the wheel and they raced towards it.

A Centurion leapt into the trailer, reaching for her.

"Brake!" she ordered the driver.

The truck skidded sideways and screeched to a halt, sending the Centurion flying into its roof. She let go of the handle and climbed down, just as three more Centurions landed in the trailer.

The driver grabbed the gun beside him, left the wheel, climbed out of the truck, reached the ground and ran over to Kimie. Together, they turned and backed up to the cement mixer, firing relentlessly.

"Gotta plan?" the man asked.

"Sort of," she answered. "More a gut feeling. Trouble is, life has a way of kicking you right in the guts when all hell's breaking loose." She placed a hand on the cement mixer's side. "Thing's warm. Thought so. Looks like someone tried to ditch this place in it and didn't get far."

"That's a good thing?"

"Hell, yeah."

She ran ahead. He followed, bolting after her for some way.

The Centurions had barely reached the cement mixer when Kimie grabbed the man's gun off him, whirled around and snapped, "Economic resistance is a bitch!"

She fired.

The shots hit the cement mixer, blowing it outwards and hurtling masses of searing cement over the golden army in mighty dollops. She recoiled with the man as they shielded their eyes from the billowing fire-balls of black and gold flames. Most Centurions dropped under the cement's sheer weight. Others struggled on, in staggering steps.

"Nice shot," the man quipped.

Kimie nodded. "Thanks."

Only three Centurions were left, closing in.

"Got another plan?" the man asked.

"Not really," she replied. "You?"

"God, no."

She shrugged. "Spent my whole life winging it, so what else is new?"

She handed the gun back to him, raised her flamethrower and tensed.

Thuk!

A heavy pole rammed into the Centurion's chest, shoving the golden being into a mass of flames.

Mysti.

She stood tall as another Centurion surged in, lashing out at her. She blocked the blow and hurled the being into the flames after the first, then sent the last Centurion flying in after it.

"Good stuff!" Kimie called.

"You too!" Mysti called back. "Kinda threw my plans out the window 'cause I had to ditch 'em and save your butts, but it looks like things paid off."

More Centurions emerged from the shadows.

"Yeah, right," Kimie said grimly. "This lot are still coming to collect."

Mysti's face hardened. "Last stand, kid."

"Yeah," Kimie agreed. "For them."

A Centurion swept in for Mysti. She tensed, ready to let loose, when a hook suddenly burst through its chest and swung the being into a dump-ster where the lid banged down with a resounding boom.

Barbie Q stepped out of the shadows, grinning slyly. "I always love a little bang for a buck."

Kimie saw that her maniacal gaze had changed. Now, it was replaced by a human spark, courtesy of the Stargazer, though shades of her old presence still flickered.

More Hookers appeared behind her, raising their arms to the Centurions, ready to let loose.

Others beat them to it.

A high-pitched squeal pierced the night as thick steel nets flew over several Centurions, pulling them to the ground. Louder squeals erupted as a wave of Alley Cats and Sewer Rats surged in, led by Alley-Money, to join the gleeful Hookers in a full-blown rumble.

Mysti dived right in too, smacking a Centurion's head with her gun.

"Thanks!" she called to Alley-Money. "How'd you find us?"

"It was not hard," Alley-Money replied. "You were making enough noise."

"Guess so," Mysti agreed, bashing her Centurion to the ground. "No, seriously, you found us way too easy."

"Our Queen is within a station of power," Alley-Money explained. "The Stargazer assisted her in sending us a message."

"How'd you get it?"

Barbie Q raised her hand. "Guilty as always! Just hooked up with his signal."

Alley-Money continued. "More of our enemies are in a radio station. They are trying to work their evil upon our realm."

Barbie Q spoke up. "Yeah, and I've just sent a few of my girls down there to hook up with 'em too."

The Centurion she'd thrown into the dumpster emerged, pushing up the lid.

She ran over, pulling the lid up fully. "I love talking trash." She climbed in eagerly. "Let's get down and dirty!"

Her hooks fired, followed by the Centurion's hisses as it tried to absorb her but failed miserably.

"Can't do that," she said smoothly. "I'm already worth my weight in gold."

The Centurion hissed angrily as she reached in and took away its inner cents.

Platinum stepped onto the roof.

She'd emerged from one stairwell to find herself facing another several metres ahead. It hadn't appeared on any building plans when she'd gone through the schematics, and if two opposing stairwells weren't curious enough, this one's doorway was bathed in a dim red glow. She stared into the red mist wafting from it, breezing eerily into the night. Her head tingled. The hideous presence was enflaming her mind again, snarling hungrily whilst trying to worm its way into her psyche. It didn't get far. It couldn't. She was too strong for that, courtesy of her superior.

She took a step, then stopped, rooted to the spot. She tried moving, but couldn't. The City's feral essence clutched her too tightly for that. At least it was out in the open, right where she wanted it, but she knew that *it* wanted her here too, or else the Centurions would have attacked by now.

The infectious presence in her mind pulsated sickly, attempting to envelop her. She couldn't move her body. It couldn't move her mind.

Stalemate.

The Stargazer observed the readings on his terminal screen. The City's energy reserves were almost back online, care of the Centurions in the radio station. Another screen showed several Hookers in the street, trying to batter that building's front door in. They weren't having much luck. It was sealed too tightly.

Yushera, however, was gazing at a third screen, horrified.

The Stargazer noticed her reaction to the Sky Scrapper's image upon it. "What's up with you, scaredy-cat?"

She was almost too shocked to speak. "A demon! There is evil in the tower!"

Gilwain analysed the readings. "Indeed. I've never seen a Freakquency spike on this scale."

The Stargazer peered in. "That's a bio-organic compound. See how those wave particles are turning? They're in unison."

Gilwain frowned. "That would mean it's coming from—"

"You got it," the Stargazer cut in. "An energy-based life form that seems to have been dwelling in the Sky Scrapper for some time."

"A demon," Yushera confirmed.

"That's one way of putting it," he agreed, "although I'm not sure if *it* caused the System or was caused *by* it." He twisted a dial. "I'm also detecting someone on the building's roof."

He flicked a switch. The radio station's image changed to the Sky Scrapper's peak where a blonde woman stood before a doorway, swamped by a heavy mist.

"My lady!" Gilwain said, astounded.

Yushera was unimpressed. *"That* is your superior?"

He nodded.

She made a face. "Too clean to be a Queen. A spotless one can never be trusted, for she hides the blood on her hands. That is why we in the sewers never clean ourselves. If there were blood on our hands, you would see it."

The Stargazer mused thoughtfully. "I think it's safe to say she's on our side. Look at the way that angry strobe light's got her. She's frozen. Our dragon must have a nest egg tucked away up there. Looks ready to hatch."

"Is there a way to aid her?" Yushera asked.

"Oh, yeah," came the reply, "but first we gotta blow the butt out of our Nuclear Fusion GenEarator so it'll never crap on anyone again."

He resumed his work with Gilwain.

Kimie gazed up at the Sky Scrapper's ominous red glow at its peak. "Okay, what's that?"

Several murmurs of "demon" and "evil" came from the Alley Cats and Sewer Rats. Now that they'd subdued the Centurions, all eyes were focussed on the building.

Alley-Money spoke gravely. "The System. It bleeds."

Mysti stepped forward, staring up at it. "Means we've made an impact. The City's gone into the red."

"Our beast is wounded," Alley-Money observed.

"Which makes it dangerous," Mysti warned.

The surrounding youths whimpered.

"Wimps," Mysti muttered, then indicated the tower. "That's the trouble with bosses. They play in their towers too long and lose sight of the ground. Let's bring 'em down to Earth."

She ran through the crowd to the monster truck.

"Hey, wait up," Kimie called.

"Not this time!" Mysti called back. "You're in charge!"

Kimie looked around at the Hookers, Alley Cats and Sewer Rats and grimaced. "Gee, thanks."

Mysti reached the truck, climbed to the door, entered, revved the engine and sent the vehicle roaring ahead. Cries went up as everyone leapt out of the way, leaving her to veer down the street, picking up speed as she made for the Sky Scrapper.

The Stargazer spoke proudly. "One Nuclear Fusion GenEarator out of operation. That thing's stuffed for good. Now we need to get the Hookers into that radio station to stop the golden soldiers getting the City back in business." He saw Yushera frowning. "Typical. I get online, you get feline. What's up?"

She seemed confused. "I know not. A voice sings to us on the wind."

The Stargazer observed the terminal screen. "So we've got one threat coming from the Sky Scrapper, another from the radio station and now …" He hit a button. "Another wavelength's started resonating from *below* the City."

Gilwain examined the readings. "An enemy?"

The Stargazer shook his head. "I doubt it. This is a whole different frequency altogether."

Gilwain zeroed in on the image. "Interesting. It's so deep that it might be from *before* the economic takeover." He pressed a button.

Soft, gentle harmonies rose from the speakers, filled with more joyous depth than the trio ever thought possible. They listened, captivated, and for the first time in what seemed like forever, the Stargazer felt whole, Gilwain elated, and Yushera saw something higher than the glory of the sewers.

She spoke softly, entranced by the music's soaring bliss. "It is beautiful."

"Indeed," Gilwain agreed. "It was always my family's promise to create perfection such as this."

The Stargazer's jaw dropped. "Trust you to take credit for anything good as soon as it shows up." He huffed and worked the terminal. "At least it offers us far more than the City can anyway, 'cause its purpose is way higher. That's what happens when you see the bigger picture. This baby's a shift upwards from an economic target to an astronomical one. If it can counteract the Sky Scrapper's heavy Freakquency, it's impressive."

Yushera was in awe. "It is fitting that this miracle should come from below the ground where the sewers are."

"And it can only be dwarf-made," Gilwain added.

"Enough with that," the Stargazer retorted.

"Jealous, are we?" Gilwain shot back.

"You don't even know what you're listening to."

"I know what's in a dwarf's heart."

"Where is the magic coming from?" Yushera cut in.

The Stargazer stopped and blinked. "Ahem—yes. It's resonating a little *below* your sewers actually. Tucked away snugly."

She spoke resolutely. "I feel as if I know it. It can help us."

"Of course," Gilwain said. "It's dwarf—"

"Garbage," the Stargazer interjected, then addressed Yushera. "We need you to get down there, your Majesty, to take a look at it. You know the territory, and a few tunnels are so narrow that podge belly here couldn't fit through 'em if he tried. We'll assist you from here, *if* you're willing to wear a COM link."

Yushera's face hardened. "A Queen does not take orders."

"Not even when her sewer kingdom's about to be shot to the stars?"

She sighed. "This is most undignified. Very well, I accept, but I shall go with all the dignity and grace fitting to that of a Sewer Queen."

She composed herself and then opened her mouth, letting loose with a piercing squeal. Several rats scurried out from various holes and came to a halt before her.

"Which way?" she asked the Stargazer.

He indicated a broken grille in the wall.

"Go," she ordered the rats, "and pave the way for your Queen."

The rats dashed to the grille, vanishing down it.

Regally, she sat on a chair with her back to the Stargazer. "Place the device on me."

He pushed part of her grimy hair away and fitted the COM link around her neck. Once it was secure, she rose and approached the grille.

"Remove the obstacle."

The Stargazer glanced at Gilwain. "You'll have to do that."

Gilwain went over, placed his hands on it and pulled it from the wall.

Yushera nodded, satisfied, then knelt down and crawled in after the rats.

The Stargazer examined the terminal's readings. "She'd better hurry. Whatever's in the Sky Scrapper's growing, and the Centurions in the radio station aren't helping either. The City's almost back online." He inhaled sharply. "Things are heating up out there."

Chapter Thirteen

Mysti rose to the Sky Scrapper's peak, care of a Roverboard she'd swiped from a DeciMaul.

The monster truck's rear end half-hung out of a window some way below, right where she'd left it after ramming it into the building. The truck's alloy was so tough that it had withstood the impact. Two Hookers were using anti-gravity devices they'd pinched from a lab to extract it, no doubt to have fun with later, Mysti guessed.

The dark red aura from the building's peak prickled her skin as she ascended. A whispering presence slithered into her mind and the closer she came, the more it grew. She focussed on memories of her old dog to keep its hideous taunts at bay, but the higher she rose, the greater the whispers became.

"Fall, fall, fall, why don't you fall?"
"Drop! It'll be easier that way …"
"You've always been a failure …"
"You were bred to be a killer …"

She tensed uneasily. Luckily, Bluey's presence gave her the strength to go on, along with her faith in Kimie and everyone else below. She resisted the whispers defiantly, rising against the fierce odds to reach the building's peak. Finally, she made it, to find two stairwells facing each other. Both had open doors that led into the Sky Scrapper's belly, but only one had a cloudy red glow. Before it, stood a blonde woman.

Mysti recalled Kimie's words. *"She's called Platinum."*

Clutching her gun tightly, she leapt onto the roof's flat surface, leaving the Roverboard to automatically move in and land behind her.

The voices in her head grew louder.

"You're a failure!"

"Failure …"

"Failure …"

Her first instinct was to shoot the blonde woman. She didn't know what this freakzilla was up to, or even if she was behind all this, but Bluey's spark held her back, giving her insight. Platinum was under attack.

"I've had enough of this crap!"

She aimed her gun at the door and fired. The shot flew into the doorway, enflaming the glow. Still, it was enough, and Platinum shook her head, free from the sickening force but totally indifferent. She nodded and spoke coolly to Mysti.

"Thanks for that."

Mysti was baffled. "What the crud have you been up to?"

"Careful," Platinum warned. "Our dark patch thrives on negative energy. Better behave or it'll suck you right in."

Mysti ignored her. "Is this crap down to you?"

"Pretty much," Platinum answered.

Mysti was taken aback. "You admit it?"

"Oh, yeah," came the reply. "Well, the good stuff is anyway."

"Good stuff?" Mysti cried, throwing an arm up. "Where?"

Platinum shrugged. "Open your eyes. I used that kid to lift you out of your SORE Point. I also reprogrammed the Symbiotechs to take out the City and expose the real enemy. That was a little tricky from miles away, but it worked, and here we are."

"And how many people have died because of that?" Mysti snapped.

"None," Platinum answered simply.

"You're nuts …"

Platinum stayed cool. "Did you see anyone killed? No civilian bodies are lying in the streets. Not a single one. Why?" Her tone rose confidently. "'Cause the whole attack was an illusion. The Symbiotechs were protecting people, not killing 'em. They were really rounding 'em up like sheep to be shipped to the Mountain. There were DeciMauls cut down, sure, and a few Hookers got blown apart, but as far as people go, no casualties. I guaranteed that when I hacked into the Mountain's systems and threw in my own chunk of chaos. Couldn't do it till the last second though. Got delayed by something just as big, or I'd have led the attack on the City myself *and* got a much cleaner outcome. Still, random factors are always the best." Her face fell. "Except when there *is* a casualty." Red shades from the doorway drifted over her face and she spoke softly. "I couldn't save the Orion Sentry."

Mysti was aghast. "What? You—!"

A whoosh came from the doorway as a searing fireball swept at them. Mysti ducked.

Platinum remained still, letting it miss her by inches, whilst staying calm as ever. "Dragon's breath. It's waking up."

"How?" Mysti wondered. "I just shot it."

"No, it released me when you arrived," she corrected. "Probably 'cause it sees a better investment in you."

"So that's what's controlling the City?"

"You bet," Platinum confirmed. "It overtook it in the only way it knew how—*system*atically—until everyone ended up serving it, unconsciously of course. It disguised itself well, keeping hidden as a malignant force under our sugar-coated economy. The Moneyarch thought he was in control. Bosses always do when it comes to any system, but he was as much of a slave to it as anyone. Now our System really is a monster."

A taunting laugh rose from the doorway. Mysti peered into it. Three silhouetted figures stood there. The outer ones were Centurions, but the middle figure was taller than either of them. Over seven feet.

Hundred dollar bills wafted out from the building's depths, flying into the night. Platinum stayed motionless, letting them sweep past her. Mysti batted a few away whilst keeping her aim on the newcomers who stepped out into the open. The middle one, she saw, was a man who wore a top hat and tailcoat, whilst holding an old-fashioned cane. He was like something out of the olden days, she thought, or would have been if not for his gothic white face. Long strands of his jet-black hair danced on the wind, and in many ways, he resembled the Stargazer. Then again, Mysti reasoned, the System had seduced the Stargazer, turning him into an image of itself. The Moneyarch too, for that matter, for since he'd also looked like both of them. The only difference with this weirdo, apart from the white face, was his red halo, and a blood-red dollar sign on each cheek.

Wasting no time, Mysti fired. The blast rippled through the man like he was a ghost, shooting into the doorway and sending it flaring bright red, like salt pouring on an infected wound. A hideous scream pierced her mind, then faded.

"Damn!" she hissed.

Platinum wasn't surprised. "Yep. Only scored the mouthpiece. Probably a power saver for the EconoMe."

"Like what?" Mysti pressed. "An Econo-Mist?"

"Totally," came the reply. "Shady as hell."

The Econo-Mist spoke without moving his lips. His voice pierced their minds as he tapped his cane.

"*Ra-ta-ta-ta … rap-ta-ta-ta … ra-ta-ta-ta …*"

The tension mounted, then he lifted his cane high and swung it down hard. The doorway behind him erupted with a primal cry.

Mysti fell to her knees, clutching her temples. She winced, resisting the foul presence trying to burrow into her brain.

Platinum stayed motionless, defying the malignant pressure against her own mind.

"So …" she began.

The Econo-Mist aimed his cane at her. "*Enough! Too many voices in the EconoMe makes it unprofitable. Democracy's bad for business.*"

He swiped his cane. A heavy force rammed into her, smacking her back off the building and plummeting into the sky.

Kimie stood in the street with the Alley Cats, Sewer Rats, Hookers, Symbiotechs and several battered people who'd all gathered at the Sky Scrapper's base. She'd been wary of the Symbiotechs at first, but knew they were legit when they'd started helping people. Three were even flying up to the Sky Scrapper's peak on Roverboards, having pinched them from the DeciMauls.

She kept her gaze on the building's roof, wondering what was happening up there. She got her answer when a body flew over the edge.

Kimie gasped, thinking it was Mysti.

Platinum gave a wry smile as she fell through the clouds, loving the stakes.

A whizzing noise came from below, a glow engulfed her, and she halted suddenly in mid-air. A short way below, two of her Symbiotechs on Roverboards, held her in position, care of two anti-gravity beams.

She grinned triumphantly as they all descended.

Mysti leapt at the Econo-Mist.

A wave of banknotes swept in, cutting her face. She recoiled, letting the money tide fly past.

"Arrgh! Screw you!"

The man clenched his fist. An invisible force wrapped around her throat, making her choke. She dropped the gun, letting it clatter onto the roof as she desperately tried breaking free of his hold. Her attempt was futile and she was lifted into the air, watching helplessly as he swung his cane at her Roverboard, sending it up in flames.

A whirr came from the building's edge as a Symbiotech ascended on another.

"*Resistance?*" the man mused. "*Good. We're long overdue for a merger…*"

Throughout the City, the Hookers and DeciMauls all tensed as the Econo-Mist's will bypassed the Stargazer's signal, overtaking them. Barbie Q's head rose, knowing she was once again under the System's control, now joined by the Symbiotechs.

She beamed delightedly. "I'm a working girl again!"

Her fist clenched, churning the concealed hook in her wrist as she focused on Kimie. The oblivious girl was heading away from her to get a better view of the action above.

Barbie Q followed hungrily.

The Stargazer's face fell at the terminal's readings.

"Ballop!" he swore. "The City's Freakquency's raging at full strength. It's looped its dogs and Hookers back into itself. The Symbiotechs have joined 'em too."

"Our work's still unaffected," Gilwain pointed out. "Thanks to *my* calculations."

The Stargazer's face hardened. "I know, but this is bad. Unless …" He worked rapidly.

Gilwain's jaw dropped when he saw what he was doing. "No! You can't—!"

"Got no choice," the Stargazer cut in. "I would have done it from the ol' car ages ago if I'd had the tech. Now I've gotta make up for lost time."

Gilwain was aghast. "You're about to commit murder. The Symbiotechs …"

"Yeah, and if we do nothing then it's mass murder," came the adamant reply. "The fewer allies the big bad's got, the better."

Gilwain reached for a keyboard. "We do this together."

The Stargazer raised a hand, stopping him. "No, this is down to me. I created this mess, I'll fix it. You'll have to rustle up our power reserves before the System sucks 'em up. Go!"

Gilwain got to work, scowling bitterly.

The Stargazer stared glumly at the terminal.

"I wouldn't wish this on anyone," he said softly, and activated a sequence.

Barbie Q raised her hand, targeting Kimie. The girl had come to a halt, right out in the open. Her hook whirred as she relished the moment, preparing to let loose. She grinned gleefully, before her metal body suddenly erupted with a piercing whine and she shook violently. Somehow, through her anguish, she saw that the other Hookers were doing the same.

Kimie whirled around and ducked as Barbie Q's hook shot over her head, hitting a wall. She recoiled as the Hooker staggered back, clutching her steel temples. Nearby, the DeciMauls howled as their collars erupted with high-pitched squeals, while the Symbiotechs too, groaned in anguish.

Kimie jumped as a Symbiotech's head blew into a bloodied mass and its body slumped into the gutter. A DeciMaul went next, splattering down from a Roverboard. The Info-Maniac followed, ignited by the rogue frequency.

Kimie watched, astonished, as one by one, the Symbiotechs, Deci-Mauls and Hookers all exploded into devastated masses of blood and circuitry.

Barbie Q winced amid the chaos. Her sisters were gone, leaving her as the last of her kind. Looking miserable, she said glumly, "I am so over this whole bang for a buck thing."

Then she exploded.

A small blast erupted from the Stargazer's terminal, making him and Gilwain recoil.

Gilwain picked up an extinguisher and doused the flames, then moved in to look at a cracked screen. "The City's Freakquency's growing. We can't hold out much longer."

The Stargazer bit his lip. "At least Hell's army's gone down slightly, so that helps."

Gilwain nodded. He hadn't liked the Symbiotechs fate one bit, but things were panning out. He worked the terminal rapidly, doing his best to resist the City's might.

Mysti heard the Symbiotech on the Roverboard cry out.

She turned her head slightly, struggling against the force that held her. From the corner of her eye, she saw the Symbiotech clutch his head, fall back and plummet into the clouds.

She grinned cockily, with Bluey's spirit, as she focussed on the Econo-Mist. "Things not going to plan? Didn't predict that, did ya? So is your System still perfect, or what?"

He wasn't fazed. "*So the spoilt child mouths off at her sire. We're one and the same, my dear. The mystical girl and the Econo-Mist. You're only resisting what created you. Now you're engulfed by it. The air you breathe, the food you eat, the clothes you wear, it's all owned by the System, leaving you as a minuscule cell in its service.*"

He tapped his cane rhythmically, walking around her.

"The Moneyarch was aware of that, right up until he ceased being of value to the System and stopped being prophet-able. Naturally it finished him off. He was hit by the flames of its command and, in effect, fired." His tone darkened. *"His vacant position must now be filled. You've no choice in the matter."*

Mysti seethed fiercely. "We'll talk again when I'm burning your bank-notes!"

He dismissed this. *"You thrive on hypocrisy. Who do you lead? Not a System that works, but a bunch of chaotic children. The broken new girl. The scientific genius who wasted his potential on alcohol and Hookers. Alley Cats and Sewer Rats who cower in the underworld, knowing they're nothing but the scum of the earth."*

She averted her gaze.

"LOOK AT ME WHEN I'M TALKING TO YOU!"

He swung his cane at her, smacking her head to one side with an invisible force, making her wince. She glared daggers back at him as he continued.

"The System brings order, control, prevents wars …"

"We're locked in a prison!" she snapped.

"Of your own making," he corrected. *"You're all conceivers who became subordinates. Those who resisted were assimilated or destroyed as the System took a life of its own. It started off as a child, then became mother, father and finally, God."* His voice rose, along with the doorway's red glow. *"You're merely an advertisement for its image, and it's only when you wake up that you finally stop fighting and then …"* He paused, savouring the moment. *"You become the System!"*

His ferocious will lashed out, striking her hard. Her head arched back and she growled, clenching her teeth. The colour drained from her face, turning deathly white, as her resistance lowered. Her gaze dulled to compliance, before two dark circles appeared around her eyes, morphing into dollar signs.

The Econo-Mist chuckled. *"Now you see your true value. We're all just products of life, aren't we?"*

Satisfied, he walked past his new Moneyarch to the building's edge, gazing into the night at the City's outskirts, and the power station there.

He sneered cruelly, then nodded.

Kimie stepped back, shaken.

The red glow at the Sky Scrapper's peak had expanded, forming an enormous halo. She was still baffled as to why the Hookers and other freaks here had suddenly gone feral and then exploded. Was it Mysti's work? Or the Stargazer's? Whatever the case, she was grateful. Her only intention now was to find a Roverboard, fly to the Sky Scrapper's peak and help Mysti out.

The air tingled and she felt her hand ripple. She looked down, turned it over and gasped. A black dollar sign had formed, darkening her skin. She trembled, knowing what the System was turning her into. "Oh, you bastard." She gazed up at the tower. "Guess I'm really noteworthy after all."

Her thoughts churned. So the EconoMe wasn't hiding anymore. Yes, the Hookers, DeciMauls and Symbiotechs were gone, but the System was fighting back big time. She shuddered as more dollar signs grew rapidly over her body. There was no way to fight them, leaving her screwed.

A slimy, wet tendril shot up from the ground, slapping around her arm and digging into her flesh. She winced and saw that it was comprised of banknotes. What's more, they had multiple images of a face staring up at her.

Mysti's, glaring at her dully.

Kimie's heart thumped in horror, knowing what that meant.

Mysti was the new Moneyarch.

"No …" she whispered.

The tendril's dark energy rippled through her veins as the dollar signs on her flesh grew rapidly.

More tendrils rose from the ground, embracing the Alley Cats and Sewer Rats, ready to transform them into units of City currency.

Kimie seethed. "So money really is the root of all evil. Typical Money-Tree crap."

The tendrils pulled harder.

She growled, refusing to be sucked in by anything. Sheer defiance gave her the strength to break out of the MoneyTree's hold and she wrenched herself free, staggering to the side. She grinned cockily, then yelped, tripping over a large chunk of rubble by the open street chasm. Helplessly, she toppled over, plummeting headfirst into the darkness below.

Gilwain scowled, staring at the terminal screen. Giant MoneyTree tendrils were rippling through the City streets, consuming its people in a hunger that would never be satisfied. The power station's floor shook fiercely, indicating they were on their way. To make matters worse, he and the Stargazer were struggling to hold out against the City's Freakquency, meaning they'd soon lose control of the terminal.

A beep came from it.

The Stargazer flicked a switch. "Gimme good news, your Majesty. You okay down there?"

"*I am now,*" came the reply, "*for I have discovered the source of our song. I heard it coming from my kingdom's river. When I gazed into the heavenly waters, I found a piece of scrap covered in sludge. Naturally I thought it was priceless so I took it.*"

"And …?" Gawain pressed.

"*When I clasped it I saw … saw …*"

"Saw what?" Gilwain pushed irritably.

She spoke in awe. "*A revelation!*"

The station floor rumbled louder.

The Stargazer worked the controls rapidly. "What kind of revelation? Talk fast, your Majesty."

Yushera continued. "*All I know, is that, when I touched it, I felt a joy that has slept in my heart since the days of old. Whatever I hold is of great power. So simple, yet so strong, for it is merely a bound cross, made up of two musical instruments.*"

"You mean," the Stargazer concluded, "that what you're holding … are drumsticks?"

Gilwain thumped the panel irritably.

A piercing, high-pitched whine erupted from it.

Yushera hissed in pain.

The Stargazer smacked Gilwain. Gilwain smacked him back. The Stargazer was about to smack him again when the terminal's speakers suddenly flared with the uplifting resonance they'd heard earlier. They listened, entranced, as the ground tremors softened.

Yushera spoke eagerly. "*That is what happens when I tap the cross against the wall. The City does not like it.*"

The Stargazer blinked, bringing himself back to reality. "Of course it wouldn't. It doesn't like anything with a bit of heart. I'm starting to see the picture."

The floor tremored again, care of the City.

"Then fill us in," Gilwain huffed. "And quickly!"

The Stargazer resumed his work on the terminal. "I'm sure the cross is from our ol' Village's sacred Vault. I never saw inside but did hear about it. The Vault held everyday objects moulded by the Sages of Old. They were pros at transforming divine energy into regular items which they'd then hide in plain sight should worse come to worst."

"*I have not heard of this Vault,*" Yushera said.

"Oh no, you're too young," the Stargazer replied.

Gilwain looked sternly at him. "And it's classified information."

"Then how do you know about it?" the Stargazer pressed.

Gilwain coughed and looked away, mumbling.

The Stargazer submitted. "I hacked into the Moneyarch's private channel a while back and heard everything. The Orion Sentry took a few treasures to his inn when the Village was sealed off. He must have flushed some down the drain when the place went under, but the City took the rest. One treasure was a vase, I believe." He examined the terminal readings "Thank the stars you found those sticks, your Lowness. They have the right notes to change the Freakquency, so you'd better get up here. If there's any trouble on the way, just smack 'em together in a *cymbolic* gesture of peace. The EconoMe can't stand anything louder than itself."

Yushera's response was sullen. "*I am still confused.*"

The Stargazer changed the screen's setting. Another image appeared, showing several Centurions running across town, making for the power station and getting closer by the moment.

"We've been spotted by the big bad," he reported, "so the sooner you get your treasures here your Majesty, the better, 'cause if there was ever a time to band together, it's now."

Kimie pushed herself up with a groan, finding herself in the sewers.

The air was cold. Way colder than it should have been. Her eyes adjusted to the dim light. A stream lay nearby, flowing with gunk over a drain cover. She was just figuring out what to do when …

Whoosh!

A giant MoneyTree tendril swooped in, screeching furiously. She scrambled back, bracing herself for the worst. Its cries grew and then …

Bang!

The drain cover suddenly flew up and a grimy hand rose, clutching a cross bound by a dirtied cloth. To Kimie's sheer disbelief, both were illuminated by a golden halo.

"Talk about the total random," she murmured.

The halo pulsated, latching onto her heart's wavelength. Her spirit glowed, filled with the most beautiful song she'd ever heard. This cross, whatever it was, enflamed a concealed beauty in her hidden depths. She watched, illuminated, as the cross brightened and the music grew to a heavenly climax. Just when the harmonies reached their joyous peak, the hand slammed the cross onto the slimy floor.

The booming crescendo of sheer divinity erupted through the sewers, filling her with awe. Despite being in this dark, disgusting dump that stank of god knew what, *and* facing death in the face from this sick beast, she felt unshakable. All her life, she'd had to put up with nothing but crap, but right now, down here, in a place that was meant to be filled with nothing *but* crap, her heart was elevated above everything. Its glow overtook her body, purifying her as the blood of life flowed back into her features, banishing the dollar signs and lifting her human spark right to the forefront of her very being.

The tendril halted, shaking violently. The cross was banged again, much harder this time, lifting Kimie higher than ever as the tendril struggled to hold itself together. A swift throw flung the cross into its mass of banknotes with a heavy stab. A mighty shriek erupted from its MoneyTree source far down the tunnel, then part of the tendril exploded.

The cross flew back at Kimie who ducked as it hit the wall. She peered through the billowing wave of banknotes as the severed tendril's remaining half retreated into the darkness. Baffled, she looked at the drain. A hand emerged, taking hold of the fallen cross, before Queen Yushera ascended proudly.

Kimie grinned, astounded, amid the mass of flying notes. "Good stuff, your Majesty. Now *we're* in the money!" She grabbed a handful, ready to pocket it.

Yushera cat-spat loudly, repelled by the very thought.

Kimie jumped and tossed the money away. "Yeah, guess you're right." She indicated the cross. "Whatcha got there?"

"What I was sent to find," Yushera answered proudly. "I was returning to a station of power where my subjects are assisting me in fighting the evil above …"

"You mean the Stargazer and Gilwain?" Kimie cut in, recalling their earlier plan. "Yeah, they're not exactly *your* subjects. Let's see what you got there."

Yushera presented the cross with outstretched hands.

Kimie took it. Her hand tingled in its touch as the celestial choir sang louder than ever. At last, she saw the inner black clouds that she'd carried for so long and been oblivious to. They'd engulfed her slowly, and she'd magnified them to the extreme. She pushed with her will, sensing their remains shrink and fade. Insight kicked in. The drudgery of everyday living had covered her in its garbage, just like the sewers had done to the treasures down here, yet there'd always been hidden surprises, just waiting to be awoken.

She unbound the cloth, letting the cross fall apart in her hands. The two bits of wood fell into her palm, tickling it lightly. She gazed at them astonished, seeing that they were a pair of glowing drumsticks. Her head rose as she looked at Yushera. "These are awesome. Where'd you find 'em?"

Yushera indicated the gunk in the sewers. "In the river."

Kimie grinned. "The river Styx?"

Yushera frowned, confused.

"Forget it," Kimie said. "Like calling 'em the Stix though. We could have a lot of fun here."

Yushera nodded. "Their strength has opened my heart too. Even now I feel I were destined to be more than a Sewer Queen."

Kimie examined them curiously. "Who knew something so simple could be so powerful?"

"The greatest of powers are always hidden in plain sight," Yushera explained. "My people call such things, the secrets of the invisible. They can either hinder or help."

"You got that right," Kimie agreed. "We'll need to use these on Mysti. Just look at her face on the cash round here. She's gone to the dark side."

Yushera spoke resolutely. "If she has, it is not by choice. I know the child of old. She would never indulge in such treachery."

Kimie believed her and was about to respond when the COM link on the Queen's neck buzzed, and the Stargazer's voice came through. *"Indulgence is overrated anyway."*

Kimie smiled, recognising the voice. "Let me guess, getting the Stix was your idea?"

"Yuh-huh," he answered. *"You saw what happened when the City's people started believing too much in maths without music. Sure, maths tames, solidifies and grounds us. It gets things done, but without music, it's only a structure without heart. Music, on the other hand, is the bliss of the heavenly spheres, but without mathematical focus, it sinks, growing dark, heavy, needy and wild. Music and maths both need to rely on each other to keep things in balance."*

Kimie concurred. "You got me on that."

He continued. *"Our ol' Village was overcome by corporate forces, throwing things out of balance. I believe the term some City demon used was 'phased deregulation'. The System's heavy presence either forced us underground, corrupted the weak, or sent the resistant to sleep. We all had meltdowns to the City's toxicity. Good thing is that time allows everything that's pushed down to rise back up again. Music always returns to counterbalance the maths. That's where you come in."*

Kimie nodded. "You're right, Starman. We need to change this place's tune. The beat gets boring when people only get the killer instinct for dollars. God, sometimes I wish we'd all just turn off our screens and forget about the alerts and messages on our phones and the *chi-chings* of the cash tills. Nobody listens. *Really* listens, I mean. Time and reality are a whole lot bigger than the City's ego. It's time we told it that."

Yushera's gaze fell upon the Stix. "Then we should give them something to listen to, should we not?"

Kimie felt the Stix's pulsating rhythms flow through her. "Yeah. We should."

The sewers rumbled.

"Now would be a good time …" the Stargazer said grimly.

The Stargazer and Gilwain watched as the Centurions entered the power station, raising their arms.

"*Incorporate!*"

The Stargazer turned the terminal's speaker to the max and called to Kimie, "Hit it!"

Kimie smacked the Stix together.

The speaker erupted with a bellowing resonance, captivating the Stargazer and Gilwain and stopping the Centurions in their tracks.

The resonance grew, then faded.

The Centurions started moving.

The Stargazer shook his head, returning to reality. "Again!"

The speaker blared once more, louder this time.

The Centurions froze.

Seizing the moment, Gilwain ran in, swiped his axe and sent them clattering to the floor as nothing more than piles of rusty coins that he kicked away.

Kimie's voice came through the speakers. "*You okay?*"

"Oh, yeah," the Stargazer replied, looking over the terminal. "The City's Freakquency here's dropped, thanks to you."

Gilwain tapped another screen and said to the Stargazer, "The Centurions in that radio station are no more either, thanks to that psychic blast, meaning we can hack into it now."

The Stargazer chuckled. "Only goes to show that pumping money into everything never guarantees perfection. It's the spirit of what's behind it, and there's always a higher power to answer to."

Kimie tapped the Stix against her hand, feeling their warmth.

"Totally," she agreed. "So how about we give this EconoMe a wake-up call?" She looked upwards resolutely. "'Cause it's about time the System faced the music!"

Chapter Fourteen

The Econo-Mist gazed down from the Sky Scrapper. The street was alive with his new investments. The faces of all who resisted him were white, plastered with dollar signs, and staring open-mouthed in dull worship of the tower.

He turned away, passing Mysti who hovered nearby, still held by his will. Despite how well things were going, he was concerned. An undefinable force had pinched a small portion of his economic value. This defiant anomaly was emanating from a power station on the City's edge.

Mysti wasn't giving him any reassurances either. Yes, she was subdued and looked like the Moneyarch he wanted her to be, but it was only superficial. Her rebellious glare told him that she was still her own person.

He observed her curiously. *"Resistance? Hmm, I think you need a push in the right direction ..."*

He waved his cane, propelling her to the building's edge, swung her around, pushed her over the side and brought her to a hovering halt. Far below, were the specks of people, once again under the System's control. *"You see, my dear, they're what you'll become. An economic unit. You've no say in the matter. Nobody ever does. All it takes is a little division, some bait here and there, and total desire overtakes the world until only the Alley Cats and Sewer Rats remain. I've always believed that it's best to keep the human dregs in their place. That way there's no threat to the System's survival. Give people meaning if they ask for it, as long as it's profitable for you. Just make sure they stay entertained by amusing delights while you bleed them dry.*" His hand rose to the Centurion beside him. "*Make a note of that.*"

A twenty-dollar bill emerged from the Centurion's hand.

"*Thank you.*" The Econo-Mist put it in his mouth and swallowed it, satisfied with his economic consumption. He addressed Mysti again. "*No opposition from anyone, no accountability for you. Order, peace and working together as one. Isn't that what we all strive for?*"

He twitched his head sideways. Mysti's arm rose, propelled by his will, which rippled through her body. She winced as her limb rose higher, making a fist over the crowd.

The Econo-Mist smiled.

Mysti summoned her strength, defying his hate through Bluey's inner glow which still, and would always, remain untouched. She turned her fist on its side, her thumb protruded, and she tensed proudly, in an open gesture of rebellion to the City.

The Econo-Mist's face dropped. Despite being too far up for anyone to see her, it was enough to annoy him. He tipped his cane at her.

She jolted and fell slightly, refusing to cry out as his sizzling wrath rippled into her body. She writhed in agony as she was turned around in mid-air and brought back over the concrete rooftop to once again hover before him.

He scowled angrily. "*When will you learn that you are in the System?*"

She summoned her strength, speaking defiantly. "When will you learn that you're in *life*? It'll go on with or without your crappy little System."

He observed her, unimpressed. "*Hmm. Since you remain economically resistant, I'm clearly wasting my time investing in you. You're not as profitable as you first seemed and are therefore without value. As a result, your title of Moneyarch shall be relinquished.*" He prodded his cane at her. "*You're fired.*"

A fierce blast of his will hurtled her over the Sky Scrapper's edge, sending her plummeting.

Satisfied, he addressed his Centurions. "*That's what happens when your investment's unbalanced. Time for some more budget cuts, I think.*"

He turned and strode to the red doorway, pleased with his work.

Tap! Tap! Tap!

He stopped dead. The taps were similar to his cane's rhythms. They held just as much power, but on a different frequency. That kind of rogue strength didn't make him feel comfortable at all. His cruel features twisted with hate. *"Something's out of order …"*

Tap! Tap! Tap!

This anomaly was being openly defiant in a declaration of war.

Tap! Tap! Tap!

Prickling sensations grew.

He clicked his fingers at the Centurions who all headed to the rooftop's edge.

Tap! Tap! Tap!

Bang!

A sudden psychic blast sent them recoiling.

The Econo-Mist regained his balance, shaken in more ways than one. Nothing should be able to touch him, but this thing, whatever it was, had power, resonance, colour, vibrancy and, worst of all, independence.

This angered him.

Yet deep beneath that anger was fear. This was an entity that hadn't yet been assimilated but needed to be. Anything not on the market for his financial growth was a threat. He hated that.

He raised his arm, resisting the hideous waves of this brazen anomaly, and pushed his way to the building's edge. There, he looked over the side, and snarled at the sight below.

'Well, speak of the devil!'

Mysti hovered by the building, held by the very force that dared to defy him. He peered past her, into the force's source. His keen vision zeroed in on a lone girl in the street. She stood before an oil drum, holding a simple pair of drumsticks. The wretched girl, he realised, was the City's newcomer who'd evaded him for so long.

His thoughts whirred, searching the System's internal records. He found his answers easily. The items this pathetic girl held were treasures from the old Village Vault, powerful enough to resist his will. His hatred grew tenfold. The System survived on its own rules, accounting to no one. Everyone either obeyed it or were deemed as a threat and destroyed. That was his code of conduct.

He braced himself as the drumsticks smacked down hard again. Their resonance reached him rapidly, shaking him to the core, only now he wasn't shaken physically. To his disgust, the dollar signs on everyone's faces in the street faded. They were no longer profitable economic units to ensure his survival. Now they were … human.

What's more, the Alley Cats and Sewer Rats, the scum of the earth, were also conscious again. With the blood of humanity flowing through their faces, they, and everyone else down there, now held a growing spirit forbidden in his domain.

Individuality.

Along with the one thing he despised more than anything: a heartbeat.

His lips curled into a flicker of a smile, admiring Drummer-girl from afar. If she was like this as an enemy, he pondered, she'd be impressive as an ally.

He tapped his cane, creating heavy ripples to counteract her drumbeats.

Mysti dropped into the sky.

To his annoyance, she didn't go far. Drummer-Girl kept her hovering.

He lashed his cane out furiously.

A manhole cover near her burst open as a MoneyTree tendril erupted from the sewers. Undeterred, she bashed the drum again and, to the Econo-Mist's disgust, the tendril wavered and blew apart, becoming nothing more than paper on the wind.

He seethed, then nodded to the street corner far below where several Centurions were approaching the girl. Sensing his command, they picked up speed.

The girl's powerful beats shattered their spirit, sending them crumbling into the pavement as chunks of rusty metal. Any other Centurions were easily felled, either by the drumsticks or the City's people.

Strangely, there was no sign of the blonde woman with sunglasses who he'd cast off the Sky Scrapper. She'd vanished. No matter, he thought, there was enough to deal with for the time being.

The drumbeats grew louder, rising on the wind and raising Mysti to new heights as she ascended before him. Gone were the dollar signs on her face, replaced by a cocky smile, telling him she wasn't his hot property anymore. If anything, she was cool.

Mysti Cool.

Fuelled by the raw power of the drumsticks below, she struck out with a lightning blast, blowing his holographic hat off. His long, dark hair billowed in the wind as countless bank notes flew up rapidly from the surrounding buildings and decimated MoneyTree tendrils in the street, only to be sucked into the red doorway behind him. Many notes were blank, and countless more were blanking out as the System lost its value, as its people had determined. Other notes, still with economic currency, swept in after them as the System tried to reclaim what it could.

He slammed his cane down and roared.

A MoneyTree tendril shot out from the doorway, racing in for Mysti and ready to run her right through. Just before it reached her, it suddenly halted in mid-air and froze, held at bay by the force below. Another tendril emerged from the doorway and it too stopped dead. A third followed, freezing as well, before the System finally got the message.

Mysti descended, stepping onto the Sky Scrapper's roof. Coolly, she leaned over, picked up her gun and said, "Let's remember who made who." Her gun whined as she charged it. "I think it's time for the System to be held accountable."

The Econo-Mist wasn't discouraged and merely leaned on his cane; one hand clasped over the other.

"*I see*," he said simply. "*Little Bluey's all grown up and putting the world to rights now, is she? All while our downtown Drummer-girl plays David and Goliath with two little sticks.*"

She aimed her gun at his head. "Ah, shut up!"

He raised his hand. "*You don't think I hold an ace up my sleeve?*" His fingers snapped.

A silhouetted figure appeared in the doorway behind him.

"*Including —*" he finished, "*—my million-dollar man.*"

Mysti aimed her gun at the newcomer. He stepped into the light and she froze at the sight of him. "Satan's slag-whore!"

Mysti shuddered, wondering if what she was seeing was real, or just some sick illusion.

The newcomer spoke. "Take a shot on your dream, Blue Cloud."

She trembled at the mention of her old codename. The gun shook in her hands as she stared at the only person who'd ever affected her so deeply. Her heart dropped through her chest and her stomach churned as the full horror of their betrayal hit home.

For before her stood the Dragonfly.

The Econo-Mist smirked. *"Yes, kill him and find out. You've nothing to lose. Only your sanity if he's the real deal."*

Mysti ignored him, glared at the Dragonfly and snapped, "Is it true? Is it?"

"What do you think?" he answered.

Her jaw tightened and she swung savagely with her gun, clubbing him fiercely. He fell onto the rooftop as she swept in with a yell. He rolled out the way, dodged a strike from the gun, then leapt up, wrenched it from her grasp and cast it to one side. She lashed out with her fist, he blocked the strike, grabbed her by the throat, tripped her up, threw her onto the concrete and held her there.

She struggled wildly and hissed, "You're dead, man! Dead! I'll kill you!"

She smacked his hand away, grabbed his collar, pushed her foot into his stomach and flipped him over her head. He thumped heavily onto the concrete behind her and was barely down when she scrambled in, striking him repeatedly. He blocked the blows, rolled over, threw her to the ground and held her tightly as she sobbed like a broken child.

"Why?" she whimpered. "Why'd you do it? You think it was worth all this? You make me sick!"

The Econo-Mist grinned, delighted. *"You've always denied yourself any pleasures. What is this persecution complex you have, hmm?"* He walked around them. *"You never used to be like this. Once upon a time you weren't afraid to take risks. Don't you remember the last hours of your childhood, right before you hit your SORE Point?"*

She flinched at the memory.

He savoured her discomfort. *"It started innocently enough, if you recall. Your final blow to the City brought about a celebration. You went into the cellar to fetch something or other. He was there. Your recent victory had made you cocky. You two bantered, threw streamers, and then you, little girl, jumped up and kissed him, taking him by surprise. He broke away, you got scared and ran."* He cackled. *"So much for someone who wanted, and still wants, to bring the City to its knees. That's why it's here. Systems work. Humans don't.*" He glanced at the Dragonfly. "*Without me, this poor soul was all over the place. I merely gave him some 'cents' of self-worth by providing a focus, with perks on the side.*"

Mysti stared tearfully at the Dragonfly. "You sold out, man. What for? Money and Hookers? Was that it?"

The Dragonfly looked away.

She shuddered, knowing she was right. "Oh, you sad suckhole. So you got into that crap and—" Realisation dawned. "You were working for the System the night I kissed you! Maybe even before. You baited me so I'd make a move on you, knowing I'd freak out when you didn't react, and that I'd run to my hidey-hole that the star freak had eviled up. At least he regretted what he did and tried to fix things, but you …!" Her voice rose. "You're an infected scab on the butt of a pig!" She indicated the Econo-Mist. "The pig being him!"

The Dragonfly spoke coolly. "Now you see what reality is, Blue Cloud."

Mysti tensed. "Don't call me that, you butt scum-sucker! You got into those rebel groups with your sleazy crap and then bang! You called in your Hookers. Bet I wasn't the only girl you screwed over, right?"

The Econo-Mist chuckled. "*No, there was also your replacement. Our new girl.*"

Mysti's face dropped at the mention of Kimie.

He continued. "*She was all set to take him downtown, and I do mean down. Straight into the sewers. We'd have cleaned up nicely if we'd found that rodent lair. Alas, a Symbiotech interfered at the last second, preventing our descent. He fought it off, but only just, and more ran in. They veered him away from the sewers so he couldn't follow the girl. Didn't help matters for the resistance in the long run, did it?*"

Mysti ignored him and kept her focus on the Dragonfly, addressing him bitterly. "Thing is, you moron, by selling out the City's so-called slaves, you were only attacking what you thought was the nutsack. Waste of time, man. That's him!" She nodded at the Econo-Mist.

The Dragonfly didn't react. "You denied yourself everything the System offered and look where you are. Broken and nowhere."

"While you're such a great role model for kids," Mysti scoffed. "Let's have 'em all grow up to be sleazy, Hooker-loving scum who act like snobs. You'd be so proud to have a kid and think that in thirty years' time he's gonna be a droned-out product of a System that's screwing everyone over, including you!"

The Econo-Mist sneered. "*Who wins in the law of the jungle? Why, the jungle of course.*"

Mysti ignored him, pushed the Dragonfly off her, rolled over, grabbed her gun and raised it high, ready to strike him down hard. She tensed fiercely, then stopped. The distant drumbeats had grown louder on the wind. Their impact was strong. Her heart glimmered as she lowered her hand to her pocket, clutching her dog leash. That, and the ethereal drumming, were the only things making sense right now.

The Dragonfly scrambled away and rose to his feet.

Mysti did the same. She noticed the Centurions and realisation dawned once more.

"I get it," she said to the Econo-Mist. "You can't touch me, thanks to the street music. You tried throwing me off the building and failed, so shooting me'll only make the shots rebound in your face. *That's* why you're using this loser. You want to rile me up while you pull the strings." Her confidence rose as she stepped in. "What are you thinking now? Have me kill him and be so cut up about it that I'll join you, take his place and wipe out the City's people? Or have him kill me and then go back to selling the City out from the inside? Bet you don't even know yourself yet, huh? You're still weighing us up."

The Dragonfly frowned.

Mysti knew she was winning and glared at the Econo-Mist, speaking stronger than ever. "The *big* difference between you and me, Asset-Hole, is that I'm worth something, unlike you and your *cents* of no worth! Who are you really? Do you even know what you are without being a total *banker*? You can't exist without sucking on someone, so you've made this whole place para-cityic! You're so far up your great depression that you can't see what's bigger than both of us. Alternatives! You don't know anything apart from running, fighting, screwing, taking and killing. Anything else scares you to death. It's easy to see what you are. A total wimp!"

The Econo-Mist hissed, enflaming the fiery-red doorway behind him.

"You pretend to be strong, but that's only for show, as anyone can see. You've always doubted your abilities, so you clash with everyone, including yourself. Systems can minimise and control such clashes."

She indicated the ruined City behind her. "Well done, man!"

"It was your kind who instigated the attack!" he snapped. *"Sooner or later, you'll have to make a choice. To perish in savagery as an animal, or to protect yourself in a System."*

She clasped her dog leash tighter. Its touch had always seen her through the tough times and didn't fail her now. Her confidence rose tenfold as she recalled her younger self's clone in the sewers. The girl's words returned. *"No matter how strong a system is, there's one thing it can never fight. Time. Things always change and there's always a bigger picture."*

Mysti stared at him defiantly. "No System's gonna suck me in. You're not playing with the shallow stuff here. You wanna play with surface crap, go right ahead, but I'm deeper than you'll ever see, and you know what? I choose me. Not the EconoMe. Just me." She looked straight at the Dragonfly. "And him too." She drew a shuddering breath. "If the Stargazer can flip himself around, there's hope for this one."

She reached over, interlocking her fingers with his, and tensing nervously. To her astonishment, he clasped her hand back, equally tightly, and returned her gaze, staring into her soul.

"Always," he confirmed.

She gulped, knowing he was legit, and blushed.

The Econo-Mist spoke coldly. *"Hmmm. What you don't seem to understand, is that you're not priceless. You're merely a monetary unit with limited value that's only around for a while. Systems will last for far longer than you will. What are you going to do? Fight everything from now into eternity? Whether you like it or not, the rule of life is to dominate or be crushed. If a System's time is limited, yours is even more so. It's futile to argue with facts."*

Mysti agreed. "Facts of the past and present, no. Facts of the future, I sure as hell can, and you know why?" She stepped in, moving her face right up to his. "'Cause you're not in my future!"

He stared back at her, unfazed.

Several blank notes fluttered by on the wind.

She stepped back. "No deals. I'm taking your million-dollar man and splitting. Sure, he's stuffed up, and I mean *really* stuffed up—"

"Not helping …" the Dragonfly cut in.

She ignored him. "He's just forgotten who he is and I'm gonna make it my job to remind him." She glanced at the Dragonfly. "Come on, let's ditch this place."

She turned, leading him away.

He glared at the Econo-Mist and followed.

The Econo-Mist's red halo flickered as he spoke cruelly. "*As expected. You do know that all Systems are founded upon blood, don't you?*"

"They also go down with it," Mysti retorted.

"*Exactly!*"

Squelch!

Mysti froze, thinking she'd been struck. She looked down at her chest. There was no wound. Her head rose, confused, and to her horror, saw droplets of blood trickling from the Dragonfly's mouth.

A Centurion's tendril retracted, its golden coins stained blood-red.

Mysti cried out, grabbing the Dragonfly and falling with him onto the cold concrete roof.

The Econo-Mist snarled. "*Have that cutback on your conscience. Since you believe so resolutely in alternatives, I devised one. The System can save him, care of its medical experts—*" he motioned to the Centurion, "*—but only if you sign a contract. Drummer-girl may be able to resist me but cannot help him. Only you can do that.*"

Mysti swallowed hard, not knowing what to say. Her tears fell on the Dragonfly, merging with his blood.

"I–I'm sorry …"

He croaked painfully. "Not your fault, Blue Cloud. Not mine either. Let's blame this one on the System." He winced. "Thought I could walk away with your help. Looks like the freak hid some ugly *claws* in my contract."

Mysti shuddered. "I don't have a choice here. I have to sell out …"

"No," he cut in. "Not this time. We've been prisoners for too long. You said it yourself. Alternatives. Things have to change."

She choked back tears. "Get stuffed …"

"No deal," the Dragonfly countered firmly. "Try and fix things and you'll doom us both to a living hell. I don't want to be in a prison anymore. I want freedom, for everyone. It's the least I can do." He smiled weakly. "Isn't it, Blue Cloud?"

She sobbed and nodded. "Why the sudden change?"

He struggled against his pain. "You made me realise that I'm human after all." Unseen by the Econo-Mist, he placed an object in her hand. "This little beauty couldn't release me from my contract, but it'll give you a way out. I was planning on using it against him and taking his place. Things have changed."

She pocketed the trinket, knowing exactly what it was.

His lips rose into a final smile and he whispered, "I know when to sell out …"

She watched sadly as his smile faded, his head rolled to the side, and he drifted away.

Mysti lowered her head, sitting in silence. She bit her lip, listening to the hollow winds, the crackling flames and the surrounding chaos. Her keen hearing, care of the Stargazer's augmentation, heard the drumbeats in the street below. It wasn't only the kid beating her weapons in defiance now. Others had joined in too, with chunks of street junk. That, more than anything, brought her comfort.

She wiped her eyes, looked up at the Econo-Mist and rose, leaving her gun on the rooftop. The Centurions couldn't touch her, she knew that much, but the Econo-Mist could speak, making him dangerous enough.

"*There's still time to save him …*" he prompted.

Mysti paused, considering his offer. Her first reaction was to take it and restore the Dragonfly to life. No, she determined. That would only deny any dignity in his sacrifice, as well as betraying everybody below. There was no choice but to let him go, like so many other things in her sad life.

She gazed at the Econo-Mist, speaking resolutely. "You've just proved my point, deadhead. When things get bad, people get good. Real good. *That's* why the System, any System, needs a heart to stop it from going belly-up. All you've done is bring everyone together and make 'em stronger than ever. We haven't worked for you. You've worked for us. Which makes you—" she stepped in, "—part of *our* System!"

He held his ground, defying the growing power in the streets.

His Centurions, rattled by the drumbeats below, stepped shakily towards her. Their legs wobbled, then they too crumbled, collapsing into golden coin piles. The warm wind swept in, pushing them over as they decayed, losing all value.

"So much for your solid foundation," Mysti taunted.

The Econo-Mist snarled. "*A takeover bid? How unfortunate that you disrupt my state of unholy matri-money. Very well, if you want a clearance sale, I'll give you one, but at a very high price!*"

He aimed his cane at the Sky Scrapper's roof, letting loose. Far below, numerous gas pipes vented high over the streets, creating mammoth blasts and rocking the Sky Scrapper's base. Nearby, large windows in the neighbouring towers blew outwards, sending flaming chunks of rubble spiralling heavily into the City.

Mysti glared at him sourly, knowing what exactly he was doing. Destroying what he couldn't have. "Oh, that's real mature!"

Kimie ran from a plummeting chunk of fiery debris. Not even the Stix had worked to keep it at bay and she dived out the way as it slammed into the ground and shattered.

She rose, fleeing through the growing carnage, along with the Alley Cats, Sewer Rats and other survivors.

Part of the power station's ceiling collapsed, falling past the Stargazer.

"System's going into meltdown," he reported. "Seems the City's heading into a state of a bank-eruption!"

Gilwain viewed a terminal screen. "Wait. There's a force in the sewers fighting back. Look at this."

The Stargazer peered over.

Kimie bolted, leaping over the rubble, shielding her eyes from the numerous fires, and struggling to stay upright in the rumbling streets. The Stix tingled in her grip, unable to fight the catastrophic destruction.

Things were out of control, she figured, and her music had set it all off. Now she was sure that the Sky Scrapper's bad guys were fighting back, big time, leaving an almighty clash to shake the heavens.

Thankfully, the Stix's resonance remained strong throughout the City. Their beats had brought everyone time. What's more, they'd also triggered off another force *beneath* it. A flickering glow from a street chasm confirmed that. The golden spark told her that it wasn't from a burst pipe or anything City-related. What's more, its presence was similar to the Stix she held. Maybe they'd planted a seed down there, she guessed, which was now growing.

She stumbled around a corner, tripped on a rock and dropped the Stix. She swore and reached out for them, then swore again when they fell into a crevice, spiralling into a glowing chasm and vanishing. A fierce rumble erupted, widening the crevice and forcing her to rise and run.

"Time to ditch this place!" the Stargazer called over the power station's shaking foundations.

Gilwain stepped onto a small platform, now attached to the back of the Stargazer's hoverchair. "I don't suppose this thing has a turbo boost?"

"Locked and loaded," came the happy response. "With a few improvements here and there." He flicked a switch.

The chair jolted, nearly throwing Gilwain off. The dwarf cursed as two thrusters emerged on either side of him.

The Stargazer smacked a button. The thrusters fired and he whooped in joy as the chair shot them out the door like a bullet. Gilwain hung on for dear life as the chair's speakers blared with rock music and they soared high into the night with several fireballs from the City's chaos exploding around them.

"*You did this!*" the Econo-Mist hissed at Mysti. "*All of you! Kick over an anthill and what happens? Anarchy!*"

"Totally!" Mysti shot back. "We're not feeding you now! Shrink and die!"

"*You said it!*"

The Sky Scrapper shook harder than ever. She knew it wouldn't be standing for much longer.

A blast of rock music ignited below. She moved back, peering over the

Sky Scrapper's edge. Strangely, a hoverchair holding the Stargazer and Gilwain, was some way down but rising rapidly.

"What the crud …?" she wondered, baffled.

A violent blast burst from a nearby window, sending the chair veering to the side. They cleared the area easily, before sweeping up, continuing their ascent.

She shook her head, knowing exactly what they were up to, then glared fiercely at the Econo-Mist. "Suck on this stock market crash!"

Defiantly, she turned, ran, and leapt high, diving smoothly off the building.

The Econo-Mist roared, unleashing his fury. The roof exploded, launching a searing fireball over her head. She swung her arms and legs, propelling herself with the blast, leaving the Sky Scrapper collapsing behind her.

A heavy chunk of flaming debris shot right for her neck. "Oh sh—!"

Rock music swept in, then a hand grabbed hers, pulling her rapidly through the sky to safety.

"I didn't hear a fat lady sing!"

The Stargazer.

Gilwain grabbed her other hand as the hoverchair followed her descent. She climbed onto its rear platform beside the dwarf. The chair jolted before sweeping away.

She turned the music down. "You nerds took your time, didn't you?"

The Stargazer shrugged. "What's time in the infinite scheme of things?"

She smacked him lightly. "The pain in between."

He gave a small smile.

"The tower!" Gilwain cried, looking back at it.

The Stargazer turned the chair around, setting it to hover mode. Together, they watched the building implode, falling with a tremendous crash into a cataclysm of debris to become nothing more than a smoking junk heap in the City centre.

Mysti punched the sky and the Stargazer howled triumphantly.

Far below, Kimie leapt high, doing the same. "Yes, yes, yes …"

Flaming rubble plunged for her.

"Crap!"

She turned and bolted, dodging several other chunks. There was no time to get out of the City, she knew that much. More buildings were crumbling rapidly, making it impossible.

"Double crap!" she cringed.

An engine roar rose behind her. She stopped, turned and blinked. A monster truck was fast approaching, crunching over the City's debris and driven rather clumsily by Alley-Money. Kimie moved aside to see Queen Yushera sitting in its trailer on what looked like a hastily made trash throne that was somehow meant to represent royalty. Surrounding her were several Alley Cats, Sewer Rats and City people, all holding on tightly to whatever they could find.

The truck reached her and a slimy rope dropped. She grabbed its knot, grimaced at the slime, then yelped as she was hoisted off the ground and pulled away by the vehicle's speed, flailing against it as it tore down the street. The world blurred as the rope was pulled up, then a Sewer Rat's grimy hand grabbed hers, hauling her into the trailer. She tumbled in with a thump, rolled over, pushed herself up and looked over the truck's side. The ground behind her had split open, revealing an ethereal light below. She glanced ahead, seeing that another section of the road had formed into a high slope.

Alley-Money revved the truck, aiming for the slope, then drove upwards, flew from its peak and soared high into the night. Kimie hung on for dear life, then saw the Stargazer, Gilwain and Mysti fly beside them on a hoverchair.

"What the—?" she began, then stopped as Platinum suddenly appeared on a Roverboard. The blonde woman was as cool as ever, with her hands in her pockets and looking like she owned the place.

"Gettin' more random by the minute," Kimie muttered.

The truck dropped, hit the ground, bounced back up on its enormous tyres and sent her reeling straight into the arms of a Sewer Rat.

"Have no fear," he said. "We will take good care of you."

She gulped and pushed him away. "Not in my worst nightmare." She looked around. "And I think this is it!"

The Sky Scrapper lay like a giant grave in the centre of a once-mighty empire.

The Econo-Mist stood in its debris, having descended to the ground as a dark halo. His face hardened, scowling at the sight of his worthless bank notes, dancing on the wind.

"Time to cut my losses!"

He swung his cane upwards.

A glimmer appeared above, expanding, and then descending, to engulf the whole City in a vast blue dome.

Mysti looked up at the blue halo. "What the hell's that?"

The Stargazer followed her gaze. "Ballop! An Economic Shield Pulse."

"Meaning—?" she pressed.

The EconoMe's ESP's in control," he answered. "A downsize'll be next."

Savage lightning bursts erupted, flashing by in deafening blasts, pounding the City. He navigated the chair skilfully, weaving around the burning light tendrils, steering a path through their roaring booms.

Mysti pulled out her trinket from the Dragonfly. "Can this help, Space Cadet?"

He took it. "Where'd you get this? I've always wanted one."

"Friends in high places," she quipped.

He plugged it into the hoverchair, keyed in a few notes, and the device whirred, then hummed, as if singing.

Mysti gave a small smile, thinking of the Dragonfly. "Time to pay your debt to society, fly-boy!"

A green light shot up from the chair, ripping into the blue dome above.

The lightning ceased abruptly.

The Econo-Mist sneered as the City's dome faded, along with his control over it. His fist clenched, ready to retaliate when …

Bong!

The town clock's bellowing strike shook him to the core.

Bong!

Bong!

Bong!

It was faulty and offbeat, but boomed heavily, striking midnight. Impossible, he thought. The System ran on his time. Not its own.

A chasm in the road split open wider than ever as a giant green vine erupted, straight from a forest. More followed, defying the laws of his dark presence by wrapping their thick tendrils around his limbs, binding them tightly. Steaming wisps rose from his body as he seethed in burning agony, then roared as he was dragged into the ground by another System that would always rise higher than his own. Life itself.

He snarled defiantly, watching with sheer scorn as giant trees ascended, the towers crumbled and his cash dissipated on the wind. What's more, the rising forest didn't burn, but did just the opposite, extinguishing his EconoMe's flames, amounting it to nothing.

The natural world grew higher, swamping him, then a vine's final wrench pulled him into a gaping hole below.

"Sucked into a recession!" he hissed. *"You will* pay *for this!"*

The ground shut him up as he was swallowed whole.

Yushera pointed to a giant shoot rising from a glowing chasm. "The forest! It returns!"

The Stargazer heard her from his hoverchair.

"Makes sense!" he called. "This place needed some real growth!"

Mysti recalled the Econo-Mist's words. *"Who wins in the law of the jungle? Why, the jungle of course."*

"Got that right," she murmured. "Which makes you, you worthless piece of crap, fertiliser!"

More vines emerged, felling a tower.

Several notes swept past the truck, vanishing into a chasm. Many were blank. Others had reverted to a currency familiar to Kimie. She stared at them entranced, knowing she'd seen them from a time *before* coming to the City, and desperately searched her memories. Nothing came up. She only knew that they were valuable.

Unseen by her, Platinum glided in, grabbed a handful, flew in close to the truck and released them, letting them spin past.

Tempted, Kimie reached out, grabbed a couple and pocketed them, grateful that Yushera wasn't watching to stop her.

"What the hell?" she said with a grin. "I've earned it."

The truck sped on.

Chapter Fifteen

The Sole-Searcher watched from the forest.

He stood with the City's survivors. Their stationary vehicles were nearby, having found it impossible to continue underground, and been forced to the surface. Reports confirmed that the earlier convoys had reached the Mountain, and everyone was accounted for, save for a few that the monster truck should have picked up by now. Thankfully, there were no casualties that he knew of. Now the young, the old, those from the streets and those from the sewers were equals, all standing together as the City imploded and the horizon became visible once more.

The monster truck emerged from the City, followed by a hoverchair and a Roverboard. All three joined the crowd as the truck skidded around, braking hard, to face the crumbling remains. The hoverchair too, descended, landing smoothly, and two of its occupants stepped off its rear platform. Nearby, the Roverboard glided skilfully around in an arc, landed gently, and a blonde lady dismounted.

The Sole-Searcher saw Kimie in the truck's trailer. The poor girl was frowning, no doubt baffled by the rising plant life in the City, he thought. The giant tendrils were extinguishing the City's flaming remains, courtesy of his superior's environmental protection act.

The last of the towers came crashing down, leaving a shattered mass of debris spread over a large section of earth. There was no Sky Scrapper, no Centurions, no System, nothing.

Only a rapidly growing forest.

Kimie climbed down from the truck and stood with Mysti, Gilwain and the Stargazer. Yushera, Alley-Money and Platinum joined them too, watching the growing miracle in the distance.

Mysti stepped forward, looking into it. "So much for economic theory. That's all it is. Theory!"

"Totally," Kimie agreed. "So what's next? We go live it up in the Mountain?"

Yushera's head suddenly perked up, sensing a presence on the wind. Alley-Money did the same, along with the rest of the Alley Cats and Sewer Rats.

Yushera spoke in awe. "Our Crossing is complete!"

Excited murmurs rose from her people.

Mysti tensed, Gilwain shifted awkwardly, and even the Stargazer seemed unnerved.

Kimie was confused. "What's up with you lot? Why have you all gone apoco-cryptic?"

Yushera was entranced. "Can you not hear it on the wind?"

Mysti turned, striding reluctantly through the forest. "Oh, crap, let's get it over with."

Everyone followed.

Kimie ran to keep up with Mysti. "Why? What's up here? It's not the Mountain, and your Village is out of bounds since it's sealed off by—" Realisation dawned. "—Oooh!"

"Got it in one," the Stargazer said.

"So its shield's dropped?" Kimie continued. "Is that it?"

The Stargazer raised an instrument, examining its readings. "The City's shot to hell, so the Village doesn't need to protect itself now. There's nothing to stop it expanding into End-Time, and god knows we'll need a safety-net."

"End-Time?" Kimie wondered, sensing truth in his tone. "Are you serious?"

"Who cares?" Mysti cut in. "We're going home."

"But that's not my—" Kimie began, then stopped. The wind was tingling lightly, enflaming her spirit and indeed making her feel like she was heading, "—home."

Her curiosity rose as she moved deeper into the forest. The trees grew taller amidst the intoxicating aromas. The smell of the wood, the dew on the grass, she was amazed at how fresh everything was. Despite its beauty, however, Queen Yushera sniffed the air uncomfortably.

"You're not impressed?" Kimie asked her.

Yushera looked around. "Something is missing."

"Like what?"

The Queen made a face. "Where are the sewers?"

A bird landed on her shoulder. She spat at it like an angry cat and it fled.

Kimie's heart glowed, feeling privileged to be part of this strange group. They were all together now. Mysti, the Stargazer, Yushera, Gilwain, everyone except for—

"Where's that Orion guy?" she suddenly realised.

Mysti stopped in her tracks, lowering her head.

Kimie approached her, then stopped, sensing the answer straight away. Her hand rose to her mouth in horror. "Oh, crap!"

Mysti shuddered. "Yeah. He got screwed. Badly."

Kimie choked back the tears. "W-What about the Dragonfly?"

Mysti quivered. Her voice cracked as she spoke. "Sorry, kid."

Kimie trembled as the full horror of his fate hit home. She shivered, then came in, hugging Mysti tightly. Mysti hugged her back as tears trickled down their faces.

"Just another victim of the EconoMe," Mysti said softly. She sniffed, gave her a light slap, and pushed her away before wiping her eyes. "Think of the future, huh?" She clamped a hand on a child's shoulder, pushing him ahead. "Go."

He ran excitedly. Several children followed.

Kimie brushed her tears away. "They seem happy. Everyone does. You'd think they'd be pretty messed up after so much bloodshed."

A cool voice spoke. "No casualties on our side, except for the Orion Sentry. Unfortunately."

Kimie looked up to see Platinum walking beside her, her hands in her pockets. "Crap almighty, where'd you spring from?"

"I've always wondered that," Mysti said.

Platinum smiled mysteriously. "I was back there counting the last couple of heads. Had to make sure we got 'em all. That's why I went AWOL. Since you lot were making fireworks, I was moving the City's fired workers in another direction. There weren't too many. I got everyone."

Gilwain strode alongside her. "I daresay that wasn't the only reason you vanished, my Lady."

"You're right," Platinum confirmed. "Had a couple of other things to check up on too. Was worth it. Whole plan worked like a charm."

"Did you care to fill us in on this plan?" Mysti asked gruffly.

"Or consult your Queen?" Yushera added, joining them.

"Couldn't risk it," Platinum said. "And you're not *my* Queen. Believe it or not, there are powers higher than you."

Yushera scowled.

Platinum continued. "The Symbiotech attack was all a façade. No one was killed, only rounded up and evacuated before the City went down. I picked up those who were missed, accounting for everyone." She glanced at a tree branch where a lark sang. "The Moneyarch only saw *a* truth about the City. A superficial image of sheer perfection. He didn't realise that what lay beneath the superficial was ugly, and beneath *that* was sublime beauty, repressed for far too long. That's why the City got sick. Happens to the best of us. You too."

She elbowed Kimie's arm.

Kimie looked away, feeling awkward but knowing Platinum was right. She was about to say something when Mysti stopped, staring at a tree carving. Its finely chiselled detail showed a child with a ponytail.

Kimie moved in next to her as everyone headed past them, up a slope, save for Platinum who discreetly turned, heading in the other direction.

Kimie spoke gently to Mysti. "Self-portrait?"

Mysti's voice lowered. "I forgot how much I loved this place."

Kimie hugged her warmly. "Welcome back."

Mysti returned her hug.

Keeping their arms around each other, they made their way up the slope after everyone else.

The Sole-Searcher stood at its peak. Kimie quivered, feeling the ever-growing breeze prickle against her skin, unnerving her about what lay ahead. The higher she rose, the greater the prickling grew. Finally, they arrived.

The Sole-Searcher spoke warmly. "Good to see you've both found your way."

Mysti nodded. "Yeah. Thanks."

"'Tis I who should thank you for my name," he replied.

Kimie smirked. "*You* came up with 'Sole-Searcher'?"

Mysti shrugged. "Was a long time ago. I was cocky back then."

Kimie smiled at him, "You always pop up at the right time, don't you?"

"Indeed," he answered. His arm, and his tone, rose proudly. "Welcome to our Village. Welcome … to Sanders Crossing."

Kimie shivered, sensing the forest's deep natural resonance which wavered in her vision. This place, whatever it was, held a vast mystery with astounding depth, and everywhere she looked only raised more questions. She was no longer tuned into the low Freakquency of the System she'd been in all her life, she realised. Rather, she was connected to a much higher song.

Arm in arm with Mysti, she headed over the slope's peak and down the other side. Murmurs rose in her head. She couldn't hear their words, only their soothing tones guiding her down the slope. Soon, she reached the bottom, and her vision cleared. Buildings were ahead. They weren't heavenly or spectacular, just those of an ordinary forest village. Strangely, nothing seemed solid or fixed. It was like peering into a mask that covered a presence of mind-blowing depth. This whole place that seemed so run-of-the-mill ordinary, was staggeringly … beautiful.

The Village was empty. Understandably, she figured, having been sealed off for so long. It seemed like an old pioneer's settlement that she vaguely recalled hearing about in school while being bored to death by her teacher. There was an inn, a blacksmith's shop, a general store and an old-fashioned cart. A small stake with horseshoes around it stood on the street's edge. They must have been pretty big horses, she figured. Their shoes were massive and looked like they weighed a ton.

She raised a hand to her head. "I feel like I'm in a dream."

"Yeah," Mysti agreed, "and this is the Village on a *dead* day. You should have seen it when there was life in the place. Hides a lot of secrets too. Good ones though. Even *I* barely scratched the surface here."

Kimie blinked. "Is it getting lighter?"

"It should be," Yushera replied. "A Queen has returned."

"No, I mean it …" Kimie began.

"As do I," Yushera retorted irritably.

Kimie ignored her. "Look, over there. In that building!"

Mysti did so. "That's the barn, and you're right. I think a big secret's about to expose itself."

"That sounds *so* gross."

Mysti smirked. "I know. That's why I said it."

Kimie smacked her lightly.

They watched as a soft white glow illuminated the barn door, growing steadily brighter.

Kimie wasn't as surprised as she'd thought she'd be. Yes, it was unsettling, but something was bugging her too. A doubt that nothing could be this all-powerful. Surely this had to be a con job. A big joke, just like the City had done by screwing everybody over for so long. Her anger rose, her lips pursed, and she strode up to the barn door, grabbing its handles.

"No!" Gilwain called. "You shouldn't—!"

Too late.

She pulled the doors open.

A blinding light and an electrifying wind gust engulfed her, sending her recoiling from the immense aura within. Through sheer defiance, she resisted its raw embrace, regained her stance and peered in. Bizarrely, her eyes were unaffected, despite the glare's ferocity. Yes, the barn's dirt floor remained, but vanished halfway in, merging into a white portal. Even stranger were the various colours, dancing in rhythmic patterns to its bellowing otherworldly resonance.

Kimie stared into the sheer wonder of the void's indescribable beauty, feeling like she was returning home. Faint sounds of mystical laughter grew, touching her heart. Never had she felt an intense urge to embrace anything so powerfully. The desire had always lingered in her heart, she realised, only she'd buried it deeply. Now, it was magnified to the extreme. All she'd ever needed was the realisation to see it, and the right frequency to tune in to. One more powerful than any other.

A hovering apparition materialised in its centre, growing larger and so-lidifying, before it closed in and descended, revealing itself to be a glimmering throne. One solely comprised of intertwined vines and flut-tering leaves, all working together to create a single seat of power.

Unable to resist, Kimie stepped into the barn, watching in awe as it landed in the dirt, casting wisps of steam from its base. Everyone gathered around her, astounded by the divine spectacle, and none more so than Queen Yushera.

"The Throne," she whispered. "It has returned!"

Kimie recalled Orion's words.

The Village was special. You could say it was a Nexus point. More than that, it was part of a Vine.

Now, she realised what he'd meant. She was standing before that very Nexus point. The precious link joining the roots of the earth to the celes-tial realms of infinity and was completely and utterly …

"Awesome!" she whispered.

Mysti spoke. "Yep. Welcome to the Village's *real* Crossing. Our link with it was severed when the City rose, sucking us all up for the sake of its survival."

The Stargazer took up the story. "Shields were locked in, from both this place *and* the City, protecting each from the other. Thank the stars our Village's greatest power supply was untouchable." He indicated the light. "Since then it's been waiting for us to come home for an interdi-mensional transmat."

"Blasphemy!" Yushera hissed.

"Admit it," Gilwain concurred. "Even you can't explain it."

The Stargazer dismissed this. "I can't explain the style of your beard either but I'm sure there's an out-there reason too."

"It is best not to think about it," Alley-Money said, referring to the Throne.

"You got that right," the Stargazer retorted, referring to Gilwain's beard.

The Throne's vines crackled.

Yushera was awestruck. "Our Throne awaits."

"For what?" Kimie wondered.

"Someone to park their butt on it," Mysti replied.

Alley-Money nodded. "One of us must act as an intermediary. That was the ritual in the days of old, when we spoke with the stars."

"So whose job was that?" Kimie asked. "Any of you guys?"

Mysti shook her head. "Nah, an ol' *Sourcerer*. Least until he got baited by a Hooker and turned into fish food. It really was a fall from grace, since that was her name. Shows how powerful the System was."

"Totally," Kimie agreed. "So who gets to sit in the big seat this time? You?"

"Hell, no," Mysti scoffed. "I'm no angel and I'd probably get fried. Anyway, it's not calling to me."

Kimie tensed. "It's not calling to me, is it?"

The Stargazer smiled. "Uh, no. You ain't ready, kid. There's only one person round here it's meant for." He turned to them and said, "It's a Throne fit for a Queen."

All eyes fell on Yushera.

The Sewer Queen stood regally, having expected this honour all along.

"That *is* fitting," Kimie concurred.

Yushera was somewhat hesitant. "It is."

"So, what's your problem?" Kimie pressed. "Why aren't you jumping to get your tail on there?"

Yushera sighed. "I much prefer the sewers to the heavens. How can I be a leader in the sun?"

"Hey, you've got the grounding for it," Mysti pointed out.

"Voted most likely to succeed?" Kimie added.

"Bah!" Yushera scoffed. "A Queen should never be told what to do."

"Fine, forget it," Kimie said. "You can bow to someone else instead."

The Alley Cats and Sewer Rats ignored this and murmured with excitement.

Yushera cat-spat at them.

They shut right up.

Yushera's face hardened.

Kimie could see she was torn and spoke gently. "It's time for a promotion your Majesty, and you're way overdue."

Yushera stared at the Throne's flickering resonance, then raised her hand to it.

The Throne glowed brighter.

She frowned, considering her options. Finally, she retracted her hand and spoke reluctantly. "Very well. I thank you all for this privilege."

She lifted her scraggy dress and approached the Throne, watching it brighten with every step she took. She was halfway there when she stopped, turned back and called, "Alley-Money!"

"Majesty?" came the reply.

"I'm still taking the crown jewels!"

"Of course."

A Sewer Rat handed Alley-Money a tattered suitcase full of rattling tin cans. She took it to her Queen, bowed her head nobly and presented it. With a "Hmmf!" Yushera tucked it under her arm and waved her away. Alley-Money retreated quickly as Yushera turned to the Throne again, gazed upon it, took a deep breath, held her head high and announced, "I accept this honour to rule my new Queendom!"

"That's kingdom," Mysti corrected. "God, how did you get voted most likely to succeed?"

"All a con job if you ask me," Gilwain muttered.

Mysti was confused. "A con job in a kingdom would make it a condom."

Kimie smacked her lightly, giggling. "Shut up!"

Mysti smacked her back lightly. "You shut up!"

Gilwain clasped a hand on each of their shoulders and hissed, "Both of you take your own advice. This is her moment."

They pushed him away and watched.

Yushera approached the Throne, placed her suitcase full of crown jewels beside it, then turned to face everyone. Regally, she stepped back and sat proudly upon the heavenly seat. Her hands rested on the twisted, wooden branches of its arms, before the cleansing glow of its golden halo engulfed her and she began to change.

Her rags blurred, morphing into long, white robes. Grease and slime fell from her hair as it transformed, rising above her head, turning fresh, auburn and curly, with depth and volume. Her face cleared of grime, becoming clean and unblemished, while releasing a fresh aroma, not of the sewers, but of the forest. Bit by bit, her body changed from being a teenager into a young woman in the prime of her beauty. No longer was she filled with an Alley Cat's survival instincts. Now her spirit flourished, linked to the boundless waves of angelic firepower. Colourful flickers streamed by as she spoke with the celestial authority of a higher presence from the heavens themselves.

"Contact!"

Kimie jumped and stared at her awestruck. Somehow, she kept her nerve and murmured in disbelief, "She goes from Sewer Queen to this? Talk about holy crap!"

Gilwain smacked her lightly.

The ethereal being's head rose, speaking in a ghostly voice amidst the tingling winds. *"Our Crossing is cleansed."* Several flickering lights halted in mid-air, forming into dark spinning spheres hovering by the throne.

Kimie blinked, not even recognising her anymore, and whispered, "What *are* you?"

Gilwain gulped loudly, appalled by her gall to speak to a divine spirit like this. She ignored him and asked, "I mean, are you a Higher Power?"

Gilwain choked with horror.

The being's face brightened slightly as her tone, too, lightened. *"That view is limiting, but correct."*

Kimie thought this over. "So you're like, a Former? As in, you came before us and created the universe, right?"

Gilwain nearly died.

The newly named Former was unmoved. *"If you wish to use that term, so be it, yet it is only partially true. Yes, I existed long before any of you, but I did not create your reality. I merely cultivated the Vine, binding our two realms. Now, I am simply an intermediary."* She paused. *"You have all proved yourselves as worthy opponents to the threats which have passed ... "* Her glow darkened. *" ... And for those yet to come. The rot at the Vine's root has been cleared. That is to be praised, but the root has far to grow before End-Time."* Streaks of light rippled over her. *"For the Vine to flourish, its path must be unhindered, for its crossing into other realms remains paramount. Those seeking to feed off its raw power for their own gain must be vanquished. Therefore, your greatest warriors are needed to stay close to the Village, guarding the Vine's root, with allies from the Mountain soon to aid you."* Her arm rose, indicating the celestial kingdom behind her. *"The rest of you, who have excelled in restoring the Vine's Crossing, may ascend to the very height of its divinity."*

Murmurs of excitement rose from the Alley-Cats and Sewer Rats.

Gilwain addressed the Former, speaking respectfully. "With all due respect, your eminence, if the Vine is to grow, should some of us not journey into this child's realm," he indicated Kimie, "to forge the path ahead?"

The Former was unmoved. *"The chosen have already ventured there. They shall lay the foundations for the Vine's journey."*

"Kime!"

Kimie's head rose to the voice on the wind. Its longing call had come from deep inside the void. She didn't know who it belonged to, only that it seemed hauntingly familiar. She stared past the Throne, captivated, yearning to join this presence more than anything.

The Former spoke nobly. *"Those who have proved themselves worthy may enter."*

Kimie trembled, thinking only of the voice, but hesitant to dive straight in, wondering if she deserved it. Despite her doubts, the alluring spirit grew in her heart, drawing her forward.

"I've never had much—" she began.

Alley-Money squealed with delight, grabbed a Sewer Rat's hand and they ran past the Throne to be engulfed by the eternal glow. Together they leapt in, soaring ahead as the warm light embraced them to become ghostly silhouettes in its clasp. Their laughter grew distant, then faded altogether as they vanished from reality.

Kimie's excitement grew. "Got no memories …"

More Alley Cats and Sewer Rats ran past her, diving in ecstatically.

"Just feelings," Kimie went on, as inklings of her previous life resurfaced. "I only ever wanted to fit in somewhere."

The last of the Alley Cats and Sewer Rats dived into the light, soaring ahead to vanish amidst its vibrant colours.

The Stargazer, however, reversed his chair, hesitant to join them. Kimie glanced at him, seeing his face filled with shame. He'd sold out to the System and would have to pay for it, just not in System money.

Gilwain too, shifted uncomfortably and retreated.

Mysti, also unsure of herself, did the same. She caught Kimie's gaze, saw her hesitancy, then indicated the light and said, "You wanna go for it? So go. Nothing's stopping you. You've made a difference. Take your prize."

The Stargazer agreed. "You were meant to be a miracle, right Sealing Wax?"

Kimie shuddered. No one had affected her this way, aside from her parents, and she'd never had many friends, at least not genuinely. All her life she'd held nothing but full-on struggles against the whole world. Now, there was only a flood of welcome relief.

"*Kimie …!*" the ghostly voice called, stronger this time.

Choice made.

The warm breeze rippled against her as she turned and let loose, collapsing into the Stargazer's arms, holding him tightly. There, she wept, sobbing from the depths of her heart as he held her just as tight. Her anguish poured out of her in droves, exorcising her soul, until at last she was free. Finally, she sniffed and spoke.

"Thank you," she whispered sincerely. "For everything."

He spoke just as gently. "I should be thanking you. You're our Sealing Wax that bound everyone together, turning us from nobodies into somebodies."

Kimie sniffed, kissed his cheek, clasped his shoulder warmly and rose, facing Gilwain. The dwarf smiled kindly as she leaned down, hugging him too.

"You did good," she said softly. "Real good. We'd be screwed without you." She stood up. "Sorry for the short jokes."

"I apologise for my short temper," he replied.

"Don't be," she said. "It makes you."

"As your feistiness makes you, lass."

She punched his arm lightly, then faced Mysti.

"Don't," Mysti warned, nervously.

Kimie sniffed. "I won't if you won't."

Mysti sniffed harder. "Screw you."

"Same goes."

They fell into each other's arms, hugging tightly.

"Behave," Kimie warned, through tears of joy.

"Never," Mysti retorted. "What are you, my guardian angel now?"

"You bet. I'll be watching you."

"You better not, kid. I've got a heap of living to do."

"Then make a difference, huh?"

"You mean like you did?"

"No, like only you can."

Mysti pushed her away. "Go. Get outta here. Get up there where you belong."

Kimie turned, staring into the celestial realm. The flickering shades of a single colour rippled over her. She raised her hand, observing the light. It was, for want of a better word, bluey.

She headed towards it as the presence that she now thought of as Ghost-voice, returned. It was calling her name on the wind, albeit lightly, drawing her in. Her fascination rose tenfold, along with her heartbeat. She felt freer than ever. This place was magic, a miracle, and she couldn't wait to embrace it completely.

What's more, she was grateful to everyone who'd helped her get here. Filled with sheer joy, she stopped, turned and looked back at them all, speaking proudly. "Any time you need help, it's always there. Just look up." She shrugged, with a hint of cheekiness. "It's the only way to go."

She whirled around, elated by the realm's electrifying touch, and ran past the Throne excitedly. Ghost-voice grew closer. What's more, it was familiar, like someone she'd known long ago, before this craziness began. Her heart beat faster than ever, resonating with its call.

The world fell away as undefinable lights, shapes and patterns flew by, making her laugh and weep in sheer joy. The past didn't matter. The future didn't either. There'd be no more waking up each day to fight sheer hell until she went to sleep again. Finally, she was free, sweeping into heavenly bliss. She trusted it completely, knowing it would never screw her over.

Ghost-voice grew louder than ever, becoming clearer. Her heart leapt and she cried out excitedly, suddenly realising who it belonged to. The one person she'd always loved more than anyone. The spirit she'd longed to be with. The entity of everything she stood for and had made more of an impact on her life than anything else, creating who she was, and always would be.

"Kimie …?"

She called their name excitedly on the wind, knowing she could trust them completely. Ghost-voice, she knew now, was …

The barn rumbled.

Gilwain stepped back and the Stargazer retreated.

Mysti looked down. "What the crud—?"

She leapt to the side as the ground split open, revealing a gaping chasm. A thick, black tendril darted out, shooting past the throne in a blur and entering the light. This freaky crap wasn't plant-based at all, she realised. It was a limb. No, more than that. A long outstretched arm. She gazed into the chasm, seeing who it belonged to.

The Econo-Mist.

"Unholy sh—"

She raised her gun, firing into his snickering face, then swore as the shots went right through him.

His arm retracted rapidly, now holding Kimie by the ankle, pulling her past the Former to himself. Strangely, the Former didn't react, and merely sat watching as the wailing girl was wrenched into the chasm.

Mysti dived for Kimie's hand, just missing it. A note flew from Kimie's pocket, wavering past Mysti still in mid-dive. Mysti ignored it and crashed to the ground, horrified, as Kimie swept into the darkness with an anguished wail, fading into oblivion.

Gilwain reached for Kimie's note. The Stargazer got there first, snatching it out of the air.

A twenty-dollar bill.

The chasm erupted with a sudden wind gust, wrenching the money from his hand and sucking it inside. The ground rumbled once more as the chasm closed in on itself, then sealed tightly.

Mysti rose, baffled, gazing at the rising wisps of steam in the dirt. "What the hell?"

The Stargazer stared down curiously. "I get it. Kid got caught by the long arm of the law. She must have taken some cash from the City and attracted a power vacuum that sucked her right in.”

“Meaning it’s not over,” Gilwain concluded darkly.

Mysti’s face hardened as she turned, facing the Former. “You seem way too relaxed about this, airhead. How come?”

The Former didn’t reply.

Realisation hit Mysti. “You cow! You knew this would happen. Let her take a bit of cash, get her hopes up and then bang! Shoot her straight to hell!” She indicated the ground. “How do we get her back?”

The Former stayed infuriately calm. “*We do not. She’s quite safe.*”

“Oh really, psyche-ho?” Mysti countered. “So why not go down there and join her if it’s so good?”

Silence.

Mysti scowled. “You planned this all along to teach her a lesson! Just proves you can’t trust anyone, good or bad. Trust yourself, I always say. No one else!”

The Former’s glow lightened as she spoke gently. “*You know that’s not true. There’s always a higher purpose.*”

“Not for me!” Mysti retorted. “No more games. Screw you–” she pointed at the Former, then at the ground where the Econo-Mist had been, “—and you! I’m outta here!”

She turned, heading off.

The Former’s voice rose as her glow dimmed rapidly. “*You will be back. You cannot leave. It is written!*”

“Bite me, bitch!” Mysti snapped, making an angry sign with her fist. She strode away furiously, making for the slope on the Village boundary.

The Stargazer looked to where the chasm had been and sighed. “Another day, no more dollars. Always struggling, aren’t we?”

Gilwain patted his shoulder. With a sad smile, the Stargazer patted the dwarf’s hand back, then they too turned from the Former and left the barn, following Mysti.

Mysti’s expression was hard as she strode away, carrying the only thing she’d ever trusted. A dog leash. She inhaled sharply, recalling her best friend and putting all her faith in them.

More memories surfaced, stopping her in her tracks. Probably that

Former nutcase playing with her head to drag her back to the barn, she thought. She blinked, trying to resist them, but finding it futile. They were true, she knew that much, and had been hidden for so long. What's more, they were of her life *before* arriving at the Crossing as a kid. Unable to resist, she delved straight into them.

Most were familiar. Yes, as a girl, she'd once had a dog named Bluey, and yes, when it had gone, she'd taken its name for herself. Before that, however, she'd had another name. Once again, it wasn't her true one, but she'd loved it anyway. It was …

"Rags," she whispered.

She thought harder but found nothing. Frustrated, she shook her head. "I hate this crap. It's only made me go from Rags to Rages." She mulled this over, wondering if she should go by the name, 'Rages,' instead. She quickly dismissed it. "Nah, I like Mysti better." She recalled Kimie. "Thanks, kid."

She trudged through the Village, reached its outskirts and headed up the slope, with the dog leash dangling from her hand, and the Stargazer and Gilwain following her lead.

Chapter Sixteen

Kimie felt a cold, wet patch of dirt against her face. The air was freezing. A blanket of frost tingled across her cheek. Light raindrops followed. She blinked and the world came into focus. She was in bushland late at night, or was it early morning? Probably somewhere in between, she guessed.

She shifted. A searing pain shot up her side. She winced and shifted again, then carefully sat up, fighting her bodily aches and groaning as she stared out into this damp, horrible world.

The frosty wind breezed by. Memories came with it, confusing her more than anything. She'd been in the barn, run past the Throne, dived into the light, and then a savage force had grabbed her leg, sucking her out of Bliss Airways and straight into Hell Central. She only vaguely recalled that sickening place. There'd been a couple of ugly forces lurking about in there too, and they'd scared the crap out of her. Thankfully, a glimmering sphere with an ethereal presence had shot in, smacked into her hard and then bang, here she was.

She looked up as another light came over her. Nothing like what she'd seen in Bliss Airways or Hell Central. This was an ordinary car headlight, sweeping along a road. It was someway above her, she realised, meaning she was at the base of a slope. Only then did she grasp that *all* of her memories were back, including the ones she didn't want to recall. Of getting kicked out of school. Of the psychos in the café. Of those dodgy cops at her house and of being kidnapped. She began to doubt herself. Surely the City and the Crossing had to be real, she thought. Or else she was just a delirious nutcase.

No, she concluded, they were legit. She was sure of it. She'd only stuffed up right at the end when she'd taken a bit of cash and the City had come to collect. Now she was back home, thanks to her stupidity. This was cruel. More than cruel. Sheer torture.

"I've got all the brains of a damn goldfish," she muttered, feeling like one just returned to a bowl. "This place is feral. No wonder I went nuts here."

Despite everything, she knew she'd have help now. Platinum would be around somewhere. She'd just have to find her.

She rose to her feet and staggered painfully up the slope. The road was empty when she reached the top. Bizarre, she thought. Those dodgy cops weren't here, nor was their car. Then again, she figured, they were probably following Platinum's orders and taking her to fantasyland anyway. They'd have no reason to stick around once she was in.

Two sets of headlights appeared ahead. She raised her arms, prepared to take a risk by flagging them down, knowing that nothing could be as bad as the City's crap.

Neither car stopped for her. Several more passed by, refusing to pull over, until an off-duty ambulance came to a halt. The driver was more than a little curious about finding her out in the middle of nowhere this late at night. She improvised by fobbing him and his co-workers off with a made-up story that astounded even her. They went with it but didn't seem fully convinced.

Much to her relief, they were heading back to the suburbs anyway and gave her a lift. One of them offered her a phone and she tried calling home. There was no answer. Figuring that her mother must have fallen asleep, she left a message.

Kimie was dropped off in her street. She thanked the driver, promised to repay him for the ride, then headed for her house while he watched, wanting to see her safely inside.

She pushed at her rusty gate, squeaking it open. The whole place seemed different now, along with everything else round here. Unlike the

Village, it was gloomy as hell, weighing her down and getting heavier by the moment.

Her front door was unlocked, strangely enough. She turned and waved to the ambulance driver, who nodded and drove off. She watched him go, then entered her house.

The clock's dull monotone was the first thing she heard. It ticked loudly from a mantelpiece overlooking a coffee table where her mother sat wearily, her head in her hands. Kimie guessed that she'd woken up, heard the recorded message and was waiting for her.

"Mum!" She hurried over, knelt down and hugged her. "Oh god, Mum! It's okay. Everything's fine."

Her mother spoke wearily. "Is it? Where have you been, Kimie?"

"I—" Kimie began.

"Your principal called," her mother cut in. "I know what happened at school. You were kicked out."

"Well, yeah …"

"It's six in the morning, Kimie. The police were here. Where were you?"

"I … can't say."

"God help us!" She hit the coffee table hard.

"Mum, it's okay," Kimie pressed. "If I can find the woman I met in a café earlier, she'll help. She's on our side. I didn't think I could trust her at first but now I know I can."

Her mother drew a heavy sigh. "Where do I begin with you …?"

"Listen, Mum, we don't have to live like this. There's another way—"

"With what, Kimie, what?" She rose to her feet tiredly as Kimie followed. "Do you want to guess what happened to me today? Go on, Kimie, guess!"

Kimie didn't know what to say.

"I lost my job!" her mother snapped. "That's what happens when a company downsizes. *You* get kicked out of school and now this? How the hell are we going to live? On peanuts?"

"Can you hear me out …?"

"Why?" her mother cut in. "What have you got yourself into? Drugs? Is it drugs? Or worse than drugs? What's your escape plan for us?"

Kimie's mind raced, thinking desperately.

Her mother was exasperated. "Tell me what it is and fast, because I don't think I can take much more of this. I'm sick, I'm tired and I don't know what's going to happen now, so please stop carrying on and give me something useful. Give me anything, just help me out here."

Kimie tensed, wondering how the hell she could explain the City and the Crossing without sounding like a lunatic. Nevertheless, her heart tingled, still alive with the barn's raw power. That overrode everything, bringing up a memory of—

"I saw Dad," she blurted out.

She blinked in astonishment, realising what she'd just said, and knowing it was true. She'd been too in awe to take it in when she'd dived into Bliss Central, and couldn't recall it after waking back up in this hellhole either. Now she knew, she finally understood, that the heavenly voice that had called to her on the wind, belonged to her father.

Her excitement rose. "I saw him! Well, heard his voice anyway. It was Dad ..."

Smack!

Her head snapped sideways from a heavy blow. She recoiled, clutching her searing cheek. "Cow! Why'd you do that? I was trying to help!"

"How dare you!" her mother hissed furiously.

"I heard him!" Kimie cried. "I heard Dad!"

"From where?" her mother cried back. "Some magical fairyland? How could you, Kimie? How could you, when he ..." Her eyes welled with tears, " ... died an hour ago?"

Kimie's heart missed a beat. A sickening shiver rippled through her, along with rising dread. "What?"

Silence.

"No, that's not right, Mum. You can't be serious."

More silence.

"Mum, I heard him. He can't be gone."

Her mother shook her head, speaking bitterly. "Ring the hospital and find out. Go on."

Kimie choked back the tears.

Her mother drew a shuddering breath. "This is reality. Whatever

"Thank god!" she cried. "And thank *you* for coming back!" She stepped away, speaking quickly. "You *have* to come in and talk to my mum. She's in a bad way."

Platinum shrugged. "Sure. Let's tip her over the edge. Live dangerously."

Kimie sighed, feeling like crap again. "Yeah, I get it. Taking you inside'd only freak her out, 'specially since we've just—" She shuddered, "—lost Dad. Forget it." She ran a hand through her hair. "I *know* I heard his voice in the barn. I—" She stopped. "What are you? A magic go-between?" Her eyes lit up. "Doesn't matter. You can take me back to the Village. Let's get my mum and go."

She grabbed her hand, pulling it. Platinum didn't budge. Kimie pulled harder, unable to shift her. "What's up with you? Why are you so rooted to the spot?"

Platinum's reply was just as steadfast. "'Cause the root holding me in place comes from a big mother of a Vine."

"Screw that!" Kimie retorted.

"And end up sick and alone like the System? Go for it."

Kimie got ready to blow. Reason kicked in and she relented. "Least you've admitted that crazyland's real. That's a start."

Platinum indicated their surroundings. "I thought this was crazyland?"

"You are the biggest pain in the—" She drew a sharp breath, then everything fell into place. "I get it. I'm just a tool to play games with. You saw me in the café and made me a puppet. You set things up from the start, shooting me into the City, showing me god knows what in both heaven and hell and then *wham!* I'm back here. Bet you made that cash fly by the monster truck so I'd take it. Was that something you and freakzilla in the barn thought up? I'm right, aren't I?"

Platinum stayed silent.

Kimie pushed on. "I bet all that stuff you told Mob-guy in the café about stealing two million for a cyber attack was all for show. You wanted to bait me!"

Platinum stayed cool. "Totally, but not just you. Him as well."

Kimie was startled. "You admit it?"

"Fully," came the reply. "There was never any plan to steal two million.

He chickened out after you left the café and couldn't go through with it, like I knew all along. Seeing a power bigger than his ego rattled him. He'll lie low now and stay that way, while I bury his sick career completely."

"And your career's not sick?" Kimie retorted. "How'd you even see me in the bathroom?"

Platinum lowered her head a little, showing her sunglasses. "Great shades, huh? Didn't need 'em in the café though. Saw you spying on me from miles away, so I kept Mob-guy occupied. I'd have got you out of the bathroom when things had calmed down but you pulled a surprise move and split. Would have come for you sooner but got tied up in another mess, so I had to use my boys instead. Believe it or not, the City wasn't the only thing I was dealing with. There are some real doozies out there. Barely got out of that one." She inhaled sharply. "When I finally reached the Mountain, your lot were launching a City attack. Worked out well. I needed a distraction while I went in for the big bad bosses, and you surprised everyone right from the word go."

Kimie suppressed her admiration. "So you saw me in the café and recruited me, huh?"

"No," Platinum answered. "Before that. Had seen you around and was impressed."

Kimie was astounded. "You were spying on me *before* the café?"

Platinum gave a hint of a smile. "Always knew you had potential. When I heard you got kicked out of school, *and* that Mob-guy was in the area, I killed two birds with one nest egg, but you were the bigger prize. You're a rebel with heart, and just what I needed."

"And you're a stalker!" Kimie shot back. "Why didn't you come up and talk to me?"

Platinum's tone didn't waver. "I just called you a rebel. What would you have done?"

Kimie's lips pursed. "You gotta point, lady. Your backup here's pretty useless, too. Who are they? Dodgy cops?"

"Not quite," Platinum answered. "Yes, they're on the force, but no, they're not corrupt. They answer to me. I call 'em Affirminators, with my boss being the '*Firm*' keeping us busy."

Kimie pressed on. "So how'd I get into fantasyland? Magic?"

"Gateway," Platinum corrected. "The ol' Boss liked how you stood up to my boys by taking matters into your own hands. He gave you a little push into the City. Well, a big push actually, 'cause it took a lot of pushing to get your buttload of negative energy in there. He also got the Sole-Searcher to show up once you landed, but if things had gone right, you'd have entered the System without losing your memory. Sure, it's a Gateway side effect, but that's also the trouble with systems. They suck away who you are and take over. With Bluey down we needed someone else to kick things off."

"Oh, I'm ready to go off right here," Kimie cut in. "So where were your dodgy cops when I needed a ride home just now?"

"Long gone by the time you came back," Platinum responded. "There's a temporal lapse between here and the Village, 'specially since it ran on System time for so long. That'll sort itself out soon, thanks to your work. Running from the café, fighting off my boys, getting into the City, spearheading a Mountain of an attack on it, that's impressive. You got spark."

"It's about to blow up in your face!" Kimie snapped. "Throwing a kid into a warzone's an insane gamble for everyone."

Platinum was resolute. "Your fiery instincts changed a sick System for the better."

"And where does that leave me?" Kimie retorted.

"Back in another cesspool," Platinum replied. "You can help change this one too."

"That's the plan, is it?"

"We're all here for a reason."

"Get stuffed!"

Kimie turned and walked away.

Platinum followed, her hands in her long, dark coat pockets. "Sorry to hear about your dad. Your mum and her job too."

Kimie whirled around, seething. "You are lower than a dung beetle's butt!"

Platinum wasn't fazed. "Makes for fertile ground, and we both have a good track record for raising new growth."

Kimie sensed the calm in her voice. It was almost hypnotic.

Platinum continued. "From what I hear there's been a few people fiddling the books at your mum's workplace. I can make 'em fully accountable. They'll be relocated and she can take their place."

"Hang on," Kimie cut in. "You've been stalking me, messing with my head and throwing me into things I have *no* control over. I hate that. What do you get out of it?" She stepped away. "No, I bet you want something in return. How do I know you're not screwing me over? Forget it, lady. I don't need any favours and I *don't* belong to you!"

Platinum pulled a handkerchief from her pocket, letting it unroll and releasing two objects. "You won't need these then."

Kimie caught them as they fell, feeling their tingling resonance as she gazed at them in awe. "The Stix!"

Their essence was only minuscule compared to what she'd felt in the barn, but enough to pack a sacred punch. Their raw energy swept into her mind, illuminating the dark patches that had been hidden for so long. She flinched as they were touched, then exorcised, as Platinum spoke.

"It was a hell of a job getting 'em back, and with the depth they fell, a *real* hell of a job. Thank heaven for Roverboards."

Kimie wanted to rise to the heavenly heights with them, and would have done so, if a hideous dark patch hadn't latched onto her brain, rooted itself in firmly and refused to budge. The Stix's glow dimmed as her psychic nightmare grew, bringing ugly memories to the forefront of her mind. She shivered at their revelation and murmured, "I don't think we're out of the woods just yet."

Platinum stared at her curiously.

Kimie continued. "When I was sucked from the barn into Hell Central, I passed something freaky. Made me sick, like when you see a doco of a serial killer on TV and walk away feeling yuck. This was a thousand times worse. It was … sheer, raw hate."

Platinum paused, like she was about to grimace, but stood firm. "That's another ugly job on my sludge bucket list. The City's big bad, who we call the Econo-Mist, went underground when it fell, stirring up another dark asset."

Kimie frowned. "Like what? A giant … psychic worm?"

"Corpse," Platinum corrected. "She's reverting to the witch she once was."

"Real witch?"

"You've no idea," came the reply. "He'd known about her for a while. One of his projects was to use the City's energy to wake her up for his own economic gain. We shut the City down first, but he succeeded to a point, and she's awake, just not under his control like he planned. You'd have been trapped in Hell Central with them both if my Boss hadn't sent in help to get you out. The Witch needs to be dealt with and fast, 'cause she's woken up hungry. Trouble is, she's smart too, and getting smarter now that she's working with the Econo-Mist, meaning that the Village is in trouble again."

Kimie sighed. "Can never win, can we? There's always a bigger problem ready to blow." A thought struck her. "Hey, what about Mysti? Can't she go in and blast the crap out of psychella or whatever she's called? The Stargazer and Gilwain could help."

Platinum dismissed this. "Mysti's doing her own thing right now. Like you, her memory was sucked dry when she first hit the Village, years ago, as Bluey. Going into the SORE Point didn't help either. She still doesn't have a clue about her life before the Village, apart from her ol' name and that dog of hers. She bolted into the woods right after you were sucked into Hell Central. Luckily, she's got the space man and the dwarf with her. They'll make for the Mountain."

Kimie nodded. "I bet she'll get some backup, go to the Village, and blow up the crap that's dropped out of hell's latest bowel movement." She raised the Stix. "These'll help."

"We wish," Platinum replied. "The Witch is way older than 'em and cancels their frequencies out. She's ready to rumble the Mountain, big time, and the stakes'll be much higher than what you've just dealt with. It's too dangerous for you to go back."

Kimie tensed, sensing how bad things were. Platinum's tone suggested she was freaked, majorly, but wouldn't admit it in a million years. No, Kimie concluded, Blondie's mind was made up. The Village was out of bounds.

She felt the Stix's glow waver along her arm. Somewhat coolly, she raised them and changed tack. "So what's the deal? You gave me these for a reason. You offering me a job?"

"No," Platinum answered. "The Boss is."

Kimie was taken aback and raised her eyebrows. "You mean … whatever Yushera turned into?"

Platinum showed no reaction. "The Former's only part of the Boss. Their past. Thing is, the Boss has two other spheres. A present and a future."

Kimie shook her head. "A real Holy Trinity, huh? And with Sewer Queen caught up in it too."

Platinum gave a little smile. "No, she was only the mouthpiece. When Mysti and the others turned their backs on the Former and split from the Village, the Throne released Yushera and returned her to the world much cleaner. 'Course as soon as she saw a reflection of herself in the river, she spat one hell of a hissy fit, dived straight into a mud pool and now's much happier, at least until she's called to the Throne again. That won't be anytime soon, since she's also fled the Village and is making her own way to the Mountain. Nothing's ever easy."

Kimie drew a deep breath. "Tell me about it. So what am I meant to do? Clear out the bad guys round here to make way for your Vine? The Former mentioned ambassadors. Is that what I am now?"

"Uh … no," Platinum countered. "You're not *from* there, but you can help out by keeping the ones we have on the right track. They tend to get distracted. Very much so." She pursed her lips, slightly annoyed. "You'll form part of a network that links you, me, them and the Boss, to everyone here."

Kimie shifted uncomfortably. "How?"

Platinum's head rose. "The Boss wants the café where you first saw me. I've made sure its owner's been promoted to a restaurant downtown. Our ambassadors'll go in and set up the café as a new Crossing for the Vine's growth into this world."

Kimie was impressed. "You've taken multitasking to a whole new level, haven't you?"

"Wit a little help from above," Platinum quipped. "The Vine needs a clear path to prepare for End-Time."

"There's that stupid word again."

Platinum's tone lowered as she continued. "One ambassador's gone rogue. If only my fangirl in the group had spotted the bad egg first. You'd think so, since I trained her up personally, but no. She's so focused on the bigger picture that she misses the smaller details. Good thing is that another ambassador's compensating for that. Now I'm working on our bad-egg's replacement."

Kimie bit her lip. "I'm guessing you've got someone in mind? Come on, I can tell it's not meant to be me."

Platinum spoke coolly. "They need a frequency to balance them out and yours ... doesn't fit."

"Great," Kimie muttered.

"Yeah, but you'll outrank 'em, kid."

Kimie was startled. "Huh?

"Hey, you did a good job with the City, you get promoted," Platinum said simply. "You'll keep an eye on the café once it's up and running. My girls'll answer to you, and you'll report to me. My cop buddies'll help out too, when they're not busy."

Kimie was uneasy about her promotion. "I don't know. I mean, how do I live in the meantime? Can't go home with Mum like she is."

"You're an artist, aren't you?"

Kimie was confused. "No."

"You did well at art in school, at least until that fight in the art room. Saw your reports. You did better at it than anything."

"You know we *really* have to talk about your stalking ..."

"You've been watched for longer than you think," Platinum stated. "The Boss likes potential."

"Just keep messin' with my head, lady ..."

"There's an arts centre," Platinum cut in. "In the hills. Good one too. They'll give you an apprenticeship and a place to stay. You can do what you love. Pottery, painting, sculptures, the works. They're eager to have you. They called and told me when I was being shot at going into the Sky Scrapper. I couldn't talk at the time and got back to 'em when I was less busy. I hate to see good art go to waste."

"You're a freak," Kimie scoffed. "No, seriously, you're a freak." She looked at the Stix. "I know I can trust you, but don't want to be locked into anything either." She paused. "Thing is, I don't have a choice, and you're way too smart for anyone. I never know what your game is."

"It's not a game," Platinum corrected. "We're all merely insects on a Vine."

Kimie made a face. "Ugh! Can't you come up with anything better?"

"It's true," Platinum said, "but we encourage growth, not spread rot." She reached into her pocket, pulled out a crumpled bit of paper and slapped it into Kimie's hand. "Well earned."

Kimie opened it. Inside was a card. A—

"Platinum card!" she whispered in wonder. Her excitement grew as she held it up. "How much is on it?"

"As much as you want," Platinum answered simply.

Kimie beamed. "Seriously?"

"Seriously," Platinum confirmed. "So long as you stop focusing on *more* and focus on *morality*. If you want something, then *it* will decide if you need it or not. Try and exploit it and it won't work. Everything's run by the Boss. Less trouble that way."

Kimie nodded. "Fair enough. Sucks, but fair enough."

"Your operative's name's Sealing Wax …"

"Fitting …"

"…And the paper you're holding has the art gallery's address."

Kimie smirked. "Planned it well, didn't you?"

"No," Platinum replied. "The Boss did. I'm only a mouthpiece."

"You're more than just a mouth, lady. *You* need to believe in yourself too. You're cool, y'know that?"

Platinum's lip twitched uneasily. Unsurprisingly, she quickly regained control and said, "Well, the Stix are rubbing off on you, aren't they? That's what happens when they're itching to make music."

Kimie glanced at the street. It looked stranger than ever, making her feel like she was in another country. Another world even.

She ran a hand through her hair in disbelief. "God. So much can change in a day."

Platinum concurred. "You have no idea … yet. So you didn't end up in heaven. Least you're not in hell anymore. That's a step up."

"A *big* step up," Kimie agreed, more confident than ever.

"Totally," Platinum said. "Leave your Mum to me. Call it a favour for all your help. I'll bring her round."

"I know you will." She took a deep breath. "Y'know, for the first time in forever, things are finally going okay, apart from my dad—"

"He's in a good place," Platinum cut in. "You've seen it. Now go make him proud. Your mum too."

A whine rose behind them.

"Bus is coming," Platinum indicated with a nod. "Goes near the arts centre too."

Kimie smirked. "That another thing you fixed? Bet you did, huh? With your Boss's help."

Platinum changed tack, looking around. "Now if I could just track down that vase. I *know* it's round here somewhere. It did good in getting you out of Hell Central, if only the Gateway hadn't hurled it so far ..."

Kimie blinked. "What—?"

"Hurry or you'll miss your ride," Platinum cut in. "The arts centre's just off—"

"I know the place," Kimie said quickly. "Catch ya!"

She smacked Platinum's shoulder lightly with the Stix. Its energy tingled, elating her, then she turned and ran for the bus, flagging it down. The bus slowed, its door opened and she boarded. The driver seemed tired and cranky. Probably his first run of the day, she figured. She moved past him, scanning her Platinum Card on the way. It let her on with a beep. She grinned, made her way to the backseat and sat down.

The bus geared up and headed off. She looked outside. There was no sign of Platinum. No surprise there, she thought.

She nestled into her seat. Strange how things worked out, she reflected. Yesterday she'd been on a school bus and all hell had broken loose. Today she was on another bus, and everything had worked out well. She'd made a difference. People now believed in her, leaving her feeling valuable. That blew her mind completely, giving rise to a whole future full of possibilities.

A girl, a little younger than her, sat nearby, gazing glumly out the window.

Kimie knew exactly how she felt.

"Bad day?" she asked.

The girl nodded wearily. "You've no idea."

Kimie shrugged. "Think I got some. Things'll get better."

The girl scowled. "You're off your face! You can't change the system."

"Not straight away," Kimie countered. "Can change yourself, though. Changes within bring changes without." She blinked at her sudden influx of wisdom and raised a hand to her head. "Whoa! Freaky!"

The girl scoffed irritably. "Get stuffed."

Kimie ignored her, knowing it was pointless to argue. The girl felt trapped at the bottom of a well with everyone looking down on her. She was beyond reason, for the moment anyway.

Kimie sighed and rested her head against the window, feeling the bus's gentle rocking motion as it trundled along. Only then did she realise just how tired she actually was. She couldn't recall how long it had been since she'd slept, and spiralling back and forth through the Gateway didn't count. Before she knew it, she'd drifted off into a light sleep.

When she opened her eyes again, the bus was driving past a familiar café. The place where everything had begun, she realised. At this hour it should have been opening up. Now, Counter-Guy from yesterday, was walking out carrying a box. Several more were in the moving van he was heading for. Platinum had worked fast in getting him out, she thought. Through her sleepy gaze, she saw a sign on the door that said, *"Closed."*

Sanders Crossing was growing. Into Sanders Café.

The bus drove on. She closed her eyes, snuggling dreamily into her seat amidst the day-to-day garbage of the so-called 'real world.' Time stopped until …

Crash!

The bus braked with a sudden whine as horns wailed. Doors slammed and yells exploded, along with furious swearing.

The girl near Kimie stood up, horrified. "Crap!"

"What's up?" Kimie asked, calmer than usual.

The girl shuddered. "Bad news. I know these guys. They're animals."

The yells grew louder.

Kimie rose from her sear. "Leave it to me."

The girl grabbed her arm. "What are you, insane?"

Kimie listened, then pursed her lips. "God! Can you believe what they're crapping on about. It's kids' stuff." She clutched the Stix tightly and strode to the front of the bus. "I wish everyone'd stop having melt-downs. I got this."

"You're dreaming!" the girl called.

"Just the opposite," Kimie said back. "I've woken up."

She tapped the Stix against the door. It opened with a hiss and she emerged onto the street, striding towards a small group of people. Two men stood out; knives pulled on each other.

"Oi! Apeknobs!" she called.

She raised the Stix, slamming them onto a car boot. A heavenly resonance blew throughout the street, engulfing everyone and shaking them to the core. They went silent, then their heads rose in awe, immersed in the ghostly echoes of the celestial drumbeat, unsure of where it came from and relishing a presence higher than themselves.

Sirens rose as a couple of police cars swept in, came to a screeching halt and four cops emerged. Two ran up to the street fighters and cuffed them. The men didn't resist. If anything, they were startled as they were taken away.

Everyone else shook their heads, baffled, before the so-called real world took over and the remaining cops dispersed them all. The gangs hurried off, while several passersby took photos of the police cars on their phones. No one thanked her for what she'd done. Maybe that was down to the Stix, she sensed. Their powers probably wiped people's memories, which was good, otherwise they'd be pinched in no time. Of course it was just as likely that these deadheads were too far up their own butts to care.

The bus behind her took off with a hiss, leaving her alone in an empty street.

"You're welcome!" she called into the wind.

The Stix tingled in her hand, soothing her spirit and filling her mind with possibilities. Maybe she could cure the whole world by beating the Stix relentlessly, she thought. No, that would have to be on a large scale. For the moment, she'd simply have to use them to beat the toxic crap out of the people round here, like Bus-girl, to make a difference.

The air shimmered as she sensed the Vine's presence creeping into the neighbourhood. Her head rose as she embraced its raw power and spoke firmly. "No more meltdowns. Only grow-ups. For everything."

Clutching the Stix tightly, she headed down the street as its daily rubbish swept around her, readier than ever to make the world face the music.

dreams you've been having, whatever drugs you're on, this is home, it sucks, and we're screwed."

"But things change …" Kimie protested, thinking of the Village.

"Really?" came the harsh reply. "I don't know what's happened to you, but going by things up till now, I expect the worst."

"Can you just listen …?" Kimie pleaded.

Her mother grabbed a picture of them and furiously hurled it against the wall, smashing it. The frame splintered as she slumped to her knees, sobbing. "Go, Kimie, just go! You've done enough! Get out!"

Kimie whimpered through her own tears. "Mum …"

"I said *get out*!" She grabbed a folder and hurled it at Kimie, who dodged it. "Now!"

Kimie trembled, feeling more alone than ever. She raised her hand shakily to comfort her mother, then stopped. "I'm sorry, Mum. I'm … sorry."

Tearing up, she turned and left, leaving her mother crying profusely.

Kimie walked away from her house, wiping her eyes and sniffing.

"Great!" she said tearfully. "Just great. No school, dead dad, and no job for me *or* Mum." She gazed at the sky. "God, I could have had it all. Everything. Just got greedy for a couple of bucks!"

She kicked over a garbage bin. A cat screeched and fled.

"Alley Cats and Sewer Rats, scum of the earth," she sobbed. "Now they're doing better than I am."

She slumped against a tree, slid down it and sat on the footpath, listening to an early morning garbage truck trundle by.

She smacked the ground miserably. "So unfair! I shot a whole crapped-up System to hell and what do I get?" She sniffed. "I get to question my sanity. I swear I'm going nuts. That's all I need."

A figure emerged from behind the tree, speaking coolly. "Yeah, but nuts come from family trees. Least we can grow out of 'em and move on up in the world."

She looked up, seeing a silhouetted figure in a streetlamp's glow. Platinum.

Kimie leapt up, hugging her as the Village's magic returned tenfold.

About the Author

Sam Silver is an up-and-coming and yet-to-be bestselling award-winning author. He has three university degrees, all in the interests of literature, education and information management, but puts his writing first in the interests of his true legacy.

He has been part of various literary festivals, writing groups, and stalls, and has written daily for the last twenty years.

Meltdown is his second literary fire-work after his first novel, Burning Embers.

He lives in Perth, Western Australia.